Prairie Schooner
Book Prize in Fiction
EDITOR: Hilda Raz

Jesse Lee Kercheval

The Alice
Stories

University of Nebraska Press | Lincoln and London

Acknowledgment for previously published material
appears on p. vii, which constitutes an extension of
the copyright page.

Library of Congress Cataloging-in-Publication Data
Kercheval, Jesse Lee.
The Alice stories / Jesse Lee Kercheval.   p. cm.
ISBN-13: 978-0-8032-1135-3 (cloth : alk. paper)
ISBN-10: 0-8032-1135-X (cloth : alk. paper)
1. Family—Fiction I. Title.
PS3561.E558A78 2007
813'.54—dc22   2007013218

Designed & set in ITC New Baskerville by A. Shahan.

Contents

Acknowledgments

I would like to acknowledge
with gratitude the magazines
in which the following stories
first appeared:

"A Story Set in Germany":
London Magazine

"Family Portrait," "Honors,"
and "Mary": *Prairie Schooner*

"Alice in Dairyland":
The Missouri Review

"Beasts": *Ploughshares*

"Scarce" appeared as "Going
into Hiding": *Good Housekeeping*

The Alice Stories

Alice in Dairyland

W hen the phone rang, I was still in bed under the covers trying to stay warm though it was nearly noon. As I ran to answer, I saw it was snowing again. It was January, 1989. I'd been in Wisconsin, America's frozen dairy land, nearly six years so I should have been used to it, but I was still a Florida girl at heart and each flake seemed to take me by surprise. "Alice Anne?" a voice said. My name came out slurred, like it was *Allison*.

"Mom?" I said. My mother had flown up from Jacksonville to spend Christmas with me only to collapse in the airport, a dozen tiny bottles of Bourbon rolling from her purse. Since then she had been in a special university clinic for her various addictions—alcohol, valium. Until now, though she was only a couple of miles away, just across the lake at the far end of the campus, she had not been allowed to call or have visitors.

"Can you talk? Is Anders there?" my mother asked. Anders was my boyfriend. I was talking on his phone. I was in his apartment. I had a room in a graduate student scholarship house but, even to my mother, I did not pretend to spend much time there. My mother was suspicious of Anders because once, in an uncharacteristic fit of honesty and confession, I'd told her Anders disapproved of her drinking.

"Anders!" I called. There was no answer, but even so I lowered my voice as I said, "Listen, Mom, couldn't I take you home? Check you in someplace there? It's going to be *below* zero here tonight. Couldn't . . ." Somehow, as irrational as this was, I believed it was her coming north, leaving Jacksonville, and not the alcohol or pills that had caused her collapse. She had fled winter and her native Munich when she'd married my father and had a horror both of cold and anything German. If only I could get her someplace warm, someplace far less German than Wisconsin, she would not be sick.

"I have to go, Alice," was all my mother said. "I just wanted to tell you I sent you a belated Christmas card. I made it in art therapy class. I sent one to your brother, too."

"But Mom," I started. I hadn't yet told my brother Mark our mother was in the hospital. As a matter of fact, I had outright lied, sending a Christmas present of Florida oranges to his apartment in San Francisco, telling the operator at the grove's 800-number to sign the card "From Mom." I heard a voice in the background call my mother's name. *Mrs. Stratton . . .*

"I'm fine, Alice, really." Her voice was shaking. "They say I can have visitors soon." She hung up.

After talking to my mother I had a terrible craving for Scotch, or Bourbon, or even a tall glass of gin. None of which I had had since I last visited her in Jacksonville. I'd grown up in a house stocked with tax-exempt Army liquor, and my mother still kept a mean bar. Look where it got her, I imagined Anders saying.

Oh, Lord, I would have to call Mark tonight, tell him all about Mom before he got her card with its locked-ward address. I stared into Anders's refrigerator for a while, but it held only some bottles of murky looking natural fruit juices. If he were home he would remind me that my mother's collapse was thirty years of hard drinking in the making, remind me that I was the child here—though a child of twenty-six on her way to a PhD in English—and therefore not responsible for how my mother had lived her life. But what did Anders know? It was my brother Mark and I who were there after our dad left. Mom pulling us through the streets of Madrid where we'd gone on some ill-conceived "space available" Army vacation. In the rain, lost and crying, she had kept telling us over and over to go to the American Consulate if she dropped dead. Anders had sane Lutheran parents. They didn't drink or have passports.

I settled on some yogurt, added a handful of Grape-Nuts. Ate it standing by the sliding-glass door that looked out over the lake. This was Lake Mendota. There were two large lakes on either side of downtown Madison—Mendota and Monona. Their names sounded so much alike, it had taken me six years to stop mixing them up.

Even though Lake Mendota was several miles across, it froze hard enough to park cars on. When I first moved to Madison from Florida and my new college friend Bibi told me about the cars, I thought she was kidding. How did the fish breathe under the ice? Then I got used to the solid concrete white of the frozen lakes in winter. But this winter I kept hoping for a mild spell, for a patch of blue to hold out in the center. Something my mother could see from her hospital room—presuming she had a window. But over the last month, since her complete and astonishing airport collapse, I had watched the ice creep in from the edges until now, way out in the middle of Lake Mendota, people were skating. I put my feet up on the radiator, trying to get my toes warm, and started working.

I was revising the syllabus for the freshman English class I taught each semester as part of my graduate assistantship. Each semester I took out all the assignments that hadn't quite worked as well as I had hoped. Usually that was all of them. Then, slowly, I put back the ones I still had hopes for, filled in the blank weeks with assignments I either made up or borrowed from happier, more successful teaching assistants. My feet were almost warm when the phone rang again.

"Alice, this is Anders."

"Hi," I said. "Are you in the darkroom?" Anders was a new assistant professor in the art department, teaching nearly all of the photography courses. He'd been up late the night before, taking pictures of me pretending to be asleep in our rumpled, unmade bed. Something about black-and-white film, Anders had explained, turned wrinkles into light, and shadow into art.

"Listen," he said, "I'm at Angela Mosley's apartment on Commercial Avenue, out past the Oscar Meyer plant. Do you remember where it is?" Just before my mother arrived, Anders had taken me to an end-of-the-term party that Angela, one of his graduate students, had given.

"I think so." I remembered the place as a wall of identical doors facing a parking lot, more like a motel than an apartment building.

"There's a wreath with some Christmas lights on the door." Anders sounded winded, as if he'd sprinted up several flights of stairs.

I felt a little slow.

"Are you in some kind of trouble?"

"Angela is," he said. "I'll tell you about it later. I came here to help her get some things. Now her car won't start and she needs to get out of here. My car keys are in the fruit bowl by the door. Can you bring them to me?"

"Sure," I said. "I'm on my way." He hung up. Even though I had a valid Wisconsin driver's license, I'd learned to drive in Florida and had never, in all my impoverished student years in Wisconsin, owned a car, so I was not an old hand at icy winter roads. The snow was blowing like sand across the road, and I drove very carefully. After maybe twenty minutes of this I found Commercial Avenue, then the apartment building. I spotted the lights on the wreath from the parking lot. When

Mark and I were kids in Jacksonville, my mother had made us string Christmas lights in our cabbage palms.

I waited for a minute in the parking lot, then climbed the stairs, which were outside and open to the wind, as if this were Florida not Wisconsin. Someone had scattered the steps liberally with rock salt to keep them from icing over. I rubbed my hands together, wishing I'd remembered my gloves. Even after six winters in Wisconsin I had trouble remembering the cold weather extras like hats and gloves, had trouble believing in weather cold enough to hurt. No wonder thirty thousand people a month moved to Florida, I thought. Even my thick wool coat felt thin. I knocked on the door. *Hurry up, Anders, hurry up.* But no one answered. I knocked again, then stepped back and looked at the wreath, which I now could see was plastic. A little hand-lettered card below it read

Angela Mosley and Jo Beth Kasenbaum
WELCOME FRIENDS

I knocked one last time, then gave up. Maybe Anders thought the snow had been too much for me, had called a cab.

I went back down the stairs to the parking lot, but just as I reached Anders's old Volvo a pickup truck bumped into the parking lot without slowing down, and blocked me in. A woman jumped out; it was Angela's roommate, Jo Beth. I remembered her vaguely from the party. She had come in late, sat alone in the kitchen drinking a beer. She was a big woman with short, shiny black hair. She had on a hat and gloves, a nice thick down jacket. Jo Beth saw me, pointed a gloved finger. "It was you. All the time it was you. Where is she?" When Angela had gone into the kitchen to get a corkscrew, I remembered, I had seen her kiss Jo Beth lightly on the lips.

"Angela?" I said. "I don't know. I knocked . . ." I started. Jo Beth shoved me up against the car.

"You fucking bitch!" Her breath hung in the air. She pressed a finger into my chest. I looked down and realized that what I'd thought was her finger was the barrel of a gun. She had a gun. Not a big gun, but a gun. I couldn't believe it.

"She was happy," Jo Beth was saying. "I know she was." She had the gun pressed to the middle button of my jacket. She pulled at something on a chain around her neck with her free, non-gun-holding hand. A large gold cross.

"Please," I say, "I don't know anything about this."

Jo Beth quit playing with her cross. She took a step back, the gun shaking in her hand, and I realized that—cross or no cross—she was going to shoot me. It was broad day-light in Madison, Wisconsin—a town with almost no violent crime—and I was about to get shot. No matter that her hand was shaking, the gun first pointing at my heart, now only at my stomach. It was so cold, if the bullet hit me I would fall down and lie there until I froze to death.

"She was happy. *We* were happy." I was about to be shot for stealing someone's lesbian lover. I was innocent, but maybe, just maybe my solid, reliable Wisconsin boyfriend wasn't. Would I die without knowing? Anders, you shit. If I were to get shot it would be in the papers. My mother would read about it in the *Wisconsin State Journal.* No.

I dropped to my knees. Jo Beth was startled. I closed my eyes. "Our Father, Who art in Heaven. Hallowed be Thy Name. Give us this day our daily bread." I heard Jo Beth's knees hit the icy asphalt beside me and then a noise, a gentle sucking like the drain on the side of a pool. She was crying. "And forgive us our trespasses as we forgive those . . ."

"Who have trespassed against us." Jo put her arms around me, her bulky jacket making her hug thick and clumsy. She still had the gun. I couldn't seem to remember the rest of the Lord's Prayer. Where had I learned it anyway? My family had bounced from one lukewarm Protestant church to an-other, never staying long enough to learn even the words to the hymns. "Jesus Christ," I said, "Lamb of God, whose blood washes away our sins." Jo Beth didn't seem to know that one. Maybe I was making it up. I started over. "Our Father Who art," and she said it with me, finished it when I stopped. *For ever and ever. Amen.*

"Oh, Jesus," she said, wiping her nose with her sleeve. She slipped the gun into her pocket. She had lost her lover. My mother was in the hospital, begging every day for a drink. "What the fuck," she said. I nodded, seeing clearly in that moment what she meant.

We got up. My legs were numb from the cold. I almost fell. Jo Beth steadied me, then stepped back, shaking her head. She was still shaking her head when she got in the truck, backed out of the parking lot. I waited, leaning against Anders's Volvo until Jo Beth's truck was out of sight, until the sound of the engine faded and then was gone.

I drove back to Anders's apartment. No one was there. No sign anyone had been there while I was out. I felt weak, as if I had been shot or had somehow mysteriously lost a lot of blood. How did the cops and detectives on TV do it? They got beaten and shot at every week but slowed down only for the commercials. Another fine example of the difference between life and fiction. I drew a hot bath and was about to get in when the phone rang. It was Anders. I walked with the hall extension back into the bathroom.

"Angela remembered she had a roll of quarters, so we took the bus," he said. "She was afraid Jo Beth would come home early from her shift at Oscar Meyer. They're breaking up. Angela broke down after class, she was so upset about it. What could I do? I'm her thesis advisor. I had to help out."

I could hear his Wisconsin honesty. Of course he had to help her. Of course she was nothing but his student. But part of me still thought he might be lying. My father lied to my mother right up to the day he left. "Where are you?" I asked.

"At my office."

I stuck my left foot in the tub. The hot water burned like hell. "Jo Beth has a gun," I said.

"Gun?" He pronounced the *n* very carefully, as if he thought maybe what I had said was *gum. Watch out, Jo Beth has gum.*

"Gun." I lifted my left foot out, put it back in. This time the water felt less hot.

"Are you okay?"

"Yeah." I put my right foot in the tub too, stood there. It was weird how the water felt boiling hot to my right foot but only lukewarm to the left. "I mean, I'm not shot."

"Jesus, Al, I'm sorry. I wouldn't have called you if I'd had any idea. I never imagined . . ." I shut my eyes and imagined Anders frowning into the phone, brow wrinkled. Of course he hadn't known Jo Beth would have a gun. Of course he was shocked. His parents would have been shocked. Such things did not exist in their ordered Lutheran universe. "Listen, I'm going to call campus counseling about Jo Beth. I don't want to get her in trouble, but this is serious. They'll know what to do. In the meantime I'm sending Angela to the apartment for safe keeping. Will you let her in?"

"Give her your keys," I said, angry that Anders was so calm. If he really cared he could at least act upset. Calm was acting like my father, calm was being a lying, logical heel. "I'm taking a bath."

I fell asleep in the tub, woke to find Angela standing in the door. She had flipped on the light and the bathroom fan. Now the water really was lukewarm. She was looking at me clinical-ly, then she shifted her gaze to the toilet. "I have to pee," she said. She had an unopened bottle of Stoly in one hand. Some-where between Anders's office and here she'd found a liquor store.

"There's a half bath in the hall," I said. "You passed it com-ing in. It looks like a closet." She thought about it for a min-ute, then left. I got out, put on jeans, a sweatshirt, my Ree-boks. Then I checked to make sure Angela had locked the front door behind her when she let herself in. I didn't think Jo Beth would have any reason to know where Anders lived or to come to his apartment, but it didn't hurt to be careful. I heard the toilet flush, and Angela came out of the half-bath with the bottle of vodka still in her hand. Her hair was wet, as if she had stuck her head in the sink. She held the bottle out to me. "So," she said, "do you want to get drunk?"

We sat at the table by the window, watching the sun go down over the far end of the lake, over my mother's hospital, and pouring shots from the bottle. By the time we were halfway through the Stoly it was so dark outside it seemed like midnight, though it was only five thirty. Angela lit the candles on Anders's table, something he and I never did. His mother had given them to him.

"So," I said, "how come your lover wanted to kill me?" Angela shrugged.

"Everyone acts or reacts in accordance with their social conditioning," she said.

"You mean, if you work at Oscar Meyer packing lunchmeat you are conditioned to shoot people? That's pretty classist." Angela shook her head.

"I'll put it another way. Either we become who our mothers told us to be," she said, "or who they told us not to be." She pulled her fingers through her hair, which was almost dry. In the candlelight it looked blonde and fuller than I remembered it being, and I realized she must have washed it in the sink in the guest bath. With what? I was about to ask, but she said, "I got shot once, you know. Two years ago, in San Francisco." I told her I didn't know, and she told me how she had been walking to the Museum of Contemporary Art with another woman when suddenly her friend said, 'Ouch, I think something stung me.' And there was a little piece of cement stuck in her friend's bare calf, a chip from the sidewalk. 'How . . . ?' her friend started to say.

"Then," Angela said, "I felt somebody slap me hard on the

back, but there wasn't anyone there, and blood started coming through my t-shirt. My friend screamed and I realized I had been shot. I mean, there wasn't a sound or anything, but I looked at the buildings across the street and realized that there must be a sniper up there somewhere. 'Keep walking,' I said to my friend, because I was afraid if the sniper knew I'd been hit, he'd want to finish me off. My friend kept trying to open random doors we passed but it was Sunday, so everything was closed, locked up. A window up ahead of us went *pop* and shattered into this spiderweb, then one behind us, *pop*. No sound but the glass, you know? I was *so* scared. Then, finally, we got to the corner, I saw a bus coming and my friend said, 'Can you run?' and I said, 'Yes.' So we ran and jumped on the bus, and it turned the corner. And that was that." Angela poured the last shot of the vodka into her glass. "They never caught him." She looked at me, pushed her hair out of her face.

"Or her," I said. She didn't smile.

"You don't believe me, do you?" she said, and before I could decide whether I did or not, she lifted her shirt. She was wearing a white cotton sports bra, but above it I saw a small purple scar about the size of a quarter. "That's where the bullet came out." When she moved I smelled sandlewood and realized that she had washed her hair with one of the little round guest soaps I had brought Anders that sat in a wicker basket on the back of the toilet. Who would do such a thing?

"And here's where it went in." She turned her back toward the light, and just below her wing bone I saw a small pink pucker peppered with a few grains of gray. Gun powder? I leaned closer trying to tell, but the candles flickered. "I can't see," I started to say, but suddenly it was not too dark to see but rather too bright. Anders was standing in the doorway, his hand on the light switch. Angela sat up, her spine smacking me in the nose.

"The city police picked up Jo Beth for running a red light. They found the gun," Anders said. I looked up at Anders. He had his arms crossed over his chest. Angela stood up fast, too fast, and had to grab the table to steady herself. "Go put some water on your face," Anders said to Angela, and Angela tacked across the room to the bathroom, making it to the door on her second try. Anders watched Angela's progress as if it were the most interesting and important bit of navigation going on in the world, then shifted his disapproving gaze back to me.

He lifted the empty bottle off the table. He shook his head. "Alice," he said.

"Alice-isss-isss," I repeated, quite stupidly drunk. He set the bottle down hard.

"Damn it, Alice. Do you want to end up like your . . ." He stopped himself. Angela had come out of the bathroom. She was doing much better, walking pretty straight, much straighter than I could have, which made me suspect she'd had plenty of experience.

"I think I'll go to bed," I said. Anders opened his mouth as if he was going to say something but he didn't, and he didn't stop me.

I woke up sometime in the night, drunker than when I had gone to sleep. The bed was spinning like water going down a drain. I flung out one arm, feeling for Anders to steady myself. He wasn't there. His half of the bed was cold and empty. I listened and thought I could hear his snores coming from the spare bedroom next door, where he kept an old futon we'd slept on before I moved in and he'd been motivated to buy a real bed. Just like my parents, I thought, separate beds. Then I saw that my mother was sitting beside me. I was freezing, even under the down comforter Anders had carefully arranged over me before taking to his futon. My mother was wearing her lightest cotton PJs and I could see how incredibly thin she was, even under her fierce Florida tan. She was drinking her usual, an iced tea-sized glass of bourbon, something

I'm sure her doctors at the clinic had warned her about in no uncertain terms. When I was growing up she'd always had one or two of those while she fixed dinner. She touched my wrist and her fingers were unbelievably hot. She held out her drink to me, offering me a hair of the dog.

"Stop it, Mom," I said, trying to push the drink away without spilling it all over the bed. She pulled back. I struck out, trying to knock the drink out of her hand. Didn't she know it was killing her?

I felt my fist hit home. "Hey, knock it off!" It was Anders. It was daylight and he was tangled in the cover next to me. Had he been there all night? Had I been dreaming about the futon? About my mother? His cheek was red where I had hit him. "Ouch."

"Sorry," I started, but as the adrenaline, the incredible rush of fear, drained off I realized I was going to be sick. Halfway to the bathroom it hit me that I had slept in my clothes, was even still wearing my sneakers.

I made it to the toilet. My stomach heaved and heaved again, but nothing came up. Kneeling on the tile I was so cold my teeth chattered. Anders came to the door. "Are you all right?" He put a warm hand on the back of my neck. I nodded, regretted it immediately. Anders held his ground, holding my shoulders as my stomach again turned inside out. Even my mother had never done that for me.

"Look on the bright side," I managed, when I could breath again. "They say people who have bad hangovers never become alcoholics."

After a while I felt a little better, my stomach fooled into thinking I had actually managed to throw up whatever was making me sick, though I knew the vodka had long ago made its way, for better or worse, into my body. "I'll make you some tea," Anders said. I rinsed my mouth, washed my face.

I found Anders in the kitchen waiting for water to boil.

"Where's Angela?" I asked. Maybe she was the one I'd heard snoring on the futon while Anders slept next to me. Anders frowned. The tea kettle began to whistle. He made two cups of mint tea. I blew on mine then took a sip, waiting for his answer.

"She left last night—to bail Jo Beth out. She said Jo Beth's getting a gun proved she loved her." Anders shook his head. It was not a Lutheran world. "I guess they're not breaking up after all."

"I'm sorry," I said. And I was. Guns as love seemed sad to me. So sad, that on top of being nauseated, it was almost unbearable. And I still had to call Mark and tell him the truth about where our mother had spent Christmas. I didn't want to. I didn't want life to be so goddamn sad.

The phone rang and I heard Anders say, "Yes, this is Anders Dahl. Alice Stratton?" She's right—*oh, no . . .*"

And I knew what had happened, as clearly as if I'd seen this bit of bad news coming, seen it leave the clinic and cross the lake to Anders's waiting ear. I knew who I was never going to visit in the hospital, who was not going home to Jacksonville, who I would never see again, ever, or at least in this life. My mother was dead.

Anders was still nodding into the telephone, "Yes, yes, I see . . ." Any second, he would hand me the phone. But I didn't want it. I backed across the kitchen into the dining room. I pulled hard on the handle of the sliding-glass door, and though I didn't expect it to, it gave way. This was Wisconsin. It was not even locked. I opened it, and cold air spilled over my feet. Anders felt it too. "Alice!" He dropped the phone, but I was already out the door, down the short slippery lawn, one foot on the ice. "Wait!" he called after me, but I didn't. He wouldn't catch me. I had slept in my sneakers and he was barefoot. My Reeboks skidded forward on the ice. I almost fell, but the soles caught on the snow cover and I was not just walking on water—like Jesus—but running. It felt strangely familiar, like I was, at long last, the real Alice, the one who lived her life in Wonderland, where when you fall down a rabbit hole or step through a mirror, everything changes.

As I ran my eyes began to water. Tears froze on my cheeks. As far I could see there was emptiness. This morning I was the only living soul on the ice. No one was skating or ice fishing or walking their large furry dog. A gust of wind hit me, unbelievably sharp, and brought Anders's voice with it. "Alice, wait," then took it away. In that second I knew what he was thinking—that I was headed along the edge of the lake for the hospital, but he was wrong. I was not headed anywhere you could find people. I meant to keep running until I reached the diamond heart of the lake. I would live there, at least until spring. Live where everything was white, white on white, whiter than white. Where my mother, if not exactly alive, was, at least, not officially dead.

But Anders did catch me. He threw himself at me in a full flying tackle, and we both went skidding across the ice, Anders holding me tight. I opened my mouth, prepared to shout, to be angry, but I wasn't. Anders had run across the lake in unlaced shoes with no socks to save me from myself. We lay panting, face down on the ice, Anders's arms around me. And maybe it was only the running, but for the first time in a long time I was not cold.

Damage

When the earthquake hit San Francisco, I was in the dressing room of Victoria's Secret trying on a black lace bra. The thin partitioned walls of the dressing room swayed. The white slatted doors went bang, bang, bang. "Hang on, Alice," I told myself, "hang on." The floor bucked under my feet as if I were driving my mother's old Buick over a double set of railroad tracks. It kept up. Five seconds, ten. I looked at my watch. It was 5:04 p.m., October 17, 1989.

I knew right away what the shaking was even though I had only lived in San Francisco for two months and had never felt an earthquake before. Maybe because of this I took the time to pull on my sweatshirt before I ran. I didn't want to hear a fireman yell, "Get that lady some clothes!"

Only when I reached the street and saw the other women from the dressing room, one in a transparent silk nightgown and another in jeans and a strapless bra, did I realize how less-than-universal my reaction was. By then the shaking had stopped. I stood with the other women. There were no firemen. No one cared in the least what anyone was or wasn't wearing.

I felt my heart pounding inside the sweatshirt I'd risked my life to put on. A minute passed. The ground stayed still. "Whew," the woman in the strapless bra said, "that was a big one."

"Yeah, it was big," the woman in the nightgown said.

I nodded in agreement but still found it hard to believe. I might be just a newly arrived graduate student from Wisconsin, but even I knew that San Francisco dreaded the next "big one," an earthquake that, like the one in 1906, could level the city. But had this quake been big? True, the store mannequins were on their backs in a heap, but the plate-glass window in front of them wasn't even cracked.

On my walk home most things seemed intact. It was rush hour, and the streets were full of traffic. People passed by, carrying groceries. It didn't seem nearly as strange as the time a winter storm had paralyzed the University of Wisconsin on the last day of finals with thirteen inches of blowing, drifting snow. I remembered putting on my boots, going out. Even the McDonald's was closed; its parking lot was empty. I remembered thinking *it's like the end of the world.*

Upstairs in my apartment the electricity was out, but the emergency spotlight the landlord had installed over the door more than lit up the place. In its glare I saw that all the kitchen stuff had come out of the cabinets. Grape-Nuts and Stress Tabs mingled on the floor. But, to be honest, the place didn't look much worse than it usually did. Neither Nina, the apartment's official tenant, nor I, her not-on-the-lease temporary roommate, were much for housework.

Nina was sitting at the kitchen table with her nose about an inch from the blue screen of her new impossibly miniature TV, a Sony Watchman. "You'll ruin your eyes," I said, which was exactly what my mother would have said. It always surprised me when this happened, but now that my mother was dead it seemed both sad and creepy. At least I hadn't suddenly developed an accent when I said it. *You vill rune your eyze.* My mother had been born in Germany.

"So what?" Nina said, motioning toward her Watchman. "Get a load of this, Alice," she said. I peered at the five-inch screen. I could just make out the Bay Bridge, so tiny on the Watchman it looked like a model.

"What am I supposed to be looking at?" I asked. Nina pointed, and I leaned closer, squinting. Then I saw it. A section of the bridge was missing. On the edge hung a car, its front wheels dangling in awful, empty space.

"Is there anybody in it?" I asked.

Nina adjusted the Watchman's tiny antenna. "What do you think?"

The picture of the car stayed on the screen for ten seconds, twenty. Longer than the quake itself. I thought I could see the car rocking. Or was it just the picture on the Watchman? "They're shooting this from the Goodyear Blimp," Nina said. "It was here for the World Series."

At the very moment Nina said that, the station switched to Candlestick Park. Or so the announcer said. There was only a blank gray screen and a voice.

"The players simply left the field," some sportscaster was saying over a crackling phone line. "They walked through the tunnel and out to the parking lot, got in their cars, and drove away. Everyone here was very calm."

"We've had some reports of looting," another voice, someone back at the studio, said. "Have you seen any . . ."

"I have to go now, Dave," the sportscaster said, "there are other people waiting to use this pay phone." The picture went back to the car, which possibly was slipping forward off the bridge. It was unbearable to watch. I closed my eyes. But it was unbearable to not watch. I opened them. The car was still there.

The phone rang, and Nina got up to answer. Who could possibly be calling? Nina's mother in L.A.? Surely not Anders, the boyfriend I had left back in Wisconsin. He had thought it was crazy for me to go so far away just to work on my dissertation. Would he even have heard the news yet half a continent away? Or maybe some other Wisconsinite, like Bibi, my best friend from my undergrad days—maybe she had already heard the news. She was a paper artist who tended to work with the radio on. The Watchman switched to a high shot of the Bay Bridge. Looking at the size of the hole in the cement and steel I was amazed that our phone was working, that San Francisco was still connected to the rest of the world.

"It's your brother, Alice," Nina said, handing me the phone.

"Allie, is that you?" Mark said. "Are you okay?"

"Oh God, Mark, are you okay?" I couldn't believe that I had forgotten to worry about him, just when there was something concrete to worry about. "Are you on campus?" He taught comparative lit at Berkeley, and I imagined him there across the dangling Bay Bridge.

"No, I'm at the hospital with George." Mark was gay, and George was his lover. George was a real estate lawyer, but now he was back in San Francisco General with his fourth bout of pneumonia that year. Of course Mark was there. George had AIDS. He was dying. Everyone Mark knew was dying. It was like a secret war, an earthquake that really was the "big one" but about which only people in San Francisco seemed to know or care. In Madison, on the university campus, you heard about AIDS, but not like you did in San Francisco. And in Jacksonville, where Mark and I had both grown up, I knew no one was weeping or sending money to the Red Cross for George's disaster.

"Listen, Allie, I'm fine. George is fine, but things are crazy here. Can you check on Dagwood?" Dagwood was Mark's dog. Not his dog, really. Dagwood was the family beagle, from back when our dad was still married to our mom and our mom was still alive. There had been a Blondie then, too, a Siamese cat. But she had gotten sick, gotten thinner and thinner, until she looked like one of those big-eyed kitten paintings some people had in their dens. It turned out she had feline infectious leu-kemia—the disease they said now was like cat AIDS—so Moth-er had had her put to sleep.

Mark—I knew because he told me—refused to be tested for HIV. What was the point, he said, when there wasn't any treat-ment or cure? It was an epidemic and, historically, epidem-ics meant quarantines. The government was probably already keeping lists, Mark said, and getting tested would just put his name on one.

I didn't know about that. I only knew I worried every day that he looked paler and that he was losing weight. "Don't you dare go and die and leave me all alone," I had said to him one night on the telephone not long after Mom died, the same night I accepted his offer to support me while I finished my dissertation if I would come and live in San Francisco and be near him.

"Don't die and stick you with Dagwood, you mean," Mark had said, and laughed.

"Jesus, I hope Daggie is okay," I said. Dagwood had always hated thunder; I couldn't imagine he was crazy about earth-quakes either.

"Listen," Mark said, "you're okay, right? And I'm okay. He'll be okay."

After I hung up I dug around in the kitchen drawers, all open, for a flashlight or a candle, but couldn't find anything, not even a match. That was the trouble with not smoking, I thought. My mother had always kept a big brandy snifter full of matchbooks by the door.

"I'm going to Mark's," I said, letting myself out. "I'll help clean up when I get back."

"Fine," Nina said, waving without taking her eyes off her Watchman. "No point in cleaning up yet—not until the aftershocks."

Outside it was night already, but the sidewalk wasn't as dark as I thought it would be. The cars stalled in traffic lit the way with their headlights. I heard sirens in the distance. Police or fire, I couldn't tell. But instead of coming closer or fading away they seemed to stay put, as if they too were stuck in traffic. Mark and George lived only a few blocks away in a building that overlooked Golden Gate Park, but I put my purse under my arm and walked fast, head down. If there were looters the police weren't going to be much help.

On Mark's street there was more damage. The sidewalk glittered with broken window glass. An entire marble façade of a building had fallen, come clean off the front of what was now a drab brick building. The rubble blocked the sidewalk and half the street. I imagined running from that building, feeling the weight of the marble as it hit the back of my head. I picked my way carefully around debris but, thank God, there weren't any feet sticking out so everyone had probably been at work when the quake hit. In my experience, most people in San Francisco were always at work. Especially if they lived in expensive apartment buildings like this.

Or like Mark's building. The etched glass from its door lay in pieces on the sidewalk. I stepped through not bothering to find which key fit the lock. Inside, miraculously, the power was on. In the lobby the lights—white and silver deco moons—shone as brightly as ever. Still, I took the stairs instead of the elevator. "Aftershocks," Nina had said.

I made it up the four flights and found the right key first for the deadbolt and then for the regular lock. But when I opened the door to my brother's apartment the room I saw was empty. The horse-hair couch, whose back was usually toward the door, and the claw-footed mahogany dining table were gone. Had Mark and George been robbed? It was hard to believe the first thing looters would go for was a back-breakingly heavy Victorian parlor set. I stepped inside, mouth open. Then I saw what had happened. The furniture, which Mark inherited from our mother, was all on castors—Mom, who'd worked long and hard at becoming a typical American housewife, had had an irrepressible German mania for vacuuming under things—and the earthquake had sent it all rolling like boxcars across the clean parquet floor through the arch and into Mark's study. The couch and table huddled with his desk like scared livestock.

"Daggie Dog?" I called. "Dagwoody?" I heard his tail thumping and found him stretched out on the couch, taking this opportunity to sleep where he wasn't allowed. He did not look particularly traumatized. "Good dog," I said. He gave my hand a slow lick.

I once heard Mark say he was raised by a real dog—meaning Dagwood, not our mother. Mark meant this as a joke, but it made me sad because it was both unkind to our mother and true. It was Daggie that Mark and I and our father and mother had taken turns petting when we almost never touched each other. I put my face close to Dagwood's, kissed him behind his ears like when he was a puppy. He smelled like old dog.

I straightened up. He was a tan-and-white beagle, but now the tan was mostly gray and the white mostly yellow. Great flaps of extra skin hung down from his muzzle and his stomach. But here he was, alive and shedding on my mother's couch when she had been dead nearly half a year. Dagwood jumped down and waddled off to the kitchen. It was dinnertime and he knew it.

Mark's kitchen looked like Nina's. All the cans and boxes and bottles and pots had taken this opportunity to get out of their respective cabinets and see a bit of the world. Unfortunately Mark and George had many more pans and provisions than Nina did, so it was a considerable mess. The milk had leapt out of the refrigerator and exploded across the floor. I toed through the damp debris thoughtfully but didn't see any dog food.

"We'll buy some, Daggie," I said. He looked at me doubtfully, holding his head on the slant. But when I got his leash off the peg on the back of the door, he knew I was serious. We were going for a W-A-L-K. Just as I put my hand on the door knob, it hit—another quake. Probably just an aftershock, but it was hard for me to judge. It felt bad. The couch slammed into the arch while trying to find its way back into the living room, and plaster showered down. Dogwood started barking, his voice rising into a hoarse, hunting bay. I sucked in a deep breath, and it hit me that I was still wearing the black lace bra from Victoria's Secret. A bra I hadn't paid for. A bra I couldn't afford. I had only meant to try it on—like a costume—but now, I supposed, I would have to go back tomorrow and pay for it. With what, I didn't know. Unless Dagwood and I were buried alive right now. I felt sick.

The shaking stopped. I flung open the door, and Dagwood bolted out, pulling hard on his leash. The quake seemed to have rejuvenated him, like cool weather used to do for poor old Blondie who would rise from her thin immune-deficient sleep to chase lizards across the yard.

In the street the traffic seemed as thick as ever. The light was out at the intersection, but some man in a white suit stood in the glare of headlights directing traffic, and people were mostly paying attention. Dogwood sniffed his way down a sidewalk lit by the endless line of cars. We headed for Antonio's on the corner where I did most of my last-minute grocery shopping, which is to say where I did most of my shopping. Dagwood trotted along beside me, stopping once at a leaking fire hydrant. But Antonio's was closed, dark. I knocked. "Tony, it's me!" I said, although I wasn't sure Mr. Antonio would recognize me even after two months of shopping there almost every day. I wasn't Italian or especially good looking. Mr. Antonio always remembered Nina, who was both. A face appeared at the door, as did a hand holding a lighter. Mr. Antonio. "Dog food," I said, pointing down at Dagwood, who was licking his testicles.

Mr. Antonio shrugged and unlocked the door. Inside it was too dark to see anything beyond Mr. Antonio's illuminated face. "You never know in a situation like this," Mr. Antonio said, waving the lighter. "My wife said, 'Stay open, make money,' but this kind of thing stirs people up." He nodded in the general direction of Oakland. "The wrong kind of people, if you know what I mean."

When I was kid I had thought only people in the South, in places with long, lousy histories like Jacksonville, were racist. Eight years in the liberal cocoon of the University of Wisconsin had only reinforced this belief. Sadly, during my two months in San Francisco I had learned that was far from true. "The Bay Bridge is out," I said to Mr. Antonio, trying to make him realize how ridiculous he was being, "if an invasion is really what's worrying you."

"So they say on the radio," Mr. Antonio said, picking his way back to the counter. "But still, there's boats, eh?" I skidded on something—loose spaghetti?—and banged my elbow on one of the shelves. "The dog food," Mr. Antonio said, "was on the back wall, top shelf. Now? Who knows?" I guessed Mr. Antonio was shrugging again, but he'd let the lighter go out, and I couldn't see him.

"Go for it, Dag," I said and unhooked Dagwood's leash. I heard him waddle forward, sniffing. Somewhere in the dark Mr. Antonio turned on a tinny sounding radio, some old Japanese transistor maybe, from the days before "Made in Japan" meant "the best money could buy." An announcer was talking about the World Series again. It had been postponed, he said. Then they cut to interviews of people in Candlestick saying what they had been thinking when the quake hit.

"I thought the fans above me were stamping their feet," some guy said. "It felt like somebody slugging a punching bag," said another. A woman's voice broke in. "I just kept thinking, Who's going to raise my kids?"

Dagwood found something and brought it to me. I took it from him and squeezed it. A package of Gainesburgers. Dagwood wheezed while waiting for me to break through the cellophane. Usually Mark fed Dagwood a brand of high-calcium low-fat dog food specially formulated for older dogs, but right now I figured beggars could not be choosers. I ripped open the package of Gainesburgers and fed two to Dagwood. "Bellissimo, Doggio," I whispered in his ear. Then I stood up and felt my way to the counter.

"Two-fifty-eight," Mr. Antonio said, holding his lighter up to the price sticker on the Gainesburgers, "two-seventy with tax." I opened my purse. All I had was a five. Mr. Antonio waved his hand at the new electronic cash register.

"No power, no change," he said. "Here," he said as he tore three Bic Flics off a display card by the register. "Take these." He slipped them into a bag with the Gainesburgers. I bent down to fasten Dagwood's leash to his collar. "So what do you think," Mr. Antonio said, "was this the 'Big One' or what?"

It took me a moment to realize what Mr. Antonio was really asking, but when I did, everything suddenly made sense. Mr. Antonio and the women outside Victoria's Secret *wanted* this to be the "Big One." Because if it was—and they had lived through it—then they were safe. An earthquake like that only happened once every eighty, maybe ninety years. But how could we know? I pointed at the radio. "What do they say?"

"They say 7, 6.9," Mr. Antonio said. "But what does that mean? Is that big? How big is big?" He shook his head.

I shook my head, too. I thought about Mark holding George's hand in the hospital as the bed shook and IV poles crashed down. How far up the Richter scale was disaster? How many people had to die to make an epidemic? A tragedy? I had no idea. At my feet Daggie whimpered, ready to go. "Well, thanks," I said to Mr. Antonio, picking up my bag. "I can let myself out."

Outside, the street was still full of cars stopping and going. No one seemed to have given up and abandoned their cars to head off on foot. Where did they think they were going anyway? I wondered. The Bay Bridge was closed, and I couldn't imagine driving over the Golden Gate when any minute there might be an aftershock. Or worse.

Dagwood pulled me down the sidewalk, determined to have his after-dinner walk. A young man, a teenager, stepped in front of me. "Hey," he said. He held up his hand for me to stop. Dagwood didn't want to. He kept going, but the boy put his hand in my chest and pushed. "Whoa," he said. His voice, in spite of what it was saying, was soft and polite. He had on a fresh white polo shirt. Dagwood's leash cut into the soft flesh below my elbow.

A girl stepped into the glare of the headlights and stood next to her boyfriend with her hands on her hips. I could see that she was wearing a mohair sweater. Its soft fuzzy shape was haloed by the slowly passing cars. They looked like nice, well-dressed junior yuppies. "Give me your purse," the girl said. "I need it."

I had the strangest feeling the two kids had been watching the same news reports as I had, as Nina and Mr. Antonio had, that they had gotten this whole idea from TV. *Hey*, I imagined one of them saying, *let's go loot*.

"I'm broke," I said. "Really."

"Don't give me that," the boy said. He grabbed the strap of my purse and pulled it toward him. Daggie did not come to my defense. He was still straining forward on his leash. I dropped the bag with the Gainesburgers and held onto my purse with both hands, all the while thinking *this is crazy*. I had given Mr. Antonio all the cash I had and I was probably the only person in America without a credit card, but still I hung on. There were my keys on my key ring. My address book. My mother, trying to organize my life, had given me both. The boy pulled, and I pulled. There was my Wisconsin driver's license, which I hadn't bothered to replace since I didn't own a car. I imagined having to go to the California Department of Motor Vehicles and answer all those multiple choice questions. What did a yellow sign with a wavy line down the middle mean? The strap broke.

The boy flew backward and landed on one shoulder, his head hitting the sidewalk with a thud. I fell hard against the hood of a parked car behind me. *Ooof.* I dropped my purse and heard the keys clatter in the gutter. Dagwood's leash slipped from my wrist and, with a bark, he was off and running.

"Jesus," the girl said.

"My dog!" I said. Daggy cut from the sidewalk into the now briskly moving traffic. "Don't hit my dog!" I jumped over the boy and ran after Dagwood.

"Oh, I can't watch," I heard the girl saying. "He's gonna get squashed."

I ran into the road. Horns honked. Lights flashed. Suddenly it was years ago, my mother and my father and Mark and I were taking Dagwood to the vet to be boarded during what would turn out to be our last family vacation. But Dagwood had other ideas. He'd leapt from the car and had run straight onto the Dixie Highway. Mark ran after him and I ran after Mark, while our mother and father stood screaming, screaming by the side of the road.

Now a huge black shape—a truck barreling through the damaged city—slammed on its brakes, barely missing Dagwood. Its horn blared.

Then it had been a beige station wagon that almost hit Dagwood and barely missed Mark. Both Dagwood and Mark had gone suddenly stiff, as if they were already dead. Although I was not with her when it happened, this was how I imagined my mother's death. Her heart attack appearing as suddenly as that station wagon, her body stiffening. I couldn't lose Daggie.

I dodged another car and caught the words "crazy bitch," but I did not stop. I saw Dagwood reach the sidewalk, and a few seconds later I was there too. I could see now he was heading for Golden Gate Park. How could an old dog run so fast? I chased him down the sidewalk, but he made it to the park and disappeared into the black bushes. I followed him, my shoes slipping on the damp grass. Inside the park it was too dark to see. I was Alice down the rabbit hole. I ran blind, my hands in front of me. Up ahead I could hear Dagwood barking. I tried to run faster, but my feet tangled in something and I fell.

"Hey!"

I had tripped over a couple on a blanket. "Sorry," I said, picking myself up. I limped forward. "Daggie?" I called. I had no idea which direction he'd gone. "Daaagwoood!" I passed other people on blankets, as if this was the 4th of July and they were waiting for fireworks. I guessed they felt safer outside with no tons of concrete over their heads waiting to come down. I had a dim memory of pictures from the 1906 quake—people standing next to campfires in this or some other park.

I almost tripped again, this time over a tent, the low domed kind that backpackers carried. Several of them seemed to be pitched in a row, and in front of them a party was going on. I heard a champagne cork pop, and a dog that was not Dagwood ran past me chasing a glow-in-the-dark Frisbee. "Daggie Dog!" I called. Someone near the tents laughed. "Daggie!" I kept going.

"Are you looking for a dog, miss?" A flashlight clicked on, and I saw a man sitting on a camp stool. He looked about Mark's age and was dressed in a neat white shirt, tie, and suit jacket, like he had just left the office. "This dog?" He turned the flashlight. The beam caught the front of a large old-fashioned canvas tent, and I saw Dagwood stretched out inside it between a boy and a girl, both wearing pajamas. They were petting Dagwood. Dagwood saw me, and his tail thumped the ground, but he did not get up.

"He came right to the kids." It was a woman's voice. I turned. The man swung the beam of the flashlight, and I saw the woman sitting on a camp stool not far from the man I assumed was her husband. Her hair was arranged in neat curls, her legs demurely crossed at the ankles. The boy and girl, too, must be hers.

"Have a seat," the husband said, patting an empty camp stool between his and his wife's.

"Rest," his wife said. I sat. My legs were shaking they were so tired. My breasts felt raw where they had rubbed against the black lace front of my stolen bra. I sat on the stool. Behind her I could hear the girl whispering to Dagwood.

"You're my sweetest puppy poo, aren't you?" Hadn't I called Dagwood that?

The husband struck a match. I watched as he leaned down and used it to light a small camp stove. The boy came forward holding something long and sharp in his hand. A stick. "All set," his father said. He handed him a marshmallow. Just like this was a regular camp out, a family vacation. In the distance I heard a radio tuned not to news this time but to music. "If you're going to San Francisco, be sure to wear some flowers in your hair." Was some station out there in the dark really playing that song? Or had someone taken the time during the earthquake to make sure he had this very tape? "You're going to meet some loving people there."

Suddenly I felt dizzy, more unbalanced than when the ground had actually been shaking. "What are we doing here?" I said.

"Didn't you see the news?" the husband asked. He pointed to one corner of the night, and I noticed for the first time how bright the sky was there. Something was on fire. "The Marina," he said. "Maybe our house." I stared at the red horizon. It was impossible to tell whether it was a single house burning or a whole city block, a whole city.

I stood, turning slowly until I had made a complete circle. Except for the Marina fire, the skyline was dark. There were none of the little squares of light that my eyes had been trained to recognize as windows, to arrange in rows to form buildings. We could have been in the desert or in the middle of a stretch of Wisconsin dairyland. The city could already be gone. Out of the corner of my eyes I saw a flame catch and flare up blue. The boy's marshmallow was on fire.

"Not like that, Danny," the wife said, taking the stick with the smoldering marshmallow away from her son. "Here, watch me." She scraped the black goo off the stick, took a fresh fluffy white marshmallow from the bag, and poked it on the end. "Like this, nice and slow." The wife held the marshmallow close to the flame, but not too close, rotating the stick until the marshmallow began to toast, to turn a rich gold. By the light from the stove I could see the woman's fingernails were red—red like my mother's used to be. I remembered my mother's hands on the steering wheel of her Buick, driving Mark and me to swimming lessons, to Scouts. My mother's hands covering her face on the day the station wagon barely missed first her dog, then her son.

I breathed in the warm smell of caramelizing sugar. After Mark and I carried Daggie alive off that highway, Mother and Father had hugged us, hugged each other. We had gone down on our knees in a tangle of hugging there by the side of the road. I half-closed my eyes, trying to remember how good that felt.

Years later when Dagwood was long dead and maybe my brother Mark too, would I remember this night clearly but incorrectly as a camping trip from our childhood? Our dad lighting the camp stove. Our mom handing out soft, pillowy, 100 percent American marshmallows. And Daggie guarding us all.

"There," the woman-who-was-not-my-mother said, pulling the marshmallow unburned from the flame. "Perfect." She popped the toasted marshmallow in her son's open mouth. "Now," she said, threading another marshmallow on the stick. "Who wants the next one?"

Honors

"**D**ad's dead." My brother Mark broke this news to me on the phone, though at the time we were both living in San Francisco and his apartment was only a few blocks from mine. I glanced at the clock. 6:32. For one wild moment I imagined he had heard about Dad's death on the evening news: "Walter Stratton, missing father of Alice and Mark Stratton, died today in a fiery plane crash."

"How did you find out?" I asked. We hadn't seen our father for fifteen years, since I was thirteen and Mark was sixteen. He'd sent child support checks until we each had turned twenty-one, but nothing else—not a birthday card or a graduation present, nothing. The checks came from a law firm in D.C. I don't think even our mother had any idea where he'd gone. If she had, she'd taken the secret with her to the grave when she died the year before.

"The VA called," Mark said. "Apparently he was admitted to the VA hospital in Orlando with congestive heart failure. He listed me as his next of kin."

I thought about this. He had been in Florida, our home state, in Orlando where I'd spent a long hot summer working at Disney World. He even had Mark's unlisted home phone number, but still he hadn't called, hadn't sent any kind of word. Then again, what would he have said? I imagined a postcard from Orlando: "Hi kids, I'm dying. Wish you were here."

"Okay," I said. "I believe you. He's dead. Now what?" I think I meant to say, "So what?" but when it came down to it, I wasn't cold and hardhearted. I felt like crying.

"There's more," he said, "but you sound upset. I'd better come over."

I nodded, not realizing what little good that did to Mark on the other end of the telephone, and hung up. Now I *was* crying. When we were little, my father was the one who bathed us at night, read us *The Cat in the Hat* and *Horton Hears a Who*, and who'd made his sweet, sad stab at reading me *Alice in Wonderland*. He was the one who took us to all the sappy middle-period Disney films that were what kids our age went to see. My German-born mother didn't like going to the movies, not even the cartoons. She always felt the plots and motivations of the characters were beyond her, a little too American for her to understand. Maybe that's why she was so surprised when my father left. But then, what did that say about me? When my father announced he was leaving my mother I was stunned, sacked, and flattened.

The night before my father left he sat on the edge of my bed and told me how sorry he was that he had to leave. "I have my honor," he said. "I've never been a quitter. But I just can't stay here anymore." I felt the weight of his decision, and when he cried that night I did too, and I cried for him, not me. I had no idea why he was leaving—all right, that's a lie, but neither one of us talked about how my mother drank herself to sleep after breakfast most days, how her days and nights had become an inseparable sticky blur. I wept for him because I thought he was leaving her, not Mark and me. I didn't know his children were part of what he was planning to quit, cold turkey, the very next morning. When I did realize it I felt like Lewis Carroll's little oysters who walk down the beach with the Carpenter and the Walrus only to realize they are about to be eaten for supper. "After kindness, that would be a dismal thing to do!" It turned out neither the Walrus, nor the Carpenter, nor my father was much for listening.

When Mark rang the doorbell I was in the bathroom, blowing my nose on a wad of toilet paper. As a grad student I was too broke to buy luxuries like Kleenex, and my roommate Nina was one of those calm beauties whose nose never ran. I let him in. "Sit down," he said. He sat opposite me at the kitchen table. "Here's the kicker," he learned forward. "We're not the only next of kin. We've got a sister."

"An older sister?" My father had always been vague about what he had been doing with his life, other than his career in the Army, before he met our mother.

"Younger," Mark said. "She's twelve. Her name is Evelina. She lives in Fairfax, Virginia, just outside D.C. with her mother. Apparently Dad got divorced again last year."

"What kind of name is Evelina? Spanish?" I imagined my father returning to Europe, deciding to search for a bride in a warmer place than Germany.

"I think she's Filipino."

The Philippines, that was definitely warmer.

"What was he doing in the Philippines?"

Mark shook his head. "Subcontractor, maybe." Lots of retired military did that: sold their skills back to the Department of Defense that had trained them, adding more salary to their army pensions. In that world, "subcontractor" covered everything from the people who ran the PX or who taught in the post school to the spooks who worked for the CIA and did God only knows what. I couldn't imagine my father doing anything violent or secretive. Then again, I hadn't imagined him with another family, living a new, maybe newly unhappy, domestic life half a world away.

I counted on my fingers. If Evelina was twelve she had been born just three years after my father left us. I thought about that. Was three years an appropriate amount of time to mourn the loss of one family before starting another? Or was the short amount of time some kind of odd sign that he loved us and missed us — or at least missed having a family? I did a bit more math. Dad had been forty-seven when she was born. I wondered how old her mother was. I wondered if this wife went to movies. I wondered if she drank.

"So what are we supposed to do?"

"Ah," Mark said. "Actually we are supposed catch a red-eye tonight to Orlando to pack up Dad's things. Then tomorrow, Wednesday, we're supposed to go to the funeral home and pick up his ashes—he asked to be cremated—then fly with them to Washington. He's scheduled for a funeral with full military honors at Arlington National Cemetery at two on Thursday, and they wouldn't schedule him without my assuring them we'd bring the ashes personally."

"We?"

"Well," Mark was almost smiling now, and I wondered if he were pulling my leg that Dad wasn't dead but was about to walk in the room, miraculously resurrected, and hug us both as we hadn't been hugged since the night he left, "don't you want to meet your sister?" And then I got it. Mark *was* smiling. He was proud of Evelina, proud of being a big brother to one more little sister. Evelina was, though she didn't know it yet, a lucky girl.

I shrugged. "I guess you're already packed."

Mark snorted. Since George and our old family dog Dagwood had both died within days of each other right after Christmas, Mark had perfected the art of traveling light. No sick lover to nurse, no dog to feed. He kept an overnight case packed and in the trunk of his car for the trips he took to give poetry readings and workshops and to get away from his empty apartment. His good dark suit was at the cleaners, he said.

34

We could stop for it on the way to the airport. "And you?" he asked.

"I've got the black crepe I wore to Mom's funeral," I said. "Give me ten minutes. And no sneering at the way I pack." Mark folded his clothes like a high-end store clerk. I rolled, then stuffed.

Mark waited in the kitchen while I dug under my bed for my suitcase. When Mom died, her funeral in Madison had been attended by exactly six people: the chaplain of the hospital, Mark, George, me, my friend Bibi, and Anders, my boyfriend back in Wisconsin. My mother had died while visiting me in Wisconsin. So in that sense I had left both my mother and Anders behind in Wisconsin when I'd moved to San Francisco earlier in the year. My mother's whole service lasted ten minutes, so I hadn't needed to have the black crepe dry cleaned. Anders, good Wisconsin boy, former devout Lutheran, had been the only one who wept. George had fainted, but that was because even then he was dying. George, in his will, had forbidden black at his funeral. God bless him. We'd all shown up in Buddhist white or shades of sad, light blue.

Besides the dress, I packed a toothbrush, a pair of black pantyhose (also from my mother's funeral), and a pair of black pumps I'd had since high school which made their last appearance that congested winter day in Wisconsin. I hated to think I was living the kind of life where I was ready at a moment's notice for a funeral, but the truth was, in those days I *was* living that kind of life.

I was packed in six minutes, then spent four more digging in the bottom of my desk drawer for the last picture I had of my father. It was a snapshot taken on a hot spring day at Jacksonville Beach. He was wearing his old baggy plaid bathing suit. Mark had taken the picture of him posed with a large inflatable raft shaped like a shark, as if he were an extra in one of the *Jaws* movies. He was tall and slightly balding, with a strong arched nose and soft, sometimes blue sometimes gray eyes. A man with changeable eyes. Had that been a sign? Maybe, but mostly he was just a good-looking, forty-something guy. He looked a bit like Roy Scheider, the sheriff in that first serious *Jaws*, who saves the town and its innocent, succulent swimmers from the fearsome appetite of the rogue great white. In this photo, he did not look like someone who would die of congestive heart failure at the young age of fifty-nine in the same year the president of the United States turned seventy-nine. He did not look like a man who would die alone in a VA hospital. A man who would be carried to his funeral a mere fifteen years after this Kodak moment, so much dust in a box.

But then he didn't look like a man who would leave behind the people who loved him, his wife and his children, then another wife and child, as if leaving—for this man who never smoked or drank or even drank coffee—was something weirdly addictive, like bulimia, a purging of all that sustained human life.

What he did look like was Mark, who shared Dad's thin, arched nose, though Mark's eyes stayed a steady pool-water blue without even the slightest suggestive shading of gray. I thought of Anders, who I had been living with during grad school back in Wisconsin. His eyes were blue. Did they change colors? I couldn't seem to remember.

I asked Mark, already impatiently tapping his fingers on the kitchen table's faded linoleum, for a three-minute extension on my packing time, and I called Anders in Wisconsin where, even in April, there was probably still snow on the ground. Officially, Anders was waiting for me to finish my dissertation and come back to Wisconsin. We talked nearly every day, but so far I had stayed in San Francisco, unable either to finish my last chapter or decide on a course for my life.

Anders's answering machine clicked on, and I started to leave a message, but it wasn't until I said the words, "My father died" that I realized I was now officially an orphan. I felt like one even if I was twenty-seven. I felt tears burning in my sinuses, somewhere behind my eyes. I waited, hoping Anders was there, that he would hear me and pick up. He would be upset for me, would make it seem okay to feel this pressing, ordinary grief.

Mark touched my arm. "You can try again from Florida."

We flew out of San Francisco at ten o'clock, sitting side by side in the rattling body of a United 727. We closed our eyes and pretended to be on our way to something harmless, like a dentists' convention. At some point during the night, after the movie was over, I realized Mark was holding my hand. Or was I holding his? We held onto each other through the long night over America like Hansel and Gretel dropped in the forest by their father, a man who no longer had the will to care for them.

I looked over at Mark, who was neatly dressed as always. He looked like a young lawyer. An accountant. Not a poet, whatever a poet was supposed to look like—Allen Ginsberg? Mark wrote difficult poems where words cascaded down the page in a way that always excited my imagination but rarely gave me a hint as to what the poem was about. Since George had died, though, he'd started writing poems that talked more directly about his life, the losses in it, and the AIDS deaths emptying whole neighborhoods in San Francisco. Still, I found it hard to believe that underneath the brother I knew, somewhere deep inside, was a poet.

In high school Mark had barely passed his English classes, preferring the biology lab with its meaty air of pigs in formaldehyde. I was the one who wrote for the school newspaper, who'd grown up reading every book I could get my hands on, imagining some day I'd write great fat novels like Dickens or Tolstoy did. Then somewhere along the line I fell out of love with fiction. It never told the real story.

Mark had gone off to college and written home the first semester to tell Mom and me that A) he was gay, and B) he was

37

switching his major from biochemistry to Spanish literature. He published his first book when he was only twenty-four. Becoming a poet was the shocker in all this, not his being gay; I knew he had already broken the heart of Mr. Hubbard, his high school biology teacher. At thirty-one Mark was on his way to becoming a respected senior poet, someone younger poets either imitated or rebelled against. Or so George had told me when he was still alive. My PhD work on the best ways to teach writing to struggling, unhappy undergraduates was a world removed from poetry.

Mark squeezed my hand. "You should write about this," he said to me, halfway reading my mind, the way siblings sometimes do. The cabin was dark now.

"Me?" I shook my head. "You should."

"I will," he said, "but you should too." He pointed at the small, rounded airplane window. "We look, but we don't see the same things." He closed his eyes. Outside, the darkness was infinite. There was no moon, no stars, no blinking lights from passing planes. It felt as if we had always been in this place. I imagined the plane as a kind of womb, a place where Mark and I existed without bothering to be born, without having a mother or father who would love us, not love us, die young. I looked out the window and saw nothing. What did Mark see?

He answered my question without opening his eyes. "That," he said, nodding toward the blank black outside, "is our father now."

At dawn we landed in Orlando, and though it was painfully early, the first thing we saw was Mickey Mouse. He was waiting, ears alert as radar dishes, to shake hands with deplaning passengers, most bound for Disney World. Mark shook Mickey's white-gloved paw with a great show of solemnity. "How do you do," he said, and introduced me. "Perhaps you know my sister, Alice?" Mickey bowed from the waist. I couldn't help wondering if the person inside was someone I knew from my old

Disney days, as unlikely as that seemed. Even when Mark said good-bye to Mickey by gallantly kissing his hand, Mickey did not break the iron Disney rule: No talking while in character.

When I'd worked summers at Disney, the characters were the park's true stars. All the other employees recognized them when they saw them, even out of costume, in the tunnels under the park or eating in the underground employee cafeteria. Some roles—Mickey and Minnie Mouse, Donald Duck—required very short actors, nearly dwarfs. The airport Mickey looked tall to me. No doubt he was. The standards for height eased if you were out of the park. Inside, if you were even half an inch too tall you would spend your whole professional life dancing and mugging as, say, Jocko, one of the mice who pulled Cinderella's carriage, without ever getting promoted to Mickey.

"Did I ever tell you about the time Mickey Mouse stood up Minnie to go to an X-rated movie with Cinderella?" I asked Mark. This was a true story, but he looked at me like I had lost my mind.

"Excuse her," he said to Mickey. "She's been under some strain. Come on," he said to me. He led me, luggage in hand, to the rental car desk.

We drove through the hot Florida sun into the sprawl that was Orlando. My father, who'd been stationed in Orlando in some distant part of his past before us, before my mother, certainly before we moved to Jacksonville, had once told me that in the old days you could stand in downtown Orlando and see the edge of town where the orange groves took over. Now it was one relentless round of McDonald's followed by Shoney's followed by K-Mart followed by another McDonald's. Still, it was Florida. The sky was a damp, deep blue, and the air was soft with humidity. I could feel my skin, always chapped and dry in California and Wisconsin, soaking in the moisture. My hair was getting positively curly. My body, if not my mind, said, *We're home.*

But this was Orlando, not Jacksonville, and neither Mark nor I really knew where we were going. Mark, trying to drive and follow the directions the car rental people had given him, nearly rear-ended a school bus. I took the map from him. We wound our way carefully through the older parts of the city until we found the VA hospital, a yellow brick building mottled with the same mildew that turned Florida oranges black on the trees. It was set back on a swath of lawn kept green by the chattering arcs of a dozen Rain Birds. The water from one spinning sprinkler splattered the windshield of the car as we turned into the parking lot and pulled into a spot marked "Visitors Only!!! Register at Desk!!!"

Inside, we gave the woman on duty the rental car's tag number and were instructed to follow the blue line to the seventh floor. The floor was criss-crossed with lines of different colors—red, orange, green—leading to different clinics and wards. People snaked along the lines, heads down, headed for chemotherapy or x-ray or the psychiatric ward. Some wore hospital gowns. Others, either visitors or out-patients, wore civvies or an odd combination of civvies and camouflage jackets or army fatigues. The blue line led to General Ward 7A.

I don't know what I expected, maybe a box of belongings wrapped in brown paper and tied up with string handed to us by a white-coated orderly who said, "Sign here, please." But on Ward 7A a plump blond nurse wearing a "Be Happy" button led us down a hall and past a day room full of men playing solitaire, reading, or watching TV. Most of them looked more old than sick. A few more were scooting up and down the hall with walkers. A pair in wheelchairs were parked by a big window overlooking the parking lot. All in all Ward 7A looked a lot more like a nursing home than a modern civilian hospital where all but the sickest were released into the care of their families. Vets who ended up here, I suspected, had no families. Or, in my father's case, had two and none at the same time.

The nurse took us to a double room at the end of the hall. One side was vacant with a doubled-over mattress and an open, empty closet. The other side of the room looked as if my father had just left, as though he had been sent to x-ray and would be wheeled in to greet us any minute. There was a pile of paperback mystery novels on the bed stand. On the dresser, a bottle of the aftershave he'd always used—Bay Rum. Two pairs of metal-rimmed glasses. A box of Q-tips. A pair of nail clippers. No pictures, as far as I could see—not of us or Evelina. No army memorabilia either—group shots of this command or that, plaques made as farewell testimonials. As far as I could remember he had never been into that.

"How long had he been here?" I asked her.

"Not long," the nurse said. "Six, seven months."

Mark opened the closet. It was full of our father's clothes—white short-sleeve cotton shirts and rows of dark pants. There was a red seventies-style Samsonite suitcase on a rack overhead. His shoes, neatly polished, were lined up below.

"Oh, I almost forget," the nurse said, dipping a hand into her pocket. She held out a Ziploc baggie. "His valuables." I saw his watch, a silver Bulova—after all these years I recognized it from across the room. I also saw the heavy dull gold of his West Point class ring and two smaller circles nestled in the plastic beside it—his wedding rings. I took the bag. There was a slim black leather wallet. I flipped it open. My father stared out at me from a Virginia driver's license. Walter Stratton, 5'11", 165 lbs. He had the same pale blue-gray eyes, but the little hair he had left shone a silvery white. Other than his driver's license there was a Visa Gold, a medic-alert card listing his heart medications and blood type—O negative, same as mine—and two twenties. Not a lot for a wallet. No family pictures. Not even a library card.

"He was a nice man, your father," the nurse said. "Such a sense of humor. You couldn't get him to stop with the jokes."

She smiled, perhaps remembering one, and was still smiling when she left.

I sat down on the bare plastic mattress. Had I ever heard my father tell a joke? I had a dim memory of telling my very first joke. It had been during snack time at nursery school.

"What did one banana say to the other banana?"

"Nothing—bananas can't talk."

One kid had laughed so hard chocolate milk came out his nose. Had I made that up or had my father coached me? I slid his class ring out of the Ziploc and slipped it on my thumb.

"He had a terrible corny sense of humor," Mark said, taking the suitcase down from the closet. He opened it on the bed and began taking shirts off the hangers, folding and packing them with his usual care. "What do you call the place where you leave your dog?" He finished the shirts and started on the trousers.

"I have no idea," I said.

"Try," Mark said.

I shook my head. "I give up."

"A barking lot!" he said. He wrapped a VA towel around Dad's shoes and packed those too. Mark was making me dizzy, he was moving so fast. "What does a horse call the horse in the next stall?" He looked at Dad's stack of paperbacks, then swept them, too, into the suitcase. He didn't wait for me to guess this time. "*Neeeeiiiiighbor!*" He looked at me, daring me to laugh. I held up my thumb with Dad's ring stuck on it like little Jack Horner with his plum. "Shit," he said, sitting down next to me on the bed. "The whole thing was a joke, like his saying 'I love you' and 'You can count on me, Son.'"

"He said you could count on him?"

"No," Mark said. "He didn't. But we thought we could, didn't we?"

I thought about that. Dad took me to the movies, taught me to ride my bike. He'd run behind me, holding me up, shouting "Don't worry, don't worry, I won't let go!" while I pedaled like crazy. It wasn't until I reached the end of our long block that I realized he had let go a long time before. He was so far away, I could barely make out his face. Was that being there for me? Yes. No. Still, I could ride a bicycle like a whiz, a skill that had served me well as a perpetually car-less student. "You know, Markie," a name I hadn't called him since I was three, "maybe we could just pretend Dad died the day he left. You know, one day our father wandered off and got frozen in some glacier, and they just now found his body. Can't we just go with that?"

Mark didn't answer. Instead he took the Ziploc from my hand. He unfastened his Rolex and stuck it in his pocket, then strapped Dad's Bulova to his wrist. "Motion winds it," he said. "There are little weights or counterweights or something inside. I remember Dad saying it kept perfect time." He looked down at the silver and white face. "I don't think Bulova even makes them anymore."

I looked at the empty closet. "We should pack up the stuff in the dresser."

Mark nodded but did not get up. He raised his arm over his head, put it back down, then held Dad's watch to his ear. "It's ticking," he said.

I got up and opened the top dresser drawer. Neatly rolled black socks. Folded white boxer shorts. Why were we packing this stuff? Who would want my father's used underwear? His ex-wife? His twelve-year-old daughter? I imagined driving by a Goodwill store, setting the Samsonite on a broken couch by an overflowing donation box. I sighed and scooped up the socks. Underneath were three white business-size envelopes, neatly laid out side by side. One was addressed, "To Whom It May Concern." Another, "Mark Stratton: To Be Opened in the Event of My Death." A third marked simply, "Alice: Open This." There was no fourth marked "Evelina." Did she really exist?

"Open This." Just like in *Alice in Wonderland*, I thought. Bottles and cakes labeled "Drink Me" and "Eat Me." What would

43

happen when I opened my envelope? I had a sudden vision of a potion that would turn me thirteen again, bring my father back, first from the missing, then from the dead. I opened the one marked "To Whom It May Concern" first.

Inside was the name and address of the lawyer in Virginia who had my father's will, a list of bank accounts, two small life-insurance policies. At the bottom of the column of numbers he had neatly totaled up his life: $66,000. "All assets to be divided between my three children, Mark, Alice, and Evelina." So Evelina did exist. I did the math. $22,000 dollars apiece.

Not nothing, but not much. About two thousand dollars for every year he hadn't called or written or suddenly appeared at my door. Enough to pay off my student loans. Maybe enough, if invested, to send Evelina to college. It was money Mark didn't really need. George had left him the building they lived in. He had a good job. "Mark," I said, and handed him his envelope. Then I picked up the envelope with my name on it in my father's scratchy old-fashioned handwriting, all sharp ups and downs, like the bad electrocardiograms that must be on file in his VA medical records.

The paper was bright white. Clearly the envelope hadn't been kicking around for fifteen years, dresser to dresser, since the day Dad left. It looked as though it had been written yesterday, or the day before yesterday, when Dad was alive in this room. I opened the letter.

"Alice," he had written. "My curiouser and curiouser daughter." Wrong Alice, I thought, and almost stopped reading. "I hope your love of books has taken you somewhere good. Maybe you are a librarian, like you always wanted to be." When had I ever wanted to be a librarian? For a while in grade school I volunteered in the base library, but that was just to get around the librarian—mean old crow—who would never let me check out more than three books at time. Working there I'd signed dozens out to myself under fictitious names like "Marvin Gardens." "Maybe you are a teacher, helping chil-

44

dren learn to love books like you do." I sighed. I wasn't sure I was that kind of teacher, and that made me sad. "Whatever it is you are doing, I wish you well. You were always my special girl. Love, your father."

His *special girl?* What did that make Evelina? I looked over at Mark. As I watched, he folded his letter, put it back in the envelope and into his pocket. What had his said? "I hope you went into the army? Became a basketball star? A senator?" Surely, he hadn't wished Mark the life of a librarian. Had he called him his *special boy?*

Mark shook his head. "What did it say?" I asked.

"Nothing," he said. "Take care of your mother." I could see he wasn't going to tell me. I figured he would eventually, but he never did. Years later, when I finally asked, he denied Dad had left us letters. He looked at me like I was making it up.

Mark began methodically clearing the lower drawers — pajamas, bathrobe, a plaid swimsuit that was a ringer for the one Dad wore in the picture I had of him in my suitcase. "Did you know that when we didn't hear from him," Mark asked, "I thought it was because of me?"

"Because of you?" I said. "Oh, Mark. It was because of Mom, how bad she was then. Or," I struggled to put words to what we never talked about. "Or if not because of her, it was because of Dad. The kind of person he was, he . . ."

"No, no," he said. He'd stopped packing and now was throwing things away. Into the metal garbage can went the Q-tips, the nail clippers. *Bam, bam.* "I'm not talking about why he *left.* I'm talking about why he didn't visit or call or write or even have some CIA friend check up on us. *He knew.*" He waved a hand at the mirror, at his own reflection, as if he were pointing out a slim, handsome gay man as the accused in a courtroom. "Even before he left, he knew. And he wanted to be able to go to his grave saying he *didn't.*" He slam-dunked Dad's aftershave into the trash, and the numbing scent of Bay Rum filled the small green room.

"Oh," I said. I had had no idea. "At least that makes a better story than mine." Mark stared at me.

"Yours?"

"I used to think he left because I grew up and stopped being the right kind of Alice," I said, and dipped into a curtsey worthy of a visit to the Red Queen. Mark halfway laughed. I really wasn't joking, but I wanted us to stop. Stop blaming ourselves for our father. He was dead. We were alive. Enough with the self-pity. I was tempted to rub together my forefinger and thumb and say, like we had in high school, "See this? It's the world's tiniest violin and it's playing just for us."

"You put your dogs in a *barking* lot," Mark said, and this time he really laughed. He bent double, he was laughing so hard. "*Neeeeiiiiighbor!*" he said. It was all sad. It was all funny. I was laughing too.

We packed Dad's glasses, his toothbrush. Retrieved the nail clippers and packed those too. Now, at the end of our task, it all seemed so little. I'd have rescued the Q-tips, too, except they were soaked with Bay Rum.

Mark closed the suitcase. "Now there's only one thing missing," he said.

"What's that?" I asked.

"Dad."

The nurse knew where he was, of course. He was at the Bagg Brothers Funeral Home, already cremated, ready to go. She gave us the address.

It turned out to be a low rambling white ranch house that could have been a regular family home except for the suspiciously large garage and the "Bagg Brothers Funeral Home" sign on the front lawn. In the movies, funeral directors, morticians, undertakers—whatever it was the fashion to call them—always wore black and wrung their hands in unctuous displays of mock grief. Ed Bagg, the Bagg brother in charge, seemed unaware of that tradition. Or maybe a low-budget veteran's cremation just didn't merit that level of service. He greeted us at the front door in a yellow polo shirt and white Sansabelt slacks. He waved us into his office, and we all sat down. A half-eaten tuna sandwich sat on top of a stack of papers on his desk. "Ah, here it is—Walter M. Stratton," he said, removing a paper from under the sandwich. "The government pays three hundred dollars for a cremation. You need to sign here," he pointed at a line, and watched while we did as instructed, "and initial here." We initialed. Then he waved a hand at a shelf on the wall lined with what looked like flower vases and music boxes. "You can pick out any urn we have in stock, no special orders at that rate. No engraving. But you do get . . ." he slid open the credenza behind his desk and pulled out what appeared to be a red, white, and blue triangle shrink-wrapped in plastic, ". . . a flag. It's for the funeral. You'll need to give this to the guy in charge when you get to Arlington. Along with the ashes."

Mark stood up and began lifting one urn after another from the shelf. He was frowning. Something buzzed on Ed Bagg's desk and without even an "excuse me" he shoved himself up and out of his chair and left the room. I joined Mark in his urn hunt. We pondered a small wooden box, an urn made of sinister green faux marble. Finally we picked a simple silvery vase that looked rather like a rocket ship. We tried not to look too closely at the thinness of its shiny finish.

A minute later Ed Bagg reappeared. "We want this one," I said, holding it up.

"Good choice," he said. He opened the credenza and after rooting around for a moment, handed Mark a small cardboard box. "Here you go." At first I thought the box held another silver urn, that the one in my hand was just a display sample, but the box was too small to hold an urn.

Mark turned the box over in his hands. My father's name was printed across one side in black magic marker. It took us both a moment to realize that the box held my father's ashes. "Oh, no," said Mark, handing the box back to a reluctant Ed

Bagg, taking the urn from me and pushing that into his other hand. "That's your job. You do it. We'll wait here."

Ed Bagg sighed heavily and left the room once again. "What if he doesn't do it?" I asked Mark.

"What?"

"What if he doesn't put Dad in the urn? How would we ever know?"

Ed Bagg reappeared, urn in hand. Either he had heard what I said or he knew enough about the relatives of the recently dead to guess. He popped the top off the urn and held it out for us to see. What was inside looked like the charcoal left in the bottom of a grill after a good backyard cookout—some fine ash, a few larger chunks. Bone? I couldn't help wondering. He corked the urn.

"Here you go," he said again. This time Mark carried our father in his new silver home out of the Bagg Funeral Home into the hot noon sun, and I sat with him in my lap as we wound our way back toward the airport. Our flight was at three.

"I hate to admit it," Mark said. "But I thought about eating Ed Bagg's sandwich while he was gone. I am starving."

We turned right by a large shopping center, and suddenly I knew where we were. "Turn in here," I said to Mark, and he did, the tires of our rental car squealing. He saw the sign at the same time I did. "Wolfie's."

On the one or two times a year that some school or business trip brought our family to Orlando, our father had always taken us to Wolfie's, a good old-fashioned, New-York-by-way-of-Miami Jewish delicatessen. Mark parked the rental car. After some discussion we locked Dad in the trunk, though I felt bad about it. Inside, Wolfie's hadn't changed at all. Dishes of kraut and kosher pickles sat on each table. The waiter brought a dish of chopped chicken livers and a basket of crackers as soon as we sat down. There were tall, tan cheesecakes on display in a revolving case by the cashier's desk. My father had loved this food. He ate matzo balls and knishes like he had been born to it, though he'd been raised by Scotch Calvinist parents in Idaho where most of his neighbors were Mormons.

Mark and I each had a Reuben and a slice of cherry cheesecake, and we felt dizzy with the sheer amount of saturated fat our bodies had taken in. Then I went in search of the ladies' room and a pay phone. I wanted to call Anders. I pumped the phone full of quarters and dialed Wisconsin. I got his machine again. "I'm in Orlando," I said. "We have Dad's ashes and we're flying with them to D.C. I . . ." I stopped, not knowing what else to say. I drummed my fingers in the shelf below the phone, and my dad's West Point class ring, still on my thumb, made a loud thud. I slipped it off my finger. The inside of the ring was worn smooth. On the outside an eagle stood rampant on either side of a garnet the size of a Chihuahua's eye. Like the watch, my father had worn this ring every single day. The gold felt heavy in my hand and oddly warm, like a small beating heart. "I miss him, Anders." I said to the spinning tape in Anders's distant apartment. "I've always missed him and now I am going to miss him forever. Damn," I said, putting the ring back on my finger. My father had regularly said "goddamn it to hell" when something got on his nerves, but I didn't want to wish him there. "Darn, shit. I'll talk to you soon."

When I came out, Mark was paying our bill. I heard him ask the cashier for one of the double-handled Wolfie's shopping bags they used for boxed cheesecakes to go. She frowned, like she had seen a lot of chiseling in her day, like she suspected us of leaving with our pockets full of free kosher dills. Mark gave her his best white-toothed smile, and she relented and handed him a bag.

"We need something to carry Dad in," he said, holding the bag up for me to see. "And he did love Wolfie's."

"Yes," I said, "yes, he did." As I walked to the car, my stomach round with kosher food, my thumb heavy with Dad's West Point ring, I felt closer to my father than I had in years. The truth was I was probably never going to know more about my father than that he wore his class ring on his right middle finger and loved cheesecake. I'd just have to let it go at that.

After Wolfie's, things got difficult, perversely difficult, as if we were in a play and the author, playing God, was determined to keep us on this tropical island called Orlando.

We turned in our rental car at the airport. Mark had arranged for tickets to D.C. They were supposed to be waiting for us at the Delta ticket counter. There weren't any tickets nor any record of tickets. When we arrived at dawn the airport had been nearly empty. Now it was awash in tourists. All the flights north—to D.C., Baltimore, even Philadelphia—were booked and overbooked.

It was three-thirty Wednesday afternoon. The funeral was tomorrow, Thursday, at two. Not just any funeral, Mark explained in vain to the ticket agent. A funeral at the Arlington National Cemetery with full military honors. The Old Guard from Fort Myers would be there. The Army band would be there. Unless she got us on a plane, we would not. Unless we got there, neither would Dad. She was unmoved by the thought of our father missing his own funeral.

Mark threw up his hands and turned from the ticket counter. "We'll drive," he said to me. He was looking grim. There was a smudge on one cheek which I realized with a shock must be our father's ashes. His tie was loose. I had the suitcases. Mark had Dad in the Wolfie's bag.

"Drive?" I said. "Drive to D.C.?"

Mark looked at his watch. "We have twenty-two hours," he said. "And counting. It's probably only a nineteen- or twenty-hour drive. Plenty of time, but we have to get our rental car back."

We swam through the pale, swirling crowds of newly arrived vacationers, trying to reach the Avis desk. Mark made it first, and even from fifty feet away I could see him gesturing at the woman behind the counter. She was shaking her head. Obviously one of the paleskins had beat us to our car. Then I saw Mark open the shopping bag. Saw him set Dad on the counter with a resounding thud. By that time I had reached Mark's side. "Okay, okay," the agent was shaking her head. "I'll just pretend you never brought it back. But I don't have any idea what they'll charge you when you turn it in in D.C." She handed Mark the keys.

"God bless you," he said. She made a shooing gesture with both hands, brushing both our good wishes and our peculiar urgencies out of her life.

We put the luggage in the trunk, Dad in the back seat. We stopped at a 7-Eleven for gas, a map of the United States, and two king-size Cokes, and then we hit the road north with Mark at the wheel.

"We'll switch drivers every two hours." Mark said. "George taught me that." Then we were silent for a long time, thinking about our dead.

We left Orlando just after five. Around eight we passed the "Welcome to Georgia" sign. It was just getting dark, and the sky over Georgia was a luminous purple. Just after the welcome sign the pavement changed color—from a darker to a lighter gray. Other than that it was hard to say Georgia looked much different from Florida, but still it felt like we were getting somewhere, that we might actually get to D.C. in time. I heard a pop inside my ears, as if we were climbing, though the road north from Valdosta was just as flat as Florida had been. I shook my head and I swear I heard something rattle, like something broken loose. This was the second night we'd spent sitting up. I kept driving.

Around nine, when it was good and dark, we got off the interstate at what, according to the signs, was Sunsweet, Georgia, for sandwiches at a barbecue restaurant. It was the end of my first driving shift, and when I turned off the car in the parking lot I just sat there, too tired to move. It surprised me

51

how dog-beaten-with-a-bone tired I felt. Sure, I hadn't slept much on the plane, but I'd stayed up longer than that before, cramming for exams or finishing papers. I was as tired as if I'd spent the previous four hours pushing the car with my brother and my father in it.

Mark looked trashed too. His tie was off, his suit jacket wrinkled from being used as a pillow. He slipped it on, reached into the pocket. "Here," he said, handing me a small prescription bottle. "We should probably both take a couple." I read the name on the bottle—George's. It was a prescription for Benzedrine.

"They're what truck drivers use," Mark said. "They weren't really for George. I asked his doctor for them at the end. I wanted to be awake, I wanted to be there when he died, not sacked out on the couch in the family lounge." I looked at the bottle of amphetamines doubtfully. Even coffee made me wired.

Mark took the bottle back, popped the childproof lid and swallowed two pills. I took one and held in it the palm of my hand. It was small and looked harmless enough. I swallowed it dry. I waited a minute, but when I didn't feel any different—no rush of adrenaline, no potentially fatal pounding of my heart—I took a second one. D.C. was still a good fifteen hours away. We got out of the car. I wondered for a moment about taking the Wolfie's bag in with us, but instead I locked Dad in the trunk again.

Inside the restaurant, Mark ordered us pork barbecue plates and big strong glasses of sweetened iced tea. When I was finished I got out the map. So far I'd been heading north mostly on instinct. We'd been on I-75, but now I could see that had been a mistake. It headed too far west toward Atlanta. We needed to cut over and get on Interstate 95 for a clean run up the coast—Georgia to South Carolina to North Carolina to Virginia. I jotted down highlights: Savannah, Florence, Lumberton, Raleigh, Richmond. In Richmond we would stop and plot a way into D.C. and on to Arlington, which lay sprawled on the Potomac across from the Lincoln Memorial.

While I made notes, Mark chatted up an old woman in the booth beside us. Mark waved at the plates of red meat and the bright red-white-and-blue booths. "Very patriotic, isn't it?" he said. His suit, even in its wrinkled state, helped, otherwise the woman would probably have decided Mark was crazy or some kind of foreigner and not answered.

"Well, not any more American than where I come from."

"Where is that?" Mark asked.

"Windyville," the woman said. Iowa or Ohio, I didn't quite catch it.

Mark bit. "Is it windy there?" he asked. The old woman smiled as she sprang her trap.

"Not the weather so much," she said, "as the people."

I went to the women's room to wash the sauce off my hands and splash cold water on my face.

When I came out, Mark was outside, stretching by the side of the car. Suddenly I wanted to move. I knew it was mostly the speed, but it was also my own muscles, tired of doing nothing but sitting for hours on end. Beyond the car was a pile of loose dirt and gravel, and I ran for it, scrambled up with the rocks scraping at the sides of my shoes.

At the top I stood balanced for a moment, arms raised, the king of the hill. Then the gravel shifted under my feet and I started to slide. Mark was still standing beside the car, stretching, then bending down to touch his toes. I ran down the collapsing hill toward Mark, landed one palm on the hood of the rental car and one on the hood next to it as if the parked cars were parallel bars.

I swung my body up and forward, a parking lot Olympic gymnast. I hadn't suffered through P.E. for nothing. I threw my head back and saw the stars. They were up there, hanging above me in the sky, above the cars in the parking lot and on the Interstate, and I was grateful. I twisted myself around for a flying dismount, but one of my elbows gave out. My hand slipped off the hood and I landed on the asphalt, flat on my back. My head made a thud like a watermelon dropped from a height.

"Allie?" Mark was bending over me.

"Yes?" I said.

"You should be more careful," he said. "You could get hurt." He held out his hand, but I stayed on the ground, which was not so much spinning as vibrating underneath me. I wasn't sure, but I thought I might be sick. Amphetamines chased with pork barbecue and a handstand had probably been a mistake.

"Al?" Mark was bending over me, looking pale and concerned. He looked about as bad as I felt, and he hadn't landed on his head.

I let him help me up and brush me off. I seemed to be okay. I didn't hurt anywhere, but then, for a girl headed to her dad's funeral, all in all I was feeling surprisingly little.

Mark drove, then I drove. The signs told us we were moving—Georgia giving way to South Carolina, then North Carolina. But the night stayed night and the drive seemed to go on forever. Or, even stranger, to have been going on forever. At some point I said this to Mark, who was driving.

I could see him nod in the glare of a passing truck. "There's a physicist at Berkeley," he said, "who thinks time may not exist. He says all moments already exist, like frames on a film strip. We only think the pictures are moving, we only see time passing, because we've been taught that time exists. The way people used to see the sun revolve around the earth because they'd been taught that the earth was the center of the universe."

I thought then of all the moments in my life, in my father's life, like this—as frozen snapshots in some cosmic family album. He was always being born. He was always meeting my mother. Mark was forever being born. Me too. It was comforting to think of those moments existing out there somewhere. Maybe the mystics were right: we were all thoughts in the mind of a single God.

But *no time* also meant my father was always paused on his way out the door. And he was always dying, had always been dying, in the same green hospital room, all alone.

No time also meant that the Calvinists were right. Everything in life was predetermined. There was no free will. If this were true, my struggle over whether to marry Anders was silly. I either already had or never would. And when my father decided to leave us, his choice was meaningless. He had already left. Or if that was petty stuff, what about Hitler? Or Pol Pot? No choice for them either. The dead were always dead, singularly or in the millions. Though this meant they were also always alive. It made my head ache to think about it. I pressed my cheek to the window. Outside, the white lines of the highway seemed frozen.

"It also feels like we're not moving," I said to Mark. "Like nothing is moving."

"I wasn't going to tell you that part," Mark said. "There's another physicist in the same department who thinks space doesn't exist either."

"Then either we have already arrived or we will never get there," I said.

"That sounds about right," Mark said, then floored the rental car to pass one more damn eighteen-wheeler.

I turned up the radio, fighting to stay awake. Mark had it tuned to an oldies station. Grace Slick, oh she of *White Rabbit* (an altogether different take on being Alice), suddenly cut loose from the speakers singing "Don't you need somebody to love?" "Don't you *want* somebody to love? Don't you *need* somebody to love? Better find somebody to love. You better find somebody *right now*."

Anders, I thought, *I need Anders.*

We did make it to Arlington, with nearly thirty minutes to spare. We'd even had time to stop in Woodbridge for gas, a last round of amphetamines, and a quick respectability make-over. Mark shaved and put on a clean shirt, though his jacket still looked rock star wrinkled. I pulled my hair back, wrestled my numb legs into the black hose, and slipped into the black crepe. I had forgotten to pack any lipstick or blush, but you couldn't be too pale, I supposed, for your own father's funeral.

When I pulled into the "Funerals Only" parking space at Arlington National Cemetery, Mark bolted out of the car and ran up the stairs with the silver urn shining in one hand, the tight triangle of our nation's flag in the other. I trudged wearily after him. A woman in a blue blazer appeared and, after asking the name of my deceased, led me into a small lounge filled with green government-issue chairs and sofas. It was surprisingly full, and for one moment I thought I was at the wrong funeral. Then I saw Anders, goddamn dear Anders, and I knew the long dark road had led me to the right place.

He was standing with his back toward me, talking to an elderly woman, but I called his name. He turned and saw me and I all but leapt into his arms. This is what I had learned driving my father's body north: I wanted a family. A real honest-to-God family. With no disappearances or doubts. I wanted a husband and children who would cry at my funeral without feeling as if their tears required elaborate justifications, *ands* and *buts* and *what-ifs*. Anders hugged me hard. "I thought you weren't going to make it," he said. "I was frantic with worry."

Worry. Someone had worried I might not appear. I loved this man.

Mark reappeared. Anders shook his hand, just as he had at Mom's funeral. Then Anders introduced us to the other people in the room, standing or sitting on the vinyl-covered couches. One woman, wearing a large corsage that looked for all the world like a cockatoo, was a representative from the Department of Defense. A whole couch full of gray-haired, distinguished-looking men were my father's West Point classmates, here as living embodiments of the Academy's long gray line. Last of all Anders introduced us to three small, lovely women: Evelina Stratton, my sister, Dr. Carolina Reyes, my father's ex-wife, and Mrs. Aguilar, Evelina's grandmother. Evelina was beautiful. If Alice in Wonderland had had long dark hair instead of blond, she would have been a ringer for Evelina. Mark sat next to her, took her small, pink-nailed hand in his.

Dr. Reyes looked like a well-dressed psychiatrist and, it turned out, that's what she was. She had met my father in the Philippines, but they had married here, after she came to Walter Reed for a residency and stayed on to work with veterans. "It was difficult for him," she said, "once he retired, and I was still working such long hours." She shook her head, genuinely sad. "He spent a lot of time helping my mother. She doesn't speak much English, and it was hard on her, moving here." Her mother, Mrs. Aguilar, was wearing a long starched, white linen dress that I took, rightly or wrongly, for some kind of traditional Filipino mourning attire. She and Anders were the only ones who looked like they had been crying.

The woman in the blue blazer reappeared. Family members could march behind the caisson or ride in a limousine, whichever we preferred. Mark, tired of sitting, still buzzing, said he would walk. So did Dr. Reyes and the West Pointers. I was afraid my legs might buckle.

Anders said he would ride with me, with Evelina and her grandmother. I didn't know who to talk to—Anders, to tell him everything that had happened, or Evelina, sister I'd never seen. Anders shushed me. "Later," he said. "Now's the time to think about your dad."

What was left to think? My brain felt sore from thinking about the mystery that was my father. Instead, I emptied my mind and just moved ahead. It was only afterward, that night in bed at the nearest Holiday Inn with Anders, still speeding on Mark's pills, that I closed my eyes and talked to my father, pretending, like I had when I was a little girl, that Dad was God and He could hear me.

It was a splendid funeral, Dad, I began. You'd have been proud. A company of Old Guards from Fort Myers, all six feet tall, formed the Honor Guard for you, and there was a marching band, complete with tuba. Four gray horses pulled the flag-draped caisson that held your silver urn. Behind the caisson was a tall black horse with an empty saddle, riding boots upended in the stirrups. A mount for the fallen rider, for you, Dad, for you.

The woman soldier who was the limousine driver said the horse was Black Jack Pershing and told me your funeral was his last before being retired to Virginia. "Black Jack followed President John Kennedy to his grave," she said. Evelina translated that into Tagalog for Mrs. Aguilar, who nodded, impressed.

We rolled slowly through Arlington, to a measured drumbeat from the band. On the reviewing stand in front of the Veterans' Day Memorial a hundred or so tourists watched us, the last full honors funeral of the day. They were wearing shorts, sneakers, and Minoltas, but they stood as Black Jack passed, quiet and respectful. You would have been touched, Dad.

Your grave was on the flat land near the Potomac, not a site up on one of the green hills, but a nice site, close to a tulip tree. All of us, marchers and riders alike, sat in folding chairs facing a patch of Astroturf that covered your open grave. As soon as we sat down, Evelina's grandmother, the woman you helped with her shopping, began to cry softly. Evelina, your youngest daughter, leaned close to me and whispered in my ear, "He taught me to ride a bicycle." She was crying too.

The chaplain gave a short eulogy based on your military record. "After retiring with thirty years of service," he said, "Walter Stratton went on to serve as a military advisor in the Philippines." Mrs. Aguilar bent her head and sobbed a little louder.

Anders—I wish you'd met Anders—held my hand tight. Then the honor guard folded your flag from the caisson, snapped it crisply, and the chaplain presented it to Mark. Mark, your only son. "For your father's service to his country," the chaplain said.

A lone bugler played *Taps*. The honor guard fired the twenty-one-gun salute, aiming toward the Pentagon. Then the band started playing something low and sad, like a hymn but with a touch of military march. A soldier lifted the Astroturf, and four Old Guards lowered your ashes slowly into your grave.

A soldier laid the green carpet back over you. It was over. It was done. But Mrs. Aguilar cried even harder, doubling over in her chair.

The woman from Defense stood up. The band started playing something snappy. You had been officially laid to rest with honor. The West Pointers and Evelina and your ex-wife Carolina and Anders and Mark and I stood too. The honor guard formed ranks on the road. I helped Mrs. Aguilar to her feet. The band marched off; the horses pulling the now empty caisson started after them. Only Black Jack stood still, looking our direction.

Mrs. Aguilar raised her hands toward your grave, then to the sky, and began to moan. Her voice started low, hoarse, then rose. The woman from Defense turned toward her, her cockatoo corsage looking startled. Mrs. Aguilar went down on her knees in her white dress on the Astroturf. The West Pointers turned away but the rest of us, your layers of family upon family, drew closer, not ready to let you go. Mrs. Aguilar moaned louder, shaking her head from side to side. Then I moaned too, Dad, feeling something moving deep under my funeral dress. Nothing we do, not even leaving those we love without a word, can make partings painless. To feel loss, to grieve—this is a promise we make when we love. I felt this for you. I did. And I won't unfeel it now.

"Dad," I cried, "I'll miss you." Evelina and Mark were crying

59

too. Black Jack screamed, his bridle rattling as he shook his head, but Mrs. Aguilar's voice rose higher even than that. Our sorrow rose into the air above Arlington, above the Potomac, up to meet the jets taking off from National and Dulles, from Bowling Green and Andrews Air Force Base, up to the very boundaries of time and space.

A Story Set in Germany

The fall after I finished my master's degree in English I
took a temporary job overseas, teaching on an army base
in Germany. I told myself I wanted to make a little money and
see if I liked teaching before I plunged into the years and years
it would take me to finish a PhD. I got a passport which had,
under my name, Alice Ann Stratton, a picture of me looking
terribly pale and nearsighted—clearly I had been studying too
much. I didn't tell my mother that I was going. Though she'd
been born in Germany, she never spoke of it. I didn't tell my
brother. I didn't tell anyone I was going; I didn't tell anyone
where I'd been once I got back. Later, if anybody ever asked
me what I knew about Germany, I would tell them I didn't really know anything, that even though my mother was German
I personally had spent just six months there, winter to spring,
and so knew nothing about Germany but trivial things—that
every window had lace curtains, that the phone system was the
most expensive in the world, that I was often asked for directions by strangers when I, too, was lost.

It was true that my mother's being born in Germany was no
help. By the time I was born she'd given up being German

and was an American citizen. German was never spoken in our house unless my mother whispered it to me when I was asleep and safe from its charm. German food was not eaten in our house. Mom carefully followed the month's calendar of recipes that came in her *Woman's Day* magazine—tuna casserole made with Campbell's Cream of Celery Soup, meatloaf made with Lipton's Onion Soup Mix. One year, when *Woman's Day* featured an Oktoberfest issue full of German recipes, my mother carefully went back through the magazine's September calendar—Coca-Cola cake, Dream Whip waffles.

Once, in the house of a grade-school best friend, I'd seen a picture over the sofa, a family portrait that had been folded into a dozen tiny squares and then unfolded and framed. Her family, my friend's mother explained to me. All of them died in the concentration camps during the war, but she escaped, carrying that picture folded in her shoe. I understood. My mother had pictures, too, of stiff-collared uncles and brothers and father, and high-haired dark-eyed aunts and sisters and mother. Hers were all dead, too, in the army, in the bombing, eating sugar beets in the rubble left after the war. The war had left her an orphan with no living relatives. My mother's pictures were not framed on the wall but hidden in her underwear drawer beneath her heavy stitched bras. Because even as a child I understood it wasn't the same thing, it wasn't at all.

When I was growing up I always thought it was because of my father, this Americanization of my mother. But maybe not, perhaps it was self-imposed, an act of contrition by a now-loyal ally. The day he left my mother for good, my father turned to me, his hands shaking, his mind somewhere else. "You should learn German," he said. "It's a beautiful language." And so I did, in high school and in college. I did not show any inborn aptitude for it. Still, that was no test, so I got a job in Germany teaching remedial English to American soldiers, and went to find out just how German having a German mother, even a "lapsed" German mother, made me.

The first thing I found out through teaching Americans in Germany was that I didn't really know anything about Americans at all. Once on a Greyhound bus trip from my mother's house in Florida back to college in Wisconsin, I'd been questioned by a German exchange student who had just finished reading *Bury My Heart at Wounded Knee.* He wanted to know how recently I had oppressed an Indian—last week? last year? I had never even *seen* a Native American. At the time I thought this encounter showed how little he knew about Americans, but really it shows how little either of us knew.

In my classes on the army post where I taught in Germany I had Navahos and Hopis and Cherokees and Yavapais. One-third of my students were native Spanish speakers from Puerto Rico and Cuba and Texas and California. One ex–low rider from L.A. told me how his mother and brother had been killed at the breakfast table by some kids who—just for fun—had shot through the thin walls of his father's house. The boy cried as he said this, his lower lip pouting out where he had tattooed his mother's initials inside.

Still, he couldn't wait to go back. He was going to sleep all day and then find his friends and go riding, and it would be the best, the best life could offer. Then there were the fellow Southerners, African Americans and white. Most of them had their high school diplomas, but they still couldn't read their official army job manuals. The army would bounce them out unless I could raise their reading test scores. And Samoans, from American Samoa. Huge men with names like Tulualu-alua. One of them told me that at any given time half the men in Samoa were in the U.S. Army because there wasn't much else to do. Strangely enough, the Samoans all liked Germany, learned to ski, and found its five months of winter fun for a change. The Germans I met found it faintly depressing. So there I was in Germany, teaching what was really English as a Foreign Language to American citizens, and, compared to my students, it was hard to work up a case for my not being a true

American based on as small a flaw as having a mother who had been a citizen of the Reich.

The post where I taught, Wildflecken, had been a German post built by Hitler, not by the Kaiser like most of the posts the Americans used. The U.S. Army used it as a live-fire range, and so it went on mile after classified mile beyond the solid stone buildings I saw, each with its own eagle over the door, its feet ragged where the swastika that the claws once held had been chiseled away. From the range, if there was good snow to protect the German fields, American tanks would roll out for a run between firing practices; sometimes they rolled over not only fields but houses or cars. My soldiers swore it was a German trick, driving too close behind a tank so that the army would be forced to buy them a new car. I wasn't too sure about that. I had never seen anything quite as flat as a German car run over by an American tank. It seemed a dangerous, un-Germanlike game.

In many ways the post was still a German post: Germans laid the beautiful patterned cobblestone roads, served the not-too-American food in the cafeteria, and guarded the gates against unauthorized entry by young German terrorists. All this was done mostly by German men old enough to have been stationed there during the war, and on the gate one old man wore an SS death's head ring on his hand. No American had chiseled it off his bird-like hand. The silver skull gleamed as he carefully checked my ID every day.

I lived on Ziegelhütte, a mountain opposite the post, in the basement of a farmhouse owned by a couple, Herr and Frau Fuss, who lived all alone on the mountain with only three shaggy ponies—I called them the Fusspferde—and a nervous wirehaired dachshund that Frau Fuss explained to me suffered from *hundangst*—dog fear. Frau Fuss was a huge healthy woman who, even in this heavily industrialized country, did much of the field work by hand. Herr Fuss was a dry stick of a man with emphysema so bad he could not climb out of the potato cellar without resting. His wheezing was kept company by the *angsthund*'s shrill yaps.

The Fusses were plenty old enough to have saluted Hitler, old enough to have been there when the American troops rolled in the first time. All through the war the post on the mountain had stayed hidden by the thick firs and thick snow. The Americans were down in the village, in Wildflecken, for a week before one of their patrols stumbled on the post, already evacuated. And the Fusses had been there when it became a Displaced Persons Camp and most of the firs were cut down for firewood by people just out of the concentration camps who'd been sent into Wildflecken's long white winter. They'd been there when the DPs were replaced by waves of Germans coming in from the east, when the post that had once sat in the middle of Germany suddenly was looking down the Fulda Gap at the East German border and at Germans who were now the enemy.

But I do not know how the Fusses felt about any of these things any more than I know what my mother felt about any of them. I never talked to my mother about such things. And I never asked the Fusses either, though I was sure, every day, that I would. Frau Fuss spoke a strong dialect of German and, although she smiled a great deal, I was never sure she understood anything I said to her. Or that I entirely understood her. Herr Fuss did not talk, only coughed and smoked, and did not read or write either. He would always wait until the beer truck made its delivery to ask me for my rent, so the driver could write me a receipt.

The Fusspferde alone were revealed to me as not what they seemed, not stump-legged old ponies but rare Icelandic ponies who belonged to a man who hoped the weather on Ziegelhütte was cold enough to breed them. It wasn't. In the winter they were happy, but come spring they had to be shaved naked with the lambs.

The old farmhouse stood all alone on Ziegelhütte, but the

65

isolation was somewhat broken by the whumph-whumph-thud of the big tank guns and the brat-rat-rat of the helicopters practicing their strafing. The windows rattled constantly, but Frau Fuss said if she caulked them in too tightly they would crack or, if there was a big enough boom, explode.

We were alone there, me and Frau and Herr Fuss, the *angsthund*, and the Fusspferde, until one day a man arrived in a yellow Mercedes. His name was Karl Dietrich Muller, and he had been staying at the Fusses' for years since the death of his wife, for vacations in the winter and fall. He rented the room in the basement next to mine and we shared the bathroom. My bottles of shampoo and conditioner and lotion were the only thing I ever saw that made him nervous. He was a hunter, a *Jägermeister*, and he drove his yellow Mercedes with snow chains covering its matching yellow hubcaps recklessly, as if it were a Land Rover.

Frau Fuss told me the Jägermeister was a brewer from Würzburg renowned for the quality of his beer. He brought several cases for Herr Fuss in the trunk of the Mercedes. Except, he later told me, he had been born in Berlin and had only fled to Würzburg after the war, so I suppose he, too, was a Displaced Person. When I got to know him he told me over and over that Berliners are the only Germans with a sense of humor and proportion. He had not, though, been back to Berlin since the war.

He spoke that lovely British English that is always a surprise to hear coming from the mouths of terrorists when they hold news conferences. He later told me he had learned it in a POW camp in Britain, a special camp for antifascist prisoners where everyone was given English language and history instruction—a lot about the Magna Carta and parliamentary democracy. He got in this special camp because his military record, captured along with his whole unit, said that he was to be watched, not to be entirely trusted. It said this on approximately half of the records of the men in his unit, he told me, and in his case it was because his wife had a half-brother who was a priest at the Vatican.

I got to know Herr Muller well because he wanted to brush up on his English, which I found excellent but he decided was poor because when he spoke to the Hispanic and Samoan American soldiers down in Wildflecken they didn't seem to understand him. At his request I checked out some books from the base library, which held a complete collection of the classics and which seemingly no one other than me ever checked out. The only books that did a good business were the war books, ones with foldout maps of the Blitzkrieg or full-color photos of SS regalia. Herr Muller chose Dickens. He was taught Dickens in school as a boy but had never read his books in English. The library at the POW camp hadn't carried Dickens because his works criticized the English social system.

Herr Muller read to me from Dickens every night, and he did the most marvelous English characters—each one distinct. I sometimes can hear their voices still, and not always saying lines Dickens wrote for them. The characters in *Bleak House* for me always have a trace of a German accent, as if they were continental cousins just in England for the holidays.

My father had read to me when I was little—not Dickens but *Alice in Wonderland*, in honor of the name he and my mother had chosen for me. And out of some spirit of authenticity he, too, had read in his version of a high-toned English accent that, influenced by daily exposure to my mother, sounded more than a little German. So in some way too complicated to explain, Herr Muller, the Jägermeister, took up where my father, who I had not seen since he left my mother, my brother Mark, and me when I was thirteen, had left off. My father never finished *Alice*. Herr Muller marched at a steady pace through novel after novel. If my mother had stayed in Germany maybe, maybe my father would have been someone like the Jägermeister, someone steady, someone who finished the books that he started.

True enough, but let me tell you how I felt. I looked at the Jägermeister's thick fingers turning the pages of *Bleak House* and felt they were the most solid things in the world. Listening to him each night, I felt the warmth I used to get when I was little from hugging my pillow as tightly as I could. Even when I was at work, amazing my classes by revealing the fact that apostrophes in English were not random accent marks, I felt as if two huge warm hands were cupped around my heart.

Not that I thought Herr Muller considered me his daughter. But he did take me skiing on the special skis with sealskin-covered runners he'd learned to make in Norway during the war. The fur grabbed the snow so we could walk up hills as well as slide down them. Earlier, Frau Fuss had told me that Herr Muller, Jägermeister, went out every day to feed the deer he would shoot in the fall. But instead he took me out to help him move the hay bales and salt blocks the other hunters had left.

He laughed at my surprise. It was no sport at all to shoot a pet deer, he said with a ten-kilo block of salt balanced on his shoulder. When we left he erased our tracks with a fir branch. A true Jägermeister. But nothing is that simple in Germany, not since the war. I couldn't help thinking about the Berliner Jews, so warm and so safe and so sure they were Germans—hadn't that been like shooting pets? And even if I had asked Karl Muller, and he had said yes and so stood revealed as a man who is kind to animals and who regrets the sins of the past, he would also still have been a man who came every year to shoot the deer he did not even feed in the winter. What would he have said if I had asked him about the gypsies, the Poles, the humans who had no right to expect kindness from the Reich, who went to the camps? But, you see, I couldn't ask.

What did my mother think? Why had I never asked her?

Or, if her being a woman made her innocent, what about her dead father, her equally dead uncles? Had my mother married an American solely to give her children the luxury of innocence? Standing under those dark German firs, I realized for the first time what it would have been like to grow up in Germany and to have had these thoughts all along. Or, worse, to never have had them at all, the whole thing both too distant and too familiar to feel anything at all.

Once in my fifth grade a girl had brought in some small snapshots for show-and-tell. Her father had taken them when the British liberated Bergen-Belsen. They were ordinary Kodak Brownie prints, out of focus, slightly yellowed. They were the most terrible things I had ever seen. When I first got to Germany the chief of the post photo shop said to me as he was making my ID that I should go to Dachau some weekend. The photos they have there in the reconstructed huts and in the museum, he said, are superb. Blown up to wall size and not a bit grainy.

But, even knowing all this, I couldn't help myself. Having turned Herr Muller into my imaginary German father, I found myself thinking in German, becoming more and more German. I had to translate my students to understand what they said. I had to translate the Dickens into German as Herr Muller had read it. It gave me awful headaches. One of my Hispanic students, who hadn't learned English until he was in high school, said it always felt to him like it was coming from the far side of his brain—the spare room, as it were. My memories of this period seem a little distorted, the visuals seen from an odd angle. Maybe my student was onto the truth.

One Sunday we drove in Herr Muller's Mercedes to Kreuzberg, a mountain named after the cross of St. Boniface; a statue of the Apostle of Germany was placed at its crown. We sat drinking beer with the abbot of the monastery—beer the monks had been making for four hundred years. The abbot and Karl Muller talked brewing, their voices rising and falling, chanting almost. I sat and watched the families drinking beer in the great hall that looked through a glass window at the huge copper vats. They would drink a few steins, then go climb to the Calvary that marked the site of the saint's cross, then come back for more beer. It was touching and sincere and very different than my lukewarm Protestant upbringing had led me to expect from the Sunday choice between piety and sin. Half-listening to the abbot and Karl, I caught in their malts and hops and bitters and strongs the shading and nuances of a sort of theology.

Oh, if they had set out to discuss religion they would have used more conventional terminology, but it reminded me of a lay witness, an air conditioning repairman, I'd heard one slow Sunday in church. He compared searching for the will of God in the world to looking for a coolant leak that you know in your heart has to be there. A complete philosophy—what he knew, as a metaphor for what he believed. It is a medieval concept, each small world the perfect reflection of the perfect whole, and it is a German concept. So I loved Herr Muller because he could discuss beer as seriously as he would God, and I loved German because in it a discussion on hops could open a cold Sunday to the infinity of the universe.

That afternoon, on the way back to Zieglehütte in Herr Muller's big yellow Mercedes, I felt as if I were floating, warm, sleepy, and full of beer. I sat curled with my feet under me on the big leather seat. The Jägermeister said, like a real German Papa, *Zu schlafen, gehen mein kleines Mädchen.* Go to sleep, my little girl. And I did. I slept in a Mercedes driven along the East German border by a veteran of Hitler's army as if I had been born to it.

Then, the Fusspferde escaped. That night, the night after the trip to the monastery, an ambulance came to take Herr Fuss to the hospital. He was coughing so hard he was blue. Herr Muller took Frau Fuss to the hospital in his car. No Dickens that night. I heard them come home from the hospital just after sunrise. All week the snow had been melting and then re-freezing at night, a sure sign that spring was only a month or so away. I looked out the window at the rising sun and saw a pony run by, kicking up his shaggy heels in the snow. I ran out the back door after him, yelling to Frau Fuss, who ran into the barn to fill her apron full of winter apples with which to coax the ponies, who were galloping jubilantly across the face of Ziegelhütte, back into their small paddock. The Jägermeister came into the frozen meadow too, but laughed so hard at the sight of the ponies and of me running after them that he was no good at all. I started laughing too, hardly able to stand on the steep slippery ground. The Jägermeister took my arm to steady me, then stopped my laughter with a long, hard kiss on the lips. His gray unshaven face pressed hard against mine.

My real father, my American father, whatever else he had done, had never kissed me like a lover. I pulled away and started to run, not after the ponies now but rather back toward the house, but my feet hit a patch of ice and sailed up over my head. When I landed and stopped sliding, I tried to stand—a little hurt. I looked down. A bone poked through the chapped skin of my calf like a white, dry stick of wood. The snow turned red, melting a little, as my blood ran down. Karl Muller picked me up and held me in his arms while Frau Fuss ran into the house for a blanket to cover the car seat. On the way to the hospital my fear of bleeding to death was mingled with the knowledge I was ruining the seat covers in spite of this precaution.

I was taken from the Mercedes to the post hospital. Just imagine one room—olive drab. The Jägermeister was left standing by the guard house, a foreign national on this bit of German soil.

There was a doctor, a young major, who looked at x-rays and ordered me into surgery. I woke up in my U.S. Army Hospital bed thinking in English. When I was allowed solid food I ordered a cheeseburger and ate every bite. Why, why had I ever wanted to be, ever thought I was or could be German? Herr Muller sent me a note on stiff, embossed paper in his elaborate, prewar German handwriting. I couldn't even read it.

After two days of not hearing from me, Herr Muller sent me *Bleak House* with a marker clipped to the page where we had stopped. I finished it. In the end, Caddy Jellyby, a minor character who has been given a peek at happiness, has a baby born deaf and dumb and her overworked husband's health is ruined. For the less-interesting major characters all ends quite happily. Dickens buys belief in the good with a dose of the unbearable. I hoped then, and still hope, that is not the way the world works.

I stayed in bed and in the hospital and safe on post until one day I woke to find the snow gone and I knew Karl Muller was gone too. Back to Würzburg, back to the brewery, to the life where he had plenty of employees but a dead wife and no children. When I was better I went to Herr Fuss's funeral and took flowers. I put lots of blush on my cheeks and hugged Frau Fuss hard so she could say to anyone who might ask that I seemed very well. At the end of *Bleak House* I had found this:

Herr Karl Dietrich Muller, Direktor
Würzburger Hofbrau Brauerei
Lindenstrasse 44
5500 Würzburg BRD

The Jägermeister's office address.

I left. Only on the bus to the airport did I notice how many patterns of lace curtains there were, the snowflakes, the sea shells, the delicate bent-necked cranes among delicate bent reeds. At the Frankfurt Airport, with my pockets heavy with change that in nine hours would be useless, I did not call, did not use those phones so expensive yet so excellent that when Herr Muller answered, my voice would sound so clear he would think I had come and was just down the street.

Waiting at the airport I did buy and drink a bottle of the Jägermeister's beer. I found it bitter—too much hops. But, then, my mother raised me on Wonderbread and Jell-O and cold Coca-Cola, and when I think of *home* those are the foods that I crave.

Beasts

"Thank you, beautiful," I said as my five-year-old daughter, Maude, came skipping over from the swings and handed me a warm, wilted bouquet of dandelions. Dandelions, the only flowers no one cares if you pick. Maude smiled at me and then turned and ran screaming back to the playground. Ginger Rogers, the fat, sweet, six-year-old basset we'd just recently adopted from the pound, pulled on her leash and barked.

"Stop!" she called as she ran, her voice causing Kyle, her best friend, to freeze in mid-motion as he was about to sit on the one free swing. "It's my turn."

"You shouldn't call her that, Alice," Bibi, Kyle's mom, said. Bibi was my oldest friend; we'd known each other since college.

"What?" I wasn't really paying attention. I was watching to make sure Maude didn't bully Kyle, who was small for his age, a worrier, and easily bossed. Instead Maude turned suddenly gracious and led Kyle by the hand to the playground's other swingset, where two cast aluminum ponies hung side by side.

"Damn adjective," Bibi said, raking her long black hair out of her eyes with her fingernails. "Or is *beautiful* an adverb?"

"Adverbs modify verbs," I said, English teacher that I was. "Beautifully is an adverb. As in 'Maude sings beautifully.'" Maude, as a matter of fact, took after me and couldn't carry a tune in a great big bucket.

Bibi waved away the instruction. "The point is, Alice, you shouldn't call Maude beautiful." Bibi emphasized *beautiful* in a way that held it out like a dirty sock between two pinched, disapproving fingers. I looked across the playground at Maude. As I watched, Maude's blond hair flew first forward than back as she swung her horse without mercy toward some imaginary finish line. Her eyes looked blue and big and bright even from a distance. Why shouldn't I call my daughter *beautiful?* Maude *was* beautiful.

And not because of hair or eye color. In Wisconsin, being blond was nothing special. Two-thirds of the kids in Maude's kindergarten class were blond. Kyle was so fair my husband Anders joked you could read a newspaper through him. It wasn't her neat, symmetrical little-girl chin and nose either. She was beautiful because in some way I couldn't quite prove scientifically, she glowed. She spun off energy like a hot new star.

Not a day went by that people in the street or at the grocery store didn't notice, didn't stop me and repeat that very *b* word. What a *beautiful* baby, what a *beautiful* girl. At the Mexican restaurant near our house where we often stopped for takeout, the señora called Maude "La Linda." "Beauty," Anders would say when Maude pitched a fit over some little thing, "and Beast."

"It warps girls," Bibi said, her voice shaking. She sounded like she might cry. "Take my word for it. I know." Of course Bibi knew. She was beautiful. And I, I was not. Nice looking, neat, maybe, but not beautiful. "It becomes everything to you. You end up spending all your time trying to *be* beautiful, wondering why no one has called you beautiful today, this hour, this minute. You live in fear of the day you'll get sick or old and turn so ugly no one will love you."

76

"Oh, honey," I said. I put my arm around her and squeezed her shoulder, but at the same time I thought *She's talking about her life, not Maude's.* Ginger licked the toe of Bibi's boot, adding her own dose of sympathy.

Bibi accepted the consolation of the hug, but said, "I know what I'm talking about, Alice. You should listen."

I frowned, shifting my focus from Bibi to Maude. My beautiful girl. It seemed so innocent. "Do you really think I'm hurting her?"

"Not if you stop," Bibi said.

I looked toward Maude. Was Bibi right? Maude was now spinning Kyle on the merry-go-round, her small sneakered feet raising dust. She was putting her back into it, clearly determined to go faster than childkind had ever gone before. Kyle was hanging on with both hands, squeaking *no no no* and then something that sounded suspiciously like *ssssttttt-toooopppp.* Instead Maude jumped onto the flying carousel and stood right in the middle, hands flung up to the sky, a blond whirligig, a Wisconsin dervish. Kyle let go of the safety bar and clung to her leg.

Bibi was looking not at the pale blur that was her son but at the horizon, at the tall chain-link fence that marked the boundary between playground and park—this side for children, the other for grass. She seemed, for a moment, to have forgotten we were there. She sighed.

"I'd better grab Maude," I said, giving Bibi's shoulder a last, clumsy pat, "before she breaks Kyle in two."

All the way home from the playground with Ginger and Maude I thought about what Bibi had said. Was she right about Maude? It was hard to know. I thought of Bibi, so bright and, yes, beautiful, sitting on the bench in her red tunic and purple velvet bell bottoms. I would never have admitted this to Bibi, but I picked clothes to be purposefully neutral. That way, if I wore the same sweater three days in a row, people assumed I owned three gray sweaters. Actually, I owned half a closet full.

I thought about what she'd said while I sorted the dirty clothes before dinner. One basket of whites—mostly towels and Anders's t-shirts—and one of darks—my grays and Anders's black jeans. In a college town like ours nearly everyone wore black, the house color of artists and academics. One basket of bright colors—all Maude's. Did beautiful people instinctively crave purples and oranges and reds? Maude had a weakness for chartreuse as well.

Over dinner Anders told about his trip to our neighborhood hardware store to get brass screws for an installation piece he was working on. Anders was a photographer who taught in the art department at the state university, but lately his photographs had begun to leap, rather inconveniently, off the walls. He cut and arranged them in dioramas and installed them in large impressive pieces of vaguely Victorian cabinetry. He'd even made an inlaid teak projector stand that spun in circles while showing magic lantern slides—he called them "moving pictures." I liked it. It was exciting to watch hand-colored prints of tropical fish spin dizzyingly around the room on the white walls above the furniture. It made me think about all the things I took for granted—real movies, TV, video, computers—miracles too much a part of everyday life to seem miraculous anymore.

These new pieces already took up an amazing amount of room in our small, crowded house, but still Anders kept buying sheets of mahogany, brass pulls, knobs, and screws, slowly and quietly building his private World's Fair. He hardly stopped except to take Ginger for her slow, waddling walks. "So," Anders was telling Maude, "I was standing in line when this woman comes up behind me and says, 'Aren't you Maude Dahl's father?'" And then the old guy behind the counter says, "Maude's your daughter?" Anders laughed. "'Isn't that amazing?' I thought, 'My daughter is famous!'" Maude shrieked, she was so delighted. I smiled.

The old man behind the counter must have been the owner, Mr. Vandergraff. Maude had gone with her class on a field trip to the hardware store just two weeks before and had come home with instructions for how to make bird feeders out of pop bottles. Obviously, Maude had made an impression on him. Had she been wearing chartreuse that day?

The woman was probably one of Maude's many teachers, at school, at swimming, at Sunday school, tumbling, ballet. Unless she knew Maude from Anders's pictures. Locally they were his best-known works. They'd hung in the faculty show at the university, in the biannual survey of who was who among Wisconsin artists, and in a popular coffeehouse near campus where students hung out for hours drinking lattes. Over the students' bent heads hung Maude at four months, an upside down blur swung in front of Anders's lens, the amazing flying baby. Maude at two, with a jumbo pitted olive on the end of each stubby finger like some mutant half-toddler, half-tree frog. Anders shaped his face into an extravagantly artificial frown. "Famous on five continents, but I'm nobody in this town but Mad Maudie's dad."

"Oh, Daddy," Maude rolled her eyes. She had taken to pretending offense when he called her Maudie, his baby name for her. The "mad" she didn't mind. But wasn't "mad" as bad as beautiful? I wondered, all adjectives suddenly suspect.

"When you win the Nobel Prize," Anders said, his faux frown losing out to his usual slight, mocking smile, "just remember to thank your old dad."

"Thanks, Old Dad," Maude said, kissing him on the top of his graying, old-dad head. That done, she turned to her mother. "Is there a field trip tomorrow?" she asked. I nodded. I'd signed a permission slip for Maude and her fellow kindergartners to be taken to the State Historical Society to see a new exhibit on Native Americans of Wisconsin. I had, as usual, ducked Maude's teacher's suggestion it was my turn to chaperon. I taught freshman English at the local community college and had forty student essays waiting for me in my bulging book bag. "I want to wear my straw hat, Mom," Maude said.

"Are you sure, Maude?" I said. On family trips Maude tended to start out with a sunhat and then lose interest. Usually I wound up carrying or wearing it. And none of Maude's teachers looked like the straw-bonnet type. Maude, though, looked absolutely stunning in it. When she'd worn it to the farmer's market that past weekend, half the people who passed us hurrying in their search for the perfect pumpkin or heirloom apples or aged cheddar could be heard to remark in passing, "Did you see that beautiful little girl in that lovely/ amazing/ damn big straw hat?" I was sure Maude had heard them as well.

Maude nodded. "And," she added, "if they're clean, I'll wear my chartreuse socks."

That night after Maude had been steered clear of the treacherous reefs that surrounded five-year-old bedtime and was safely asleep with Ginger at her feet, I lay in bed, trying to summon up some energy for my stack of papers. When I was engaged in my teaching, full of the kind of energy I had rarely been able to summon that fall, I gave my students what I thought of as slightly mad but challenging assignments. Compare someone you love to a wonder of the world. This time I had only told them to compare or contrast two people, places, or things. So I knew without looking I was doomed to comparisons of dogs to cats, Big Macs to Whoppers, Frisbee golf to Hacky Sack, Wisconsin to Iowa, or, at best, Illinois.

I gave up on my students' attempts to find meaning in the subtle variations of daily life and began leafing through one of the many back issues of the *New Yorker* I hadn't gotten around to reading. I glanced at the listings for photography shows. Anders was too busy building his vision of the Past/Future for gallery openings in Manhattan to interest him. I had grown up as an army brat, moving every four years. Anders had been born in Wisconsin in the same small town where his great-grandparents were buried. He'd left Wisconsin reluctantly to go to grad school in New York, serving time as if in the foreign legion until he could at last return home, return to a place where the people had the innate sense to call all cold fizzy drinks *pop*. His plan, he told me on our first date, was to be like Frank Lloyd Wright, a fellow Wisconsin native who also hated cities and who had made the world beat a path to his low, well-designed door.

When we met, Anders had been a new assistant professor. He was experimenting with color film, giddy with the extravagance of having unlimited access to the department's color processor and printer. He blew up everything he shot to poster-size. He would stay up all night printing what he'd shot, then drag it still wet into class the next morning for his students to see.

After we started dating Anders begged me to model. If I would, we could spend all our nights together. So I had agreed to pose. But first we'd gone shopping. Even then my wardrobe had been better suited to black-and-white photography, so we'd gone to a vintage clothing store near campus and bought a big red satin shirt the color of Technicolor lipstick. Then we went to an all-night drugstore and bought lipstick to match. The first night he took pictures of me leaping off a chair, a blurry, midair kiss of a woman. Then on other nights, juggling—and dropping—green apples. Then, in an artistic breakthrough, throwing lime Jell-O into the air.

Some of the shots looked like Kodak ads—all color, no content. But some, when I had tired of the games and the endless delays for moving the spots, metering the lights, and reloading the camera, when my mouth was a weary smear, my eyes were narrowed, my neck bent with fatigue into a slightly odd and painful angle, then voila! there was tension and a hint of

81

a story that would forever remain tantalizing and unknowable. There was art.

After the photo sessions we would make love on his futon, and then he would leave me to a few lumpy hours of sleep while he went to his darkroom on campus to develop that night's film, make color prints from the negatives he'd taken the night before.

By the end of the semester it was clear that I was going to move in with Anders and his futon. So when Anders asked me to pick up the four-foot party sub he had ordered for his end-of-class party, I agreed. I'd walked through the door carrying this most ridiculous of foods, and the assembled photography students looked up and cried as one, "It's her," as genuinely star-struck as if they had spotted Madonna. "It's the Jell-O Woman." For a moment, I was famous. But where was there to go after fruit-flavored gelatin? I was relieved when Maude came along to model for Anders.

But how long had it been since Anders had taken a picture of Maude? I tried to remember. Not a roll of holiday snap-shots, but an honest-to-God photo as art? I couldn't remember. Last summer? Earlier this fall? At any rate, it had been before Anders bought a table saw and began building his mahogany boxes.

Anders came to bed, crawling over me to get to his side, picking up a magazine along the way. Anders actually read the long *New Yorker* profiles of people you never knew existed until you saw the columns of tiny type about them. I propped myself up on one elbow. "Why don't you take pictures of Maude anymore?"

"What?" Anders was flipping through his issue, squinting at the cartoons. "Oh." He blinked, as if he hadn't really realized he had stopped. "No reason. Just that that last time it didn't work out. She posed too much."

"What do you mean?"

He shrugged. "She didn't know what to do with her hands

or with her mouth. She kept smiling like she thought she should smile in a picture." He turned back to his magazine. "You can't be yourself if you're worried all the time about being beautiful."

That's it, I thought, as we settled down to sleep. I was going to go cold-turkey on all words—adjective and adverb—that referred to the illusion we call our bodies, bodies that were bound in the course of things to grow sick or old. No more *beautifuls* or *lovelies*. Not even a stray little *don't-you-look-nice*.

Thursday was Bibi's and my annual night out to celebrate our birthdays, which fell a mere ten days apart. Our tradition was to go to a bar we'd never been to before, get good and drunk, exchange small gifts, and sometimes break into fits of inappropriate song or dance. Once we got bounced from a bar for doing an imitation of the Rockettes, high kicking and singing *New York, New York*, in my case shrill and off-key. Then, our birthdays duly celebrated, we'd take taxis home where families and hangovers awaited us. In other words, for one night we acted like we were still in college. Anders and Bibi's husband Lloyd had seen the ritual enough times that they kept the aspirin handy. This year we'd chosen the town's first martini bar. We found a table, then we each pulled out our presents and set them in front of us. Mine for Bibi was in a small gold gift box that had obviously been wrapped at the store; Bibi's present for me was in a red handmade paper bag pulled shut with rough twine.

Bibi and I had known each other as undergraduates, floormates in a large, rowdy coed dorm. But we hadn't started this tradition, hadn't become best friends, until we were in grad school. Bibi was in her first semester of art and I was working on my master's in English, already teaching freshman composition, though I hadn't known then that I had stumbled into my future. At that first birthday-party dinner Bibi had handed me a scroll tied up with gold ribbon. I unrolled it, expecting to see words—maybe a hand-set poem or a Zen koan done in calligraphy. Instead, the paper was blank. I turned it over, looking carefully at both sides. It was odd paper, as blue and fuzzy as dryer lint. I looked up at Bibi, trying not to look too puzzled. "I made it," Bibi said, "in my papermaking workshop. You whiz snips of old blue jeans in a blender with water and Elmer's glue, then spread it out to dry on an old window screen."

It is lint, I thought. "It's amazing," I said, knowing it had probably taken Bibi hours to make.

"I'll show you how to frame it." Bibi smiled lovingly at the first piece of paper she had ever made. She, too, had found her life's work.

I still had Bibi's first gift and her second, a blank book. I, on the other hand, doubted Bibi still had the first gift I had given her, a literary guide to Wisconsin. Bibi had flipped through it, peering at the foldout map, at the black-and-white photos of authors and their houses. I didn't know then that Bibi was badly dyslexic, could hardly read and so had good reason to prefer her books blank. It was me, crazy English major, who liked them dense with type.

The second year I made a better choice; I gave Bibi a pair of earrings. Big purple glass grapes, a bunch for each ear. That set the pattern. Every year was a paper anniversary for Bibi. I, on the other hand, worked my way up from glass to silver. Last year I'd even sprung for an odd bobbing pair of fourteen-carat-gold plumb weights. This year, though, I'd broken with tradition. Instead of earrings I had gotten Bibi a pin. A single smooth nugget of amber the size of a baby's heart bound with a band of silver, with a sharp dagger of a pin set in the back. It looked like something a Goth might have used to close his rough woolen cloak. I couldn't wait to see Bibi pin it to her bulky lime-green-and-orange sweater.

Before we opened presents we always had at least one drink. Bibi got her martini with vodka and a pickled baby Vidalia onion. I, ever the more conservative, went for gin and an olive. But after the first glass of pure alcohol I loosened up. Bibi talked me into ordering something off the specials board for my second. When it arrived it was a lovely, sad blue. What liquor turns a martini aquamarine? After one sip I felt like crying. Then I was crying, not from sadness, really, but a sudden acute sense of time slipping past me. I could hear it rushing like water. I remembered our first birthday bash—our skin had been peach perfect. I remembered Maude in my arms for the first time, a red-faced blue-eyed little radish. Where were any of us headed? Suddenly the rush of time made me dizzy. I wanted to stop the relativity train and get everyone I loved off before we all came to some terrible end.

"Are you okay?" Bibi put her hand on my arm, her concern touching and genuine though she knew from experience I was a maudlin drunk.

I nodded, wiped my eyes with my cocktail napkin.

"Hey," Bibi said, picking up her present, "may I?"

I nodded. "Tear away."

Bibi tore into her birthday gift, shredding the wrapping. She had a casual attitude toward machine-made paper. She held the amber up to the light and let out a long happy "Ooooooh."

"Be careful," I said, reaching out to touch the brooch's silver pin. In my martinied state I misjudged this distance and pricked myself. As if in a fairy tale, a single drop of red blood appeared on the white tip of my finger.

"Close your eyes," Bibi said, unknotting the string on the present. I did, and heard a soft *whoosh* like moths fluttering past me. Bibi put something over my head, placed it gently around my neck. Could you knit scarves out of paper? I opened my eyes. This year Bibi had given me jewelry. A necklace of folded paper strung on silver cord. A lei. *Aloha*, I thought, my mind ever the dictionary, *a word that means both hello and good-bye.* I reached slowly up to touch it, almost afraid the paper might startle and fly away.

"It's *beautiful*," I said.

Bibi gave a wry laugh. "Oh, I almost forgot," she said, positioning the amber over her left breast, then stabbing the silver pin into her sweater. "Can you watch Kyle for me on Saturday?"

I noticed my finger was still bleeding. It had left a red smear on my cocktail napkin and probably, though I couldn't see it, on the paper necklace as well. "Sure, what time? Maude has swimming lessons at 8:30, but we can be home by 9:15 if I tell her Kyle's coming. Otherwise she takes forever in the shower."

"No rush," Bibi said. She was signaling the waitress for our tab. "I'll drop Kyle off around 10:00. I have to go in for another biopsy—this time on my right breast. Lloyd's going to drive me. I should be home by 2:30 at the latest."

I started to say something, I wasn't sure what, but Bibi put a finger across my lips.

"Later," she said. "No matter what they find, they won't do anything. Not then."

Saturday, Maude was up before the alarm went off, digging through her drawer for her bathing suit and goggles. We had taken the summer off from swimming lessons, and now she was eager to start again at the Y. She had forgotten last spring's tears over her inability to float on her back. I made a pot of coffee and toasted a bagel. Friday morning after my night out I had been wretched, as sick as I had ever been in my life. "Think of it as nature's way of keeping you sober," Anders had said, shaking his head. This morning I still felt a little shaky. *This is what age does to you,* I thought. Throw a little party and it took a week for your liver, cranky old housekeeper, to clean up the place. Maude, a healthy five, ate a heaping bowl of Cheerios.

Maude swam with great splashing enthusiasm, cheerfully

venturing in over her head. It made me nervous to watch her, but her teacher was full of praise. He moved her up from Minnow to Fish. "The spirit's there," he said, when the class was over and the kids ran shivering for the showers. "Her body will catch up."

In the locker room Maude's class struggled into their clothes as the next class wriggled into their suits. Lockers banged and girls shrieked. A baby, sibling of some young amphibian, cried at the top of her lungs. I felt yesterday's hangover in the base of my skull, clearly planning a comeback. I was pretty sure I had some Tylenol in my purse and I desperately wanted to wash them down with Diet Coke, that perfect shot of caffeine and NutraSweet. Maude, sensing where her mother was headed, begged a quarter off me for the gum machine. I hesitated. Anders disapproved of gum. It stuck to your shoes and wasn't even food, but, then again, he wasn't there. I opened my change purse and dug out a quarter for Maude. That and a few pennies were all the change I had, but I knew from Maude's past swimming lessons that the Coke machine took dollar bills.

What was Bibi doing and thinking right then? I wondered as I dug through my wallet for a bill that wasn't too wrinkled. They wouldn't let you have breakfast, even before a minor surgical procedure. She must be starving. Bibi always ate a good breakfast. Maybe she was brushing her teeth, over and over. That was okay as long as you spat and didn't swallow. She wasn't worried, she'd told me the night before. This was her third biopsy in as many years. Her mother had been the same way, Bibi said. Biopsies every year and never anything but harmless fibroids. And now, with mammograms, every shadow made the docs jump. They'd be negligent not to follow up.

I fed a bill into the Coke machine. It sucked it in halfway, then spat it out. Damn. I smoothed it, running the bill back and forth across the sharp corner of the candy machine. I had had only one lump, one biopsy. It happened just before I met

Anders. The scariest thing had been the changing room at the university hospital, a locker room full of women coming in for biopsies, women getting the news from ones already finished, still others on their way to a dose of chemo or radiation. No privacy. In the corners women wept. Bibi said it wasn't like that now. Each woman had her own little curtained cubical with a La-Z-Boy recliner to lounge in while the nurse started her pre-op IV.

The Coke machine emphatically and finally rejected my dollar bill. I turned my back on the idea of liquid refreshment. Maude was sitting on the couch by the door, looking glum. Wasn't the gum machine working either? "What's the matter, Sweetie?" I said.

"I swallowed it."

"The gum?"

"The quarter."

I didn't know what to say. I had heard plenty of jokes over the years about kids swallowing things, about parents keeping watch over toilet bowls to get back diamond engagement rings. Surely, surely swallowing change was not that serious. Maude looked okay. We could afford the quarter. Maybe we should just go home and see what Anders thought.

"It hurts, Mom," Maude said, pointing at a place just below her heart. Now, suddenly there were tears in her eyes. "It hurts right here."

We went to the emergency room. There the triage nurse was openly concerned. "You didn't call 911?" she asked me.

I shook my head. The nurse frowned, then turned to Maude. "Tell me what happened, dear. How did you swallow the quarter?"

Maude looked embarrassed. At five she knew she was old enough to know better. "I don't know," she said. "I didn't have pockets so I put it in my mouth, then I was just standing there looking at the gumballs and I forgot and swallowed it."

It made sense, I found myself thinking, drawn in by Maude's slant logic. I had noticed how few clothes that were made for girls Maude's age had pockets. Boys' pants always had pockets. What were little girls supposed to do, carry purses?

"Did you cough or choke?" the nurse asked. She was writing all this down.

"No," Maude said. "I tried to spit the quarter out but it was too late."

"Are you having trouble breathing?"

"No," Maude said, "but it hurts." And she looked like she was going to cry again. I put my arm around her.

"It'll be okay, Sweetie," I said. The nurse, I noticed, looked less sure.

"The peds doc will probably want an x-ray," she said. She put us in a cubicle to wait for the pediatrician on call. A cubicle similar, I imagined, to the one where they would put Bibi. *Bibi.* Had I told Anders that Bibi was going to drop off Kyle? I had forgotten my watch, but surely it was ten already. There was a phone on the wall beyond where Maude lay on the narrow examination table with a paper sheet pulled up around her neck, but it was a blinking maze of buttons. I ran my hand over Maude's damp hair. "Does it still hurt?"

"A little," Maude said.

"Rest, Sweetie," I said to my daughter. "I need to call Daddy." I stuck my head out of the curtain. "Excuse me," I said to a nurse—not our nurse—behind the desk. "How do I get an outside line on this phone?"

The nurse made a sour face, as if all the indigent moms in town came in here to make phone calls. "Press nine," she said, "then your number."

"He's here," Anders said about Kyle. "He's petting Ginger and watching me stain plywood. Where are you?" I told him. "What does the doctor say?"

"We haven't seen one yet, but Maude seems better." Actually, Maude now had the paper sheet pulled over her head. "I'll call when I know something. We may be awhile." I hung up

89

the phone and peeked under the paper covers at my daughter. "Are you okay, Maude?"

Maude was crying again. "Why did you have to tell him? He'll think I'm stupid."

I sighed. We were in the adjective swamp again. And *stupid* didn't seem an improvement on *beautiful.* "I had to tell him," I explained. "He was worried. Besides, just because you do something stupid doesn't mean you are. Your father knows that. Everyone does stupid things sometimes." I patted Maude's paper-covered knee. "I certainly have."

"Knock, knock," a woman called, then flung back the curtain. "I'm Barbara. The doctor sent me to take you to x-ray." The woman spoke directly to Maude, not looking at me. *You let your daughter swallow a quarter,* I thought, *and they all know what kind of mother you are.* The x-ray technician held out her hand, and Maude hopped down off the table and took it. "Where does it hurt?" she asked Maude.

"Right here," Maude said, pointing.

"Her esophagus," I heard myself say.

The technician looked at me as if she were surprised to find me there. "Are you a medical professional?" she asked.

"No," I said. Just a person with a passing knowledge of body parts, I wanted to say, but didn't. "I'm an English teacher."

"Oh," the technician smiled. "In that case, I'd better watch my grammar." She started to lead Maude down the hall. I began to follow. The technician waved me back. "We'll only be a minute," she said. "And Maude's a big girl, aren't you?"

Maude nodded emphatically and abandoned me, the mother who had given her the ill-fated quarter, without a backward glance.

Actually, they weren't gone long. Maude reappeared with two heart-shaped stickers on her purple turtleneck. The first read *I Got An X-ray Today!* and the second *I Was Brave!* "She was super," the technician said, holding up the black-and-gray picture of Maude's insides. She snapped it under the clip on the light box. "I'll go get the doctor," she said, and left.

"They make you hold your breath," Maude said, hopping back up on the table. She was taken by her stickers. "Just like in swimming class." I wanted to sneak over and flip the switch on the light box to illuminate Maude's irradiated bones, but before I could move, the doctor was there.

"Dr. Jorgenson," he said, holding out his hand. I shook it. He looked about the same age as my students, and his palm was almost as soft as Maude's. "So," he said, "let's see where the foreign object in question, the . . ." he glanced at the notes the nurse had taken, "quarter has gotten too." He flipped on the light. And there was the missing quarter, floating like a bright, full moon in the night that was Maude's chest.

The doctor pulled at his smooth, young chin. "How long ago did she swallow this?"

I peeked at the doctor's watch. It was nearly ten-thirty. "A little over an hour."

"Hmm, it's sitting right where the esophagus opens into her stomach. A tight squeeze for a quarter," he said. "Let me go talk to the pediatric gastroenterologist on call. We may have to go get it."

"Operate?"

Maude was excited. "Will I have a scar like Madeline?" she asked. The doctor looked puzzled.

"It's a children's book. The heroine has her appendix out."

"Oh," Dr. Jorgenson said. "No, no scar. We have this long rubber tube, an endoscope. We slip it down your throat and grab the quarter. Bring it up, good as new."

"Yech," Maude said. Thinking, I imagined, about where that quarter had been, but the doctor thought Maude meant the idea of the endoscopy.

"You'll be asleep," he said. "You won't even know when it happens." Maude nodded. "Be right back," he said to me.

Maude sat swinging her legs. I wondered if now was a

good time to check in with Anders—I didn't like the "asleep" part—but Dr. Jorgenson was back before I had a chance. "Dr. Gert says Maude should rest here for a while to give her own muscles some time to squeeze that quarter through. We'll take another x-ray in thirty minutes, okay?"

I didn't like the idea of more radiation either, but it sounded better than anesthesia. "Okay," I said to Dr. Jorgenson. He patted Maude's foot.

"Relax," he said.

After he was gone, Maude asked, "What did you do that was stupid, Mom?"

I almost said, "You mean besides start this conversation with my five-year-old daughter?" But it was too late to back out now. I thought of the time I had eaten a large dose of hash in sloppy joe mix. For a week I'd thought my roommates were planning to kill me. Then of the time I slept with my Theory of Composition professor even though I knew he thought my teaching was hopeless. But those didn't seem quite the right examples for Maude. "Well," I said, "last year I backed out of the garage too fast without really looking and knocked the side-view mirror, *bam*, right off the car."

"Really?" Maude asked.

I nodded, not adding that I had told the insurance company someone had hit me in the grocery-store parking lot. Or that I sometimes dreamed a big guy in an Allstate jacket was chasing me, calling me a liar and a lousy driver. "What else?" Maude asked.

"I jumped off the garage roof and broke my collarbone." Maude nodded. She knew that story. "I swung a baseball bat without looking and hit a kid who was standing behind me in the nose." Maude lay down again.

"It's really hurting now, Momma," she said, touching the same spot under her ribs. *If only*, I thought, *I'd given Maude a dime.* Maude turned over on the examining table, clutching her wrinkled paper towel of a sheet.

92

"Shhh," I said, stroking her hair. If Maude got any worse I was going to fling back that curtain and go find Dr. Jorgenson. I put my face next to Maude's on the little paper pillow. "Then there was the time . . ." I had gotten as far on my list of stupid-things-I-did-as-a-child to the time I'd given the family dachshund a crayon to eat when Barbara, the x-ray technician, reappeared.

This time Dr. Jorgenson brought Maude back himself. He snapped the x-ray into place on the light box and flipped it on. I couldn't see through him—he was no x-ray—but I didn't have to. Dr. Jorgenson took one look then whooped and made a fist, pulling victory down from the air. "Way to go, Idaho," he said to Maude. Then he stepped back and I could see the full moon of the quarter was much lower and off to one side, no longer centered over the orderly ladder that was Maude's spine. "Into the stomach and on its way home," Dr. Jorgenson said.

Maude poked at her ribs. "It doesn't hurt anymore," she said, as though that surprised her.

"You know, kid," Dr. Jorgenson said, still admiring the x-ray. He tapped Maude's faint curving ribs. "You've got a *bea-ut-i-ful* set of bones here." He stretched out the word I had banned from our lives into four comic syllables. "You must drink a lot of milk."

"Ice cream," Maude said seriously. "The secret is ice cream."

"Really?" Dr. Jorgenson said. He stuck his hand into the pocket of his lab coat, drew out a prescription pad and some children's Motrin samples. He shook his head and tried the other pocket. "Then you'd be a good candidate for one of these." With a flourish Dr. Jorgenson handed Maude a slip of paper. It read, "Rx: one ice cream cone to be taken internally. Fill this prescription at the University Hospital Cafeteria. ASAP."

"Please, Momma?" Maude said. Part of me wasn't sure girls

who swallowed quarters for a main course deserved dessert, but I was so grateful to have Maude unsedated, unintubated, that I nodded in approval.

"Sure," I said. "But remember, Kyle's waiting to play, so we can't take all day." Would Anders have heard from Lloyd about Bibi yet?

We found the hospital cafeteria in the basement—weren't they always in the basement? It smelled unpleasantly like dishwater and overcooked broccoli, but the lunch rush, if there was one, hadn't started yet, and the large woman in the hairnet working the food line was happy to scoop Maude out a very large Cookie Dough cone. I grabbed a stack of napkins and followed Maude to a table near a row of dusty plastic plants. "Work on it a little," I told Maude, watching my daughter digging the chocolate chips out of the ice cream with her tongue. "Then we'll risk taking it in the car."

I spotted a pay phone on the far wall. "Stay right here, Sweetie. I'm going to tell Dad you're okay." I got change for my wrinkled dollar from the cashier. The quarters looked huge in my hand. Would I ever look at one the same way again? A woman with a stroller beat me to the pay phone, and I stopped short, trying to signal that I wanted to make a call but not wanting to seem like I was listening in.

Luckily it was a short conversation. "No. No. Okay," the woman said. "All right, then, pick us up out front." I smiled at the woman and looked into the carriage to smile at her baby as well. As a mother I felt obligated to do that kind of thing. But the child in the carriage was much older than a baby, would have been a toddler if he had been able to walk. Twin oxygen tubes ran into his nostrils from a tank at his side. A blank rubbery expression filled his round face. I forced myself to smile anyway. The mother nodded at me as she pushed her son past.

I felt dizzy, but I made myself pick up the receiver of the pay phone. Then I leaned forward, resting my forehead on the cool metal of the coin return. After a moment I straightened. Maude was still sitting at the table, working hard on her cone. This was the first time Maude had ever been to an emergency room. She had never had more than a cold. Anders had had nothing worse than the flu. We had been living, were living, on the lucky side of the planet. *Lucky*, another word you couldn't trust. We were lucky. The other people in this room—some trailing IVs from tall t-shaped stands, others just sitting wearily over Styrofoam cups of coffee waiting for news that was not likely to be good—they, clearly, were not.

But if beauty could desert you, then so could luck. Was Bibi, across the highway in ambulatory care, still one of the lucky ones? I thought of the boy in the baby carriage, then of blond, sweet, perpetually worried Kyle. I knew Bibi would say she had been lucky so far. Maybe that was the best any of us could say.

I dialed my own number. "Hello?" Anders said.

"We're coming home," I told him.

At the house Kyle ran to greet Maude with Ginger at his heels. No kid's idea of a good time is spending Saturday with someone else's parent. I told Anders the good news. "It might take as long as two weeks," I said, repeating what Dr. Jorgenson had told me. "But unless Maude starts throwing up or running a fever, the quarter can be considered safely on its way."

"Two weeks?" Anders said. "After that long it should come out two dimes and a nickel."

I nodded, then belatedly realized he was making a joke, and tried to smile. I hadn't done anything all morning except sit around and wait but I felt exhausted. "Did you hear from Lloyd?" I asked. "Do they know anything yet?"

"Yes," Anders said, "and yes." He looked over his shoulder. Kyle was sitting on the living-room couch. Maude was standing in front of him, tracing the path of the quarter with her finger. Anders lowered his voice. "It's malignant. Lloyd said they want to do a lumpectomy, probably tomorrow."

God, I thought, *lumpectomy.* What an ugly word. I knew, though, that there were uglier ones.

"Then," Anders was saying, "Bibi will have to choose between chemo or radiation. Apparently it's her choice. I told Lloyd I'd help him do some research on the Web tonight."

I shook my head. Printouts about odds would never help Bibi decide what to do. Bibi was Bibi. I imagined her flipping a big gleaming quarter—heads I choose death rays, tails poison cocktails.

Anders looked at his watch. "Lloyd said he'd be by for Kyle as soon as he got Bibi settled at the house."

Kyle was looking at us, looking even whiter than usual. He knows, I thought, somehow he knows. For a chronic worrier it must make a kind of perfect sense. He'd been preparing for bad news all his life, and now it had arrived.

"Dad, Dad," Maude was pulling on Anders's arm. "I need you to put on some music."

"What?" Anders said, for once not on his daughter's five-year-old wavelength.

"Kyle's playing audience and I'm going to dance."

"What kind of music?"

Maude shrugged. "Dance music." Anders put on the Supremes. Then, at Maude's insistence, he sat on the couch next to Kyle. "Stop, in the name of love." Maude was wiggling around, mouthing the words.

"No, no," I said, "like this." I spun into the routine I'd learned from Bibi in our dorm days, one she and I had done in a sports bar on the memorable occasion of our first birthday night bash.

"Stop!" I held my hand out like a school crossing guard. "In the name of love," I crossed my heart. Maude threw herself into it, wagging her finger along with me. "Before you break my heart." Ginger lifted her head and howled. I heard footsteps on the front porch.

"Come on in, Lloyd," Anders called over the wall of sound.

"Nice moves." It was Bibi, standing next to Lloyd and looking as if on this Saturday nothing had happened to her that hadn't happened a thousand times before, as if under her sweater were no fresh stitches and beneath them, no tumor, hard and hungry and growing.

"Auntie Bibi," Maude said, catching her hand, pulling her into the middle of the room. "You dance, too. We're a girl group. We're . . ." Maude paused, frowning with the effort of making up a name, "We're *The Beautiful Girls.*"

Bibi didn't flinch when Maude said *beautiful.* Instead she smiled, began making the hand motions I remembered so well from the early years of our Beautiful Girl lives. As one, the three of us pivoted and turned and mouthed Diana Ross's words as if nothing in this world could ever be less than lovely. As if there were no tragedy or loss, no unlucky quarters in stomachs, no blank-faced children who couldn't breathe or walk, no ugly cancerous lumps. As if the world were all beauty and no beasts. Kyle and Anders on the couch gaped in amazement. Lloyd, still standing, the long folds of his face damp from tears, sang along. Their girls were breaking their hearts. "Stop," we girls sang. "Stop." But, for now, there was no stopping us.

New Rooms

Gunther Schultz, architect, leaned forward and lifted the roof off our house. I watched as he held the cardboard dormer my husband Anders had so carefully fashioned, held it between his thumb and forefinger as if the roof were something small with claws, a crawfish say, that might give a finger a sharp nip. I could feel Anders's nervousness. I read the underside of the dormer— *Buster Bro*—Anders had used the box our daughter Maude's new shoes came in. "Clearly," the architect said, "Anders and Alice, you've given this project a great deal of thought." He set the roof gently back on the house, and we stood there with our arms folded, looking down at it.

Anders had given it years of thought, though the model of the proposed renovation had only taken a few weeks. We needed more room. From the time Maude had been born six years before, we had needed more room. Either we could move, trading in the two-bedroom house we'd bought from our former landlord, a sweet unworldly emeritus Latin professor, or move up to a bigger house, probably out of Madison and into the suburbs as so many of our friends had done. Or we could add on, raising the roof with dormers and turning the attic into the three new rooms we needed. Room one, a small study for me that would double as a guest room; I taught freshman composition at the local community college and always had a self-renewing stack of papers to grade. Room two, a darkroom for Anders to replace the dank one he had squeezed into the basement; he taught photography at the university. Room three, a half bath, so that when Maude was a teenager, Anders and I wouldn't have to get up in the middle of the night to get a shower.

Gunther Schultz walked to the other side of the table, stepping over our sleeping basset hound Ginger, and crouched down, taking in the house from the street level. His hair was white-blond and he looked barely old enough to be out of grad school. Anders walked to the other side, too, and stood with his head tilted to one side. I stayed put, limiting myself to squinting my eyes, trying to appear deep in thought.

I, personally, had been in favor of moving. My father had been career military. My mother had married him and left her native Germany without so much as a backward glance. I'd grown up moving every four years, hauling my life around in footlockers until he retired to Florida—and my parents promptly divorced—when I was in junior high school. When I'd moved from Florida to Wisconsin for college, I had never dreamed that I would live there—except brief stints in Germany and San Francisco—for the next nineteen years. Never imagined that I would live, first as tenant then as owner, for thirteen years in the same small, shingled house. Anders, on the other hand, came from the kind of family in which generations were born and died in the same room, in the same iron-railed bed. His parents lived in the limestone farmhouse his great-grandparents had built when they arrived in Wisconsin from Norway shortly after the Civil War. Clearly, Mother and Father Dahl planned to live there until they were moved to their side-by-side plots in the town's Lutheran cemetery. It made me claustrophobic just thinking about it.

I had tried reasoning with Anders. Why not move? This

house wasn't anyone's family homestead. It was a 1920s bungalow some developer had thrown up on former dairyland. Except for the Latin professor, we didn't know the names of the people who had lived there before us. We didn't even know the names of most of our neighbors, mere renters passing in the night. But, Anders said, look at the woodwork I stripped. Look at the oak floors I refinished. Think about the clematis you planted, Alice. All those tulip bulbs. Where else can we walk to the food co-op, the hardware store? Why would you want Maudie to have to change schools? Anders practically shivered when he imagined his daughter a kindergarten stranger in a strange land.

I sighed and wore out one real estate agent after another looking for a house in our neighborhood just like our house but bigger, a house even Anders could love. Until, one day, standing with a tired, grim-faced realtor in front of a four-bedroom house that seemed perfect to me, I finally faced the truth. For Anders, no house but the one we already owned would ever be perfect. He would never be tempted by a mere garage for our car nor a yard large enough for a swingset for Maude. Short of my threatening to leave him unless we bought a new house, we were not going to move, and I might as well get used to it.

"I'll talk to your contractor. Get him to draw up some estimates," Gunther Schultz was saying. When I first moved to Wisconsin I'd been shocked to find people my age with names that sounded like POW camp guards in a World War II movie. Or the relatives my mother, a war bride, must have left behind in Munich, never to be mentioned. But Wisconsin had been settled by Germans, with a handful of Norwegians like Anders's ancestors thrown in, and was still full of beer, bratwursts, and Gunthers. By now I was almost used to it. "I think your idea is achievable. That is," the architect lifted the roof again and frowned down into the empty, cardboard rooms, "if we can get the city to approve the plans."

"The city?" I said.

"The Zoning Board," he said. I could have sworn the architect shuddered. "You never know with them," he said. "But if you're determined, we'll give it a shot."

"Why zoning?" I asked. It wasn't like we were asking permission to turn our cramped single-family home into a gambling casino or even an extremely cozy bed and breakfast.

Gunther Schultz handed Anders a copy of the city's Unified Zoning Code. "Here," he said. "Read this, then we'll talk."

"It's complicated, Alice," Anders said, after spending most of the evening deep in the Unified Code with Ginger asleep, as usual, at his feet.

I was watching Maude, pajama clad, minutes from bedtime, play with the house model. She was marching a fingernail-size family of Polly Pocket dolls from room to room as if she were Gulliver the realtor closing an important Lilliputian sale. "Room for a piano, For a band," Maude explained to the Pocket family. "Room to dance."

"Apparently," Anders went on, "when the city passed these zoning regulations back in the seventies, they decided the same rules should apply in older neighborhoods and in new developments. It says here there must be at least twenty feet between any proposed addition and the property line."

"How far is our house from our property line?"

Anders pursed his lips. "Just a guess?" he said. "On the bedroom side, maybe twenty inches."

The other side, I knew, was just as tight. We were practically close enough to reach into our neighbor's kitchen window and borrow silver. The whole block was like that. In the summer, when all the windows were open, each time a phone rang everybody ran to answer. I sighed. "Then we can't do it," I said, trying to keep the relief out of my voice. "Even the center of our roof isn't twenty feet from the property line. Under these rules, putting up a TV antennae would be a violation."

"Thank God for cable, eh?" Anders said, and poked me in the ribs with his elbow. "It's not over yet, Al. The zoning committee can make exceptions—on a case-by-case basis."

Maude began humming loudly, something that sounded like the theme from *Sesame Street* mixed with the *Blue Danube*. Her tiny family was trying the cardboard dance floor, their daughter spinning on one plastic toe.

"They *can* make exceptions," I asked, "but will they?"

"Well," Anders smiled, his flimsy paper rooms already real to him, "we'll find out."

The dance over, Maude burst into applause. One by one the Polly Pocket family bowed. Maude had made her sale.

After Maude was safely tucked in bed with Ginger spread like a heavy dog-fur blanket across her legs, I took the checkbook and drove to the big warehouse grocery store on the edge of town. I did this whenever the house made me feel claustrophobic, which these days was more and more often. Anders hated this store with its double aisle of frozen pizzas as long as a football field. I liked the vast stretches of black-and-white linoleum, the numbing cold of the meat department, the restful quiet of entire aisles full of things I didn't need—cat food, off-brand Tupperware, disposable aluminum baking pans—or couldn't quite imagine buying—canned pasta, herring tidbits, string cheese. When he had to go there, Anders tried to race through the store with a list carefully itemized by row. It bothered Anders that the managers were always rearranging the store, moving things around according to some late-night whim or distributor pay off. He preferred our little neighborhood grocery, where anything new merited a hand-lettered sign reading *New Product!* or our food co-op, where, if things were chaotically arranged, at least it was done by the hands of politically correct volunteers.

I cruised the aisles, reading the labels on the new section of Indian foods—brinjal pickles, madras curry powder—that had mysteriously appeared just south of salsa and edible taco-salad bowls. No matter where I entered the store—through the automatic double doors near the liquor store or the photo-developing enclave or the video store or the lottery ticket window—no matter where I told myself I was headed—*milk, we need milk*—I always seemed to find myself in Aisle 16B under the sign that read "Q-Tips, Cotton Balls, Feminine Hygiene Products."

I would wheel my squeaking cart nonchalantly to the end of the aisle where the home pregnancy tests were stacked. They were expensive, ranging from ten to fifteen dollars a test. At first, when we'd started trying for a second child, I'd gone to my doctor to get tested. It was covered under Anders's insurance. But after a few months it had gotten too odd, too embarrassing. The nurses sighed when they saw me coming. Once in Aisle 16B I would grab the first test kit I saw, throw it in my cart and, my face burning, do a wheelie around the corner, moving fast until I was safe in 17B, Shampoos and Conditioners, with its dizzying array of fruit and floral scents.

Whenever I'd imagined a family, I'd always seen myself with two children. Probably this was just a failure of imagination on my part—I had one sibling—Mark—and I couldn't imagine what my life would have been like without him. Surely Maude deserved a brother or sister. And getting pregnant the first time, with Maude, had been so foolishly easy, as simple as my mother had always warned me it was when I was a teenager. Anders and I had decided we wanted a child and—*bam*—one fast round of unprotected sex later, there came Maude. Then, after Maude, nothing.

After four years of trying, we'd gotten serious and had gone to the fertility clinic at the university hospital. First a medical resident had explained the various procedures to us, and suddenly the whole thing seemed to me both more complicated and much riskier than the *Time* magazine articles on miracle babies had led me to believe. I could have a stroke. There was a small but statistically significant possibility that my hyper-stimulated ovaries might explode.

Then the head fertility doctor had come in to explain the expenses, none of them covered by Anders's otherwise excellent insurance. Each attempt at fertilization and implantation had, on average, only a thirty percent success rate, he told us. So multiple procedures were the norm. The doctor leaned forward in his chair, ready, for our sakes, to be blunt. Some couples spent as little as ten thousand dollars and still conceived, but expenses of eighty, even one hundred thousand dollars were not uncommon. "You have a daughter, right?" the fertility doctor asked. We nodded. "Then ask yourselves if your savings wouldn't be better spent sending her to Harvard." He stood up, shook Anders's hand and mine. "If you're still interested, call my nurse."

One hundred thousand dollars wasn't the kind of money we were planning on using to send Maude to Harvard. It was money we didn't have, period. But whatever we did have, we both agreed, we wouldn't spend it on this. We had Maude, lovely, healthy Maude. What happened, we both said, happened. "Kismet," Anders said. "Que Será Será," I said, and we went on until we ran out of popular song titles.

So far, though, what had happened was nothing, followed by another month of the same. Now, instead of spending money we didn't have on hormone injections and egg harvests, I found myself blowing it on home pregnancy tests.

I'll wait, I told myself, wheeling my cart with the little blue package with ONE STEP PREGNANCY TEST written on it in annoyingly large letters up to the check-out. My period, always light and erratic when I wasn't on the pill, wasn't even especially late. *I won't use it until next week*. But I knew I was lying. I had picked out a two-pack. I would use one now and when it failed to turn pink or get a plus or an extra blue line or whatever this brand of test did to show the result was positive, I would throw that one away, and save the other for later.

I did manage to wait until after I'd put into the refrigerator those groceries most likely to melt or grow salmonella if left out. Then I snuck into the bathroom and locked the door. After five minutes, this brand's instructions read, if the test was positive a blue cross would magically appear. A single blue line meant you were not pregnant. A blank test meant even though this kit was supposed to be idiot-proof, you had muffed it somehow and would now have to use the second expensive test in the pack. I peed carefully on the little white plastic stick.

I left the stick by the sink and went to put away the pasta and the canned goods, pretending not to watch the clock. Exactly five minutes later I strolled into the bathroom with a tube of toothpaste to put away. I let myself look, then let out a whoop. "Alice, honey? Are you okay?" I heard Anders call from his darkroom in the basement, directly under my feet. I slapped my hand over my mouth, afraid I would hoot again and wake Maude. *Jesus, Jesus, Jesus*, I thought, my fingers pressed tight to my lips. There it was. A blue cross that equaled baby + you.

I used the second test. Why save it? I wanted to be sure. Then as Anders sat at the kitchen table drinking his ritual glass of buttermilk before bed, I told him. Anders was toying with the cardboard mockup, testing out a new pitch for the staircase, trying to keep it from being as steep as a ladder.

"Can you trust those home tests?" Anders said, looking down at the little white sticks, the blue crosses already fading like bruises. "Shouldn't you go see the doctor?"

"Tomorrow." I said. I'd expected Anders to shout louder than I had. Maybe loud enough to wake Maude. He had a brother and a sister and thought all kids were great. I was the one who had to prod myself to ask after my friends' children.

Anders poked at the paper house. He sighed. "I just want it to be real," he said.

I lifted the roof off the house. "Well, if it is, we're really going to need these new rooms." Anders smiled, and I realized why he hadn't war-whooped at my first use of the word *baby*. He was afraid another child meant we would have to move, that I would make him sell the house. I paused. Should I? But the idea of the baby filled me with love for Anders, so sweetly blond, so good at making both art and cardboard houses. I was lucky to have met him, lucky to have married him, lucky to still have him. I made my decision. I didn't want to move either. I wanted to feather this nest. At that moment I couldn't imagine packing everything we owned. I gazed down into the partitioned sections of our new improved birdhouse. "We can turn my office into the baby's room," I said.

"No," Anders shook his head. "He can have the darkroom. The old one I have in the basement is fine. Who needs to stand up straight when you're printing pictures?"

I put my arms around Anders's shoulders and buried my face in his neck. Anders kissed the hand that held our roof. "Hey," I said, joking, "if it's a boy we can name him Gunther."

"Right," Anders laughed. "And if it's a girl, Schultz."

Anders went with me and sat patiently in the waiting room to see my obstetrician. I studied the back issues of *Baby Care*. When I'd visited this same doctor for my preliminary infertility exams, these magazines had seemed like cruel jokes. Did endocrinologists subscribe to *Dessert Digest* and leave issues out for their diabetic patients to see? Now I smiled at the hugely pregnant mom sitting across from me and gave the diaper ads my serious attention.

Yes, my obstetrician told us, I was pregnant. Nearly eight weeks. My last light period was apparently a not-uncommon false menstruation. "Let's go down the hall and take a peek," the doctor, a middle-aged man with a great mane of silvery hair, suggested. "An ultrasound will help us fix a due date." The technician ran the ultrasound wand back and forth on my stomach, this way, that way again, like a patient angler working a stream. Anders squeezed my hand so tightly I felt my knuckles grind together, but all I had eyes for was the video monitor, the screen filled with a silent movie of the fetus. Huge head, comma-shaped body. In black and white the fetus waved its arms slowly in front of its face, then turned over on its side like a fitful sleeper, life still a dream. I had had an ultrasound with Maude, too, but then the technology had been so primitive that though the technician had sworn he could see Maude's liver, heart, and head, what I had seen on the monitor looked like a Xerox of sand.

"Everything looks fine," the technician said as she checked off the organs one by one. She took various arcane measurements, her computer mouse clicking away. Then the due date appeared on the screen below the fetus, who now seemed to me to be covering its eyes—*peek-a-boo.*

"September first," the technician read.

"I'm having a baby on *Labor Day*?" I said. Anders and the technician laughed at the obvious irony.

The doctor only nodded his silver head, noting the date in my chart. "So it would seem."

The technician offered us a picture to take home, and I watched as a snapshot of this baby yet to be born curled off the printer like some fax from the future. "Don't call me on this," she said, handed the slick paper scroll to Anders, "but I'm ninety-nine percent sure it's a girl."

The first person we told was Maude, and she was wild with excitement. The words "Big Sister" meant she was being promoted, moving up from supervised to supervisor. She could hardly wait.

She stayed excited, even after several bouts of the bedtime books—*Billy Aardvark Has a Brother!* and *Sharing Your Mommy*—which I dutifully checked out of the library and all of which seemed to stress the downside. *The baby would get visitors, not you. The baby would get gifts, not you. And the baby would cry cry cry until even the moon gave up trying to sleep.* It was enough to give me second thoughts, but not Maude.

She drew picture after picture of our new soon-to-be-ex-panded family. I taped one of us as a pride of lions on the refrigerator. At the top were Momma Lion and Daddy Lion, both clearly smiling. At their feet, protective Big Sister Lion gazed down at teeny Baby Lion, who was about the size of a grape. In other words, about the same size as Maude's real sibling, hovering somewhere south of the equator that was my belly button. Meanwhile, on the refrigerator a hot crayon sun shone down on us all.

"Ouch," Bibi said after she heard my news. "I hope you remember how much the whole birth thing hurts. Kyle was like giving birth to a sea urchin." Bibi's only child, Kyle, had been born just two months after Maude. "A sea urchin," Bibi added, "the size of a fully inflated hot-air balloon." Bibi was sitting cross-legged on her basement floor, sorting through a bushel of potatoes she was saving for a garden. She'd had a lumpectomy that past fall and after a rough round of chemo she had broken out in this sudden and unprecedented desire to start a garden in her backyard by the time spring finally made it this far north. Because she was Bibi, a woman who did nothing ordinary, the potatoes weren't regular white ones, but some long purple variety, smuggled in, Bibi had confessed earlier, from Peru.

"Of course I remember," I said, though I didn't really. I remembered my pregnancy had been textbook perfect right up until the end when my water broke but I never went into labor. The doctor on call had had to order an emergency c-section. Anders still teased Maude about how reluctant she'd been to be born. Certainly I remembered there had been pain, but I couldn't really remember what the pain had been like. Amnesia, I figured, was one of Mother Nature's little tricks, designed to guarantee not everyone would be an only child.

Bibi raised a dark, painted eyebrow. She'd lost most of her hair and her eyebrows to chemo, but because she was Bibi she wore it well—hair shaved and polished to a high gleam, eyebrows wickedly penciled in. "Well, you know I am happier than happy," she said, and gave me an earthy, potato-scented hug. I hugged back, and we stayed that way for a while, two women on our knees hugging in the middle of a damp Wisconsin basement in February.

I let go first. I was feeling queasy, though it was afternoon, not morning. With Maude I'd never had any morning sickness. But from the moment the doctor told me I was, indeed, pregnant, I'd felt these waves of nausea, though I hadn't actually thrown up. Bibi handed me a small pile of potatoes to sort. "If you find one the least bit soft, toss it." I took the hint and started squeezing, tossing the questionable tubers into a pile, repacking the others in their little nests of straw. My queasiness passed. "Have you and Anders started vetting names?" Bibi asked.

I groaned. Last time Anders and I had almost been driven to blows, to divorce court, to madness by picking a name. I couldn't bear all the Norwegian Nels and Oles, and Anders thought my list of Southern names sounded like snake-handlers. Somehow, of all the names in *2000 Baby Names from 20 Countries*, Maude had been the only one neither of us vetoed. The exact reason now escaped us both. Even why we had thought a baby's name was so important seemed unclear from this distance. Maybe we had been deluded enough—naive first-time parents—to think the name we chose would determine what kind of person our daughter would be. Then Maude had come, her own self from the first moment. A baby with burning wide-awake blue eyes and a cry so loud the nurse said she sounded like a flock of hungry seagulls. Maude, by any name, had turned out to be a rose with both petals and thorns. All things considered, it was probably a good thing we'd adopted our basset—whose registered name was Dancing Doll's Ginger Rogers—from the animal shelter, name and all.

"We decided to wait before we talked about names," I said to Bibi, tucking another Peruvian tater tot in for its long night. "The doctor is going to do another ultrasound in a month. If we know for sure it's a girl, we can cut the number of names we have to argue over in half."

"Good move," Bibi said. "We don't want Maude to end up an orphan."

That night the contractor brought over his estimates. He had the plans Gunther Schultz had carefully drawn from Anders's model. There in black and white was Anders's dream house. But there were various options. Wood floors or carpet. Oak stairs or pine. Shingles guaranteed to last thirty years versus those that would last only twenty. But even if we made the cheapest choice every time, the renovation was still going to cost a stunning, numbing amount of money—close to sixty thousand dollars. More, in fact, than we had paid for the whole house seven years before. Even Anders was shocked. The color drained from his already pale Wisconsin winter face. We listened, nodding and smiling. Then we all shook hands, and the contractor tentatively penciled us into his calendar for July. He had been in the game long enough to read our stunned, polite faces and so knew better than to use anything as permanent as ink.

After the contractor left, Anders just sat there, staring first at the estimate with its neat rows of figures, then at the plans. "Maybe we could do without the bathroom," he said.

I got out the calculator. "We need the bathroom," I said. We had put close to twenty thousand aside to cover the renovation but, clearly, that was not going to be enough. Still, we owned our house free and clear. After we married, Anders had gotten into the habit of paying double what was due every month. Norwegians, even fourth-generation Norwegians, were not big on debt. Just the year before we had made our last payment. Now, if we were going to go ahead with these plans, turn paper into wood and plaster and heating ducts, we would have to take out another mortgage. Fortunately, the price we'd gotten from our former landlord had been so reasonable, I was sure we could borrow the forty thousand extra the renovation would take. We might both have to teach summer school. I might have to beg and scrounge for an extra class of freshman composition or remedial English, especially if I was on maternity leave in the fall. But we could do it.

"Look at it this way," I said to Anders, thinking of the fertility doctor and his one-hundred-thousand-dollar estimate. "We may have to pay through the nose for her room but at least the baby is free."

Two weeks after our visit with the contractor, Gunther Schultz called to tell us we had a date for our Zoning Board hearing. "March first?" I said to Anders. "That's the day I go back for my second ultrasound."

"What time?" Anders asked.

"Eleven-thirty."

"The board meeting starts at nine. Surely it will be over by then." Anders looked anxious. I knew the Zoning Board only held hearings once a month. If we had to wait, the contractor might well bump us from our July spot on his calendar. What if the work wasn't done by the time the baby came? I imagined what it would be like to have a newborn's every nap interrupted by the whine of power saws.

"It will be fine," I said. "If you can't go to the doctor with me, I'll bring you home a picture."

"So how are you feeling about all this?" Bibi asked me. Bibi had stopped by with a bag of special white fingerling carrots she'd picked up from the fancy new supermarket on the far side of town. Bibi wouldn't let anything that wasn't organic pass her red, cheerful lips. In this Bibi was like my brother Mark, who had taken up organic food like a religion after he tested positive for HIV. He told me he was sure it was pesticides that turned HIV to AIDS, though he wasn't so sure, thank God, that he stopped taking all the toxic, awful pills that kept the virus at bay.

112

"How do I feel about the Zoning Board hearing? Or the baby?" I asked, rooting around in a drawer for a peeler to clean the carrots for lunch. I could hear Maude and Kyle in the living room, tying kitchen towels on stuffed animals, pretending they were diapering babies. All the while, Maude kept up a running commentary about the various liquids and solids that could come out of a baby. Earlier that morning she had vehemently denied ever having worn diapers. Now she was telling Kyle what it had been like, back when they wore Pampers and owned, between them, not a single pair of underwear.

"Both," Bibi said.

"The hearing scares me to death. We're supposed to be there, looking respectable but politely desperate. Our architect is the one who presents the plans to the board. We aren't allowed to speak unless a board member asks us a question. I think if we give the wrong answer a chute opens and we fall— *whoosh*—straight into the dungeon of lost homeowners."

"And the baby?"

"Actually," I paused scraping in mid-carrot, "I'm feeling better. I've been taking my vitamins and drinking my milk and I haven't felt sick since the weekend. Think it was all nerves?"

Bibi bit the tiny tip off an albino carrot with one snap of her teeth. "It always stops when you get to your third trimester. That's how it was for me. I puked nonstop for the first twelve weeks then ate for the next twenty three."

Gunther Schultz met us outside the hearing room at City Hall. Anders, whose teaching attire ran to jeans and t-shirts, had on his good suit, the one he wore to academic conventions. I was in a suit as well, black skirt and jacket, knotted scarf—my first-day-of-class outfit, the one I wore so my students wouldn't have to ask who the teacher was. Gunther Schultz, too, looked like he had dug out his one good suit, and that made me even more nervous.

What if the board wouldn't grant us an exception? Realisti-

cally, Gunther had given our odds as no better than fifty-fifty.
I looked at Anders. Standing there in his suit he looked very
Norwegian, equal parts blond and grim. How would he take
being turned down? Anders was normally the calm one, but
he said all Norwegians had a dark moody side. His father had
once discharged a deer rifle at a neighbor over the relatively
small matter of the timely mowing of a ditch that ran between
their two properties.

I suddenly imagined Anders with the Unified Municipal
Code in one hand, a hunting rifle aimed at the cold, unfeeling
heart of the Zoning Board chair in the other. *And another thing,*
he was saying, *about the grass in that ditch . . .* Gunther Schultz
tapped me on my shoulder and stopped the panicked spiral of
my fantasy. "We'd better go in if we want to get seats."

As soon as we walked into the meeting room, saw the rank
upon rank of homeowners filling the folding chairs, I knew
this was going to take a while. Still, for prisoners about to face
the same firing squad, the appeals were not without interest.
The first case was presented by a man representing himself
who asked permission to build a deck onto the back of his
house, a sort of Fake Lloyd Wright set at an angle on a narrow,
steeply falling lot. Right now, he explained, his second-story
family room had double sliding-glass doors that led out into
thin air. The previous childless owner had installed the doors,
but, the current owner explained, he had small children and
pled fear for their safety as his reason for seeking a zoning
variance. The deck would only violate the required setback by
six inches, and then only at one end.

I was convinced. Unfortunately, one of the board members
noticed, while studying the man's plans, that not only would
the corner of the deck be in violation, but it appeared the
corner of the family room would be too. And, further, a quick
staff search of the records found no building permit for the
family room, an addition to the original house. For one awful
moment I was afraid the board might order the man to tear

that end of his house down. Instead, they referred the matter to the city building inspector for investigation and possible fines.

The petitions continued, the next three squeaking by on votes of five to four. "We're lucky the whole board is here," Gunther said. "Sometimes there are as few as four. And depending on which four . . ." he shook his head. It occurred to me this is what you got for living in a state run by Germans. Good schools, clean streets, and Zoning Board members with cold, exacting, Prussian hearts. Maybe that explained my mother's willing immigration.

At eleven the board had just started to hear its sixth appeal. Our appeal was number ten. I kissed Anders for good luck and slipped down the aisle of the hearing room, headed for my doctor's appointment.

My doctor was on call, and as soon as I saw the crowd in the waiting room I knew I was in for a wait. My obstetrician was clearly off delivering some other woman's baby. I checked in and picked out a much-worn copy of *Modern Maternity*, but I had barely sat down when, much to my surprise, the nurse called my name. "Aren't you lucky," she said. "The doctor just got back and he wants you to go straight to ultrasound so the technician can go to lunch."

"No need to get all the way undressed," the technician said, "as long as I can get to your belly." I unbuttoned my blouse, pulled down my skirt, and hopped up on the table. How much would the baby have grown? Or would the screen make it appear the same size even though it was larger? The technician squeezed a dab of warm jelly on my stomach to help the ultra sound wand, slim twin of her computer mouse, roll more smoothly. *Was the Zoning Board moving at the same slow pace?* I wondered. Or was Gunther Schultz even now presenting our case?

I looked at the computer screen. The fetus did look the

same size. I recognized the curved back, oversized head, luminous, nearly hollow eyes. This time, though, it was still. "Is she asleep?" I asked. Maude had always slept during the day, the better to stay awake kicking me all night.

I heard the technician suck in her breath. "I'm going to ask the doctor to step in," she said.

I felt the beginnings of panic stir in my chest, but my thoughts kept moving down my old worry track. Was the Zoning Board asking Anders questions? Were they voting? Then I looked at the screen again. Why wasn't the baby moving? Why was its heart, so clearly visible in its transparent chest, not moving?

The doctor put his hand on my leg. "It happens sometimes," he said. He looked tired and embarrassed. "For no detectable reason, a fetus just isn't viable."

Viable, I thought, seeing the word as clearly if I were writing comments on a student paper. *Synonyms you might want to consider — alive, living, vital, feasible, possible. As in, This isn't possible.* I felt my limbs on the examining table, heavy, unmoving. I felt my heart pounding, hard, in my chest. I stared at the fetus on the screen, translucent as a jellyfish in a science-class aquarium. So silly to think of this as a baby, my baby. So silly to think of it as my baby girl. Baby girl in pajamas. Baby sister in Maude's lap. I took a deep breath.

My face felt hot. I touched my cheek. It was wet. "I'm leaking," I thought. I couldn't stop it. Tears ran from my eyes, not in drops but in a steady, salty stream, and my nose ran too. The technician put an arm behind me and helped me sit up. I pressed my lips together, afraid I might sob. Right before her lunch, I was doing this to this poor technician right before lunch. And all those patients in the waiting room, I was making their wait longer still. I wanted, more than anything I could ever remember wanting, to simply stand up and walk out of this room, but I didn't trust my legs. I took a deep breath.

My doctor looked down at his shoes, clearly uncomfortable.

"Early miscarriages are unpredictable," he said. "In the first trimester we can usually say it's a defect in the fetus, but twelve weeks is really right on the cusp . . ."

"Miscarriage?" I heard myself ask. How could this be a miscarriage? When I was pregnant with Maude, Anders's great-aunt had taken it upon herself to warn me about what kinds of housework, in her experience, were direct causes of miscarriage. She regaled me with tales of Norwegian farm women hanging clothes on the line or reaching for bowls in high cupboards, who had their babies wriggle free and *plop*, hit the floor. Tiny parachutists bailing out of their mothers' over-worked wombs.

"In your case," the doctor said, "an incomplete miscarriage. If you hadn't come in today this might have resolved itself. But we really can't just wait and see, the chances for infection or hemorrhage are too great. We should schedule a D&C as soon as possible." He paused, and it seemed to me he was waiting for me to say something, but I didn't know what to say. "It's a simple outpatient procedure," he explained. "We can do it at our new ambulatory surgery center." He took a ballpoint pen out of his pocket and clicked it twice. "Can we schedule you for tomorrow?"

I tried to keep my eyes on the doctor as he spoke, but they kept wandering to the monitor, to the black-and-white picture frozen on the screen. The technician stepped behind me and turned off the machine. My unviable fetus, dead baby, illusion of a pink happy future, shrank to a white dot of light and then that, too, was gone. "Yes," I found myself saying. Yes, they could schedule me for a simple outpatient procedure. Yes, I could come in tomorrow to have dead tissue scraped from my womb. *Tomorrow.* What day was tomorrow? Was Maude in school? Did I teach? Did Anders?

"Do you want to call your husband?" the doctor asked me. He looked at his watch, clearly thinking of his other patients. "Is there a number where he can be reached?"

"No," I shook my head. I couldn't imagine calling City Hall, having Anders summoned to the phone by strangers who would have had to be told the reason in advance. "I'm okay."

The doctor sighed. "Call the ambulatory center after five," he said, "and they'll give you instructions for tomorrow." He stood up.

"Okay," I said. "I'm okay."

He nodded, a little confused, and left the room.

The technician helped me into my jacket and found my purse for me. "Are you sure you can drive?"

I hadn't thought that far. I'd been worrying about how I was going to make it through the waiting room, past all the women who were still mothers-to-be. I took my purse from the technician. "I guess I'll find out," I said.

Afterward all I could remember was holding my breath. All the way through the lobby, in the elevator, the parking garage, driving across town, climbing the marble steps of City Hall. I knew I couldn't actually have stopped breathing for the fifteen or twenty minutes the trip took. Still, I remembered it that way. Remembered not drawing a breath until I saw Anders step out of City Hall with Gunther Schultz at his side. Both men were smiling. Schultz, boy architect, was slapping Anders on the back. Clearly, we had won. The variance for our addition had been granted. Whatever our other loses, we soon would have our new rooms.

Then Anders saw me, and his face changed so quickly, I knew mine must have had *bad news* written across it in bright splotchy red. He put his arm around my shoulder, and together we sank onto the marble steps. I was choking, gulping in air.

"The baby," I kept saying. "I lost the baby." Though I hadn't, of course, and that was half the grief of it.

Scarce

From the bedroom I could hear Anders on the phone in the kitchen. "She lost the baby," he was saying. There were murmurs in reply to whatever was said on the other end. I heard him hang up and dial again. "Alice lost . . ."

I was still full of valium from the D&C after my miscarriage. I kept thinking, *I should feel empty,* but I didn't. I felt stuffed with an odd, ticklish nothingness, like a pillow too full of down. I clung to the blanket Anders had tucked in around me, afraid to roll over lest I keep rolling and fall, with a sad muffled *plomph,* onto the floor. Anders was only doing what I asked him to. In the past few weeks I had been so excited about at long last being pregnant that I'd told everyone I knew, everyone I'd run into at the supermarket or when picking up my daughter Maude from elementary school. Looking back, it seemed I'd told half the people in Madison, Wisconsin. Now I was filled with a deep fear of tiny baby gifts arriving, of running into friends, friends of friends, who would say that they'd heard the good news and ask when the baby was due. "Boy or girl?" they would ask, smiling. It *was* a girl, I imagined saying. So I had set Anders at the task of calling back my happy, too-hasty words.

I heard him punching in numbers, working his way through my address book. Poor Anders. He hated talking on the phone. Even in my current state, with time as blurred as a hummingbird's wing, I was sure each call lasted less than twenty seconds. Ordinarily I was the one who called friends, booked dental appointments, ordered heating oil. But for now it was Anders's voice going out over the wintry telephone wires. ". . . lost . . ." I heard him call his mother at the family's farm an hour north and my brother Mark in California.

I felt myself drift, feather by feather, toward sleep. *I used to be Snow White*, I thought to myself, *but I drifted.* I woke briefly as the street lights were going on, just long enough to realize Anders was still on the phone, and this time he was talking to Bibi. I pictured her standing in her bright, dye-stained work clothes in the studio her husband, a lawyer, had built onto their lakefront house. Maude was at Bibi's house, somewhere in its bright, art-filled rooms. I imagined Maude curled up on the couch in the den, watching Disney videos with Kyle. Or tearing through the high-ceilinged living room dressed up as a samurai gypsy raccoon. At age six, energy came and went in furious crushing waves. Then again, maybe energy always came and went that way.

I fell asleep again. When I woke for the second time it was after midnight. I was sweating, and my heart thumped painfully in my chest. I had been dreaming about something. But what? From the living room I heard the sound of the TV. Anders was watching something with a loud laugh track, then he channel-surfed past a music video and on to something that sounded like the D-Day invasion. Shells burst and marines hit the beach.

The emergency room. I had dreamed I was in the emergency room. Dreamed that somehow I had given birth to my baby—a baby no bigger than a bird. But, after the delivery, I hadn't been able to find her. I searched the hospital cubicle, frantically turning back the rumpled, bloody sheets. I had torn through my street clothes and Anders's coat, all piled sloppily in the corner. Doctors and nurses streamed by in the corridor outside on their way from car accident to drug overdose to asthma attack. No one but me was concerned with where one tiny, premature baby could have gotten to. I pulled on their white sleeves, crying over and over, "Help me, please. I've lost my baby."

Awake, I felt like I'd been punched. Even in my dreams I lost babies. In real life, though, I hadn't *lost* anything. That was just a euphemism, like saying *passed away*, instead of *dead*. For no reason anyone could tell me, my baby had died inside me, in my womb. Its tiny, fourteen-week-old body was carefully vacuumed out of my uterus so I wouldn't hemorrhage or grow septic with infection. But if I was being careful with the English language, my profession, after all, I probably shouldn't be saying *baby*. What I had lost was a fetus barely out of its first trimester, a staging-area for life, a vague plan for the future. Not a baby capable of living on its own, even with the help of the best emergency room. Still, I could close my eyes and see that last ultrasound, those large tadpole eyes, the tiny curled hands, the transparent heart so obviously not beating. I put my hand to my face. I was awake. This was no dream. But I was still crying.

"Hey," Anders was standing by the bed, with Ginger Rogers behind him like a long, low shadow. "I thought you were asleep." He put his palm on my cheek. "Can I get you anything? I had chicken noodle soup." He shrugged, knowing his suggestion was more appropriate for a chest cold than this heavy, wet grief.

"Where's Maude? Asleep?"

Anders shook his head. "Bibi kept her." I nodded. Tomorrow would be soon enough to tell Maude—already transformed in her own mind into that all-powerful being, the big sister—that this was not to be. The whole thing already seemed to me like some family game of dress-up. We had tried on the idea of a foursome the way Maude tried on costumes. But Maude was not a gypsy or a raccoon. And I was not going to have a baby. We would have to get used to being no one but ourselves.

I sat up. *Sit up. Get up.* I had a child—Maude. "They say soup is good food," I said. The flat simplicity of this advertising slogan had always struck me as funny.

"So they do," Anders said, and went to heat some.

The next day the flowers started to arrive. I hadn't stopped to consider that. And then cards, and friends calling to offer casseroles, or, because this was a college town where hardly anyone really cooked, to bring take-out. Maude came home. I sat with her on the couch, a blanket curled around us to keep off both the real and imagined cold. It was March, but this was Wisconsin and there was a fresh dusting of snow on the ground. Maude burrowed hard into my arms, trying, it seemed to me, to get closer to me than was physically possible, to be herself unborn, to be part of me again.

I told her about the miscarriage. Maude was silent. When Maude was little she had had the most amazing ideas about time. "When I am born again," she would say. "Or when you are the baby," as if time were a tide pool, where events moved forward, reversed themselves, spun endlessly around. Now, at six, for better or worse, she had learned to think of time, of life, as a straight line, as an interstate highway that ran relentlessly west.

There were tears in Maude's wintry blue eyes. "Why didn't she want to be born?" she asked.

I hugged my daughter more tightly. I had already stumbled through my explanation of how sometimes there was something wrong with a baby that meant it just couldn't live. What else to say? "I don't know, Sweetie," I said. "Honestly, I don't."

A week later, people were still sending cards. I bent to pick up the mail from where it had scattered across the mat after the postman shoved it through the slot in our door. *Sympathy* or *Get Well Soon!* or *Thinking of You.* Obviously it was hard for people to know quite what to send. I understood. Hallmark didn't have a line of sorry-to-hear-about-your-miscarriage cards, though considering the number of women who, since hearing about mine, had confided they had had one, two, or more pregnancies end abruptly themselves, maybe the card-makers were missing a major market, an untapped ocean of sentiment, grief and regret.

I stood in the dining room, aware Ginger was watching me in an uncharacteristic show of dog anxiety. Usually she spent nearly all her time fast asleep when she wasn't eating or being taken for a walk. I put the other mail—all bills—on the dining room table and tore open a card. A mother of one of Maude's friends wrote—"I know how you must feel. I lost a baby last year. But now I'm pregnant again and everything is going fine. If you would like to talk" . . . I closed the card and added the new ones, opened and unopened, to the pile on the old dresser we used as a sideboard. The dining-room table was bright with arrangements, vases of roses and tulips, delicate pots of paper whites. At first I had put some in the living room, in Maude's room. But they were always needing to be watered, to have the old blooms pulled, so finally it seemed easier to have them close to the kitchen.

I was grateful to the mother of Maude's playground buddy, to all the women whose losses, by and large, were greater than mine. More numerous, more painful, more dangerous and bloody. But I just didn't want to think about miscarriages anymore, didn't want any more doses of sympathy—that sticky, sad syrup. I was even avoiding Bibi. She hadn't avoided me when she'd gone through a lumpectomy and chemo earlier in the fall. We were friends. But I felt suddenly shy in my pain. When she called, I pretended I was napping and let the machine pick it up. Then I called back when I knew she would be elsewhere, teaching a workshop on papermaking or taking Kyle to violin, so I could leave short, perky messages—*Sorry I missed you! So busy! On the way out!*—on her answering machine, though I knew I wasn't fooling her.

I sorted through the pile of bills, the gas bill, the phone bill. One from the Y. I opened it. The annual ten-dollar rental fee for my locker was due. I felt guilty. I hadn't set foot in the Y in months. Not since Maude finished her last round of swimming lessons. And, to be honest, I hadn't worked out myself, used this locker regularly, in nearly four years, not since right after Maude was born when I was trying to flatten my post C-section stomach into something a bit more human and a bit less like a specimen of inept taxidermy. Why didn't I go? Maude was at school. Anders was teaching. I had another week of sick leave from the community college where I taught. Someone else was being paid to teach my freshmen that week and to grade their papers. For now, I could go to the Y if I wanted. Get some exercise. Go swimming. I could, at least, see if I still remembered the combination to my gym locker. Besides, if Bibi or anyone else called, I really would be out. I patted Ginger on the head as I left. "I'll be back," I said to her brown worried eyes, "I promise."

In the end, I had to ask the attendant for my combination. Once, in high school, I'd forgotten the combination for my gym locker, and the janitor had had to cut the lock off with a giant pair of shears. Luckily, at the Y they kept the combinations on file. From that I guessed I wasn't the only member who had ever wandered away from the exercise fold. My gym bag was still there, though dusty, along with my swimsuit and bottles of anti-chlorine shampoo. But when I tried to put on my swim cap it came apart in my fingers. I bought another from the same attendant who'd looked up my locker combination and also rented a fresh towel for fifty cents. I hated to think how long the one in my locker had gone without being washed.

In the women's locker room I stripped off my heavy sweater, turtleneck, and leggings and stood in front of the floor-length mirrors. At four months, my pregnancy had hardly begun to show, but still my middle looked thicker than I remembered. My stomach was a soft little pouch. To be honest, everything on my body looked softer than I remembered. As if, after all the years I'd spent trying to get pregnant, my body had decided the least it could do was look the part. I stepped on the scale and flinched. I needed to swim laps. Every day. Miles and miles.

I put on my suit, wrestled my hair into my cap, showered, and walked out onto the tile deck of the pool. Through the windows at the far end I could see the playground, empty and crusty with old snow. The lifeguard looked up from her clipboard and nodded. The only people in the pool were a half-dozen older women on the far side doing aquarobics. I recognized several from my post-Maude exercise kick—the woman with the terrible widow's hump, the one twisted from arthritis. But, bent or no, they were still alive and there, exercising.

I eased into the pool. The water always felt cold after the shower. The aquarobics class lifted their milk jugs full of water, kicking their legs to their young instructor's count. I adjusted my goggles and kicked off from the wall. It only took a lap for me to realize just what bad shape I was in. I had never been a competitive swimmer. I hadn't been on the swim team in high school let alone college. But, when I was little, there had always been a pool at the officer's club wherever my father was posted. After a few years kicking around in the shallow end, I had started swimming laps.

After the third lap I found myself gasping. I rolled over and did the backstroke. Then I alternated one lap of crawl, one of breaststroke. I didn't do speed turns. No one had ever taught me. But, then, it wasn't as if anyone was swimming on my heels. I had half a pool to myself. That was what I liked about this Y. I used to joke with Anders that the lanes should be marked slow, slower, and hardly moving. After Maude was born I tried swimming a time or two at the community college where I taught, but it was always full of students on the swim team. There, my slow pace had caused the swimming equivalent of a twenty-car pileup.

I finished my sixth lap and pushed hard off the side, taking the extra feet the glide gave me. I felt the muscles in my arms and legs groaning. My lungs creaked like the hinges on our old basement door. How had I gotten so out of shape? Maybe I had never been any kind of athlete, but this was ridiculous. It was a wonder I didn't fall down dead just climbing the stairs to my classroom. *Ten laps*, I said to myself, not really thinking I would make it. Then when I did, *fifteen is only five more*. I sank into a mindless rhythm. This was the part of swimming I had always liked best. No words. No time. No losses, old or new. My body was the shuttle weaving blue cloth on a loom. I stopped feeling tired, my arms and legs trusting the buoyancy of the water, moving easily stroke after stroke. Without noticing I had swum thirty laps.

I stopped at thirty-six. I felt I could have swum a few more, but I didn't want to overdo. Thirty-six laps was half a mile. I couldn't believe it. I'd swum half a mile. My legs wobbled only slightly as I climbed the ladder and walked across the deck toward the women's locker room. The lifeguard smiled down at me. "You might want to check the board," she said. "They've posted some changes in the pool schedule for tomorrow."

Tomorrow. Had the lifeguard mistaken me for a regular? Or was this something she pointed out to everyone? "I will," I said, trying not to pant too openly. "Thanks."

I did swim the next morning, another half mile. And another the morning after that. Ginger got used to me leaving the house, towel in hand, then returning, smelling of chlorine. I even took Maude to the Y for family swim time on Sunday and snuck in a dozen quick laps, one eye on my bobbing, dog-paddling daughter. On Monday, when I went back to teaching and didn't have time to swim in the morning, I found I spent most of the day thinking about when I could get to the Y. I went late that night, after Maude was in bed, with Ginger wheezing gently at her feet. When I told Anders I was headed out into the frosty, March night to swim, he looked up from the photographs he was matting, surprised.

Anders had just taken up casein printing, an early color photographic process that actually used the protein from milk powder. From Wisconsin dairies, he hoped, since he was a good Wisconsin boy. He had even driven out into the country surrounding our college town to take a few test pictures of Holsteins. It appealed to his mild Midwestern sense of irony—pictures of cows made from milk! And the process produced lovely, dreamy soft colors, I thought, rather like chalks or pastels. "Good for you," he said, and kissed me good-bye.

Swimming at night was okay, but I missed swimming in the morning when the pool was as flat and silver as the mirrors in the women's locker room. The next morning, as I fed Maude her oatmeal and Ginger her kibble, I kept imagining myself moving steadily through the cold, still water. I remembered a book I'd read once about the craze in the 1920s for long-distance swimming. There'd been black-and-white photos of smiling women greased from head to toe, ready to swim across the English Channel or from Key West to Cuba. Their training took years, their swims sometimes days. If I had lived then, if I hadn't had to work for a living, if I hadn't had a family, would I have been capable of something like that? I imagined swimming around the clock, nothing in my life but the quiet pull of my strokes in the water.

After Maude was safely off with Anders to wait for the school bus, I drove to the college, my briefcase full of papers I would have to find the time to grade before class. To my surprise, the road to the faculty parking lot was blocked by fire trucks, their lights a fit of lurid red. I stopped my car in a line of cars. The one in front of mine, a red Volvo wagon plastered with bumper stickers, was empty. I recognized it as belonging to Ted, the chair of the English department. *Eschew Obfuscation*, read one of his stickers. *Visualize Whirled Peas*, another. I got out of my car and stood looking toward the campus. I couldn't see any smoke. Students and teachers and administrators stood in small clumps on the athletic field by the side of the road. Beyond the fire trucks were police cars. A large gray van pulled up behind my stopped car, then cut heavily over the curb and drove across the grass past the fire engines. A man came up behind me. It was Ted. He was smoking one of his famous unfiltered black cigarettes, some Egyptian brand he had a friend send him. "Bomb squad," he said. "Telephone threat."

Ten years before, when I'd just started teaching at the college, someone had called in so many bomb threats in a row that the president of the college had been forced to lengthen the semester and postpone exams until after Christmas break. He even had to offer a few nervous students tuition refunds. Back then, in the post-Vietnam protest but pre-Oklahoma city, pre-Unabomber days I had never even considered that there might have been a bomb to go along with the any of the scares. These days, though, a bomb didn't seem quite so far-fetched.

I imagined my class and my life being stopped, mid-sentence, mid-worry, mid-breath, by something with enough explosive power to suck all the oxygen out of a building, imploding, then exploding it in a matter of seconds. What would that moment of airlessness be like? Quiet, like swimming underwater? I took a deep breath, let it out. "You don't think it's for real, do you?" I asked Ted, who had started teaching at the college the same year as I, had lived through that first long season of standing out on the lawn.

Ted pursed his lips, clearly turning the idea over, then shook his head. "Why go through the hassle and expense of building a bomb when a phone call gets you and all your friends out of class for a mere fifty cents?"

The dean of students—a large, unflappable woman—came over. She was originally from Newark, New Jersey, and wore the air of someone who had seen it all before. In this case, she had. She was another old-timer. Ted nodded at her. "Déjà vu all over again," he said. The dean nodded back.

"They've been at it for an hour and haven't even cleared the admin building," she said. "Shoo," she flapped both hands first at Ted, then at me. "Consider classes officially canceled." I stood there for a minute, blinking. The dean put her hands on her hips. "Don't expect me to tell you twice to take the day off," she said.

I obediently got back in my car, turned it around, and headed into town. I meant to head home, clean the oven, move the couch, and vacuum up dust bunnies. Write thank-you notes for all those flowers. To do at least a few of the thousand things that are on any working mother's *List of Things to Do*. But I didn't. I went to the Y.

After a week I was up to a mile. I stood looking at myself in the mirror, and except for a tendency for the chlorine to dry out my skin and make my hair a bit fuzzy, I thought I could already see improvement. My stomach looked flatter, less pregnant.

The only trouble with swimming a mile was that, at my speed, seventy-two laps took me well over an hour. Add the time I spent driving to the Y, showering and changing, and I was lucky to get done in two. Since Maude didn't go to bed until eight-thirty and the Y closed at ten, I kept finding myself standing by my locker in the dark after the janitor turned out the lights. I decided to try getting up really early. The Y opened at five. I flinched as I set my alarm for four thirty. Come on, I told myself, it's no earlier than you'd have to get up if you had a baby.

The first morning I made it back in time to make Maude

her bowl of instant oatmeal before Anders walked her to the bus stop, Ginger in tow. But the next day I malingered in the blissfully hot shower, and Anders had to microwave Maude's breakfast for her. And the next day I missed Maude altogether, arriving home with my wet hair half-frozen on my head just in time to see the school bus turn the corner, leaving nothing but a puff of gray diesel exhaust.

I decided trying to split my swimming into two shifts, to go early in the morning and then again after Maude was in bed. Maybe that way, I thought, I'd even have time to swim a mile and a half. But that night, when Anders saw me headed out the door with my suit wrapped in a fresh towel, he frowned.

Then, once in the pool, I found I just couldn't get my strokes right. When I stopped after a bare twenty laps, my legs felt dead. Discouraged, I sat in the whirlpool for a while, letting the tiredness seep out of my bones into the hot swirling water. The young woman next to me looked over and smiled. I recognized her as the morning aquarobics instructor.

"You put in a long day," the instructor said, nodding at me.

"You, too," I said.

The instructor shrugged. "I'm working on my master's in recreation science. Teaching at the Y is my practicum. Plus, I get paid, so it's kind of a twofer."

"Oh," I said. I didn't know recreation was a science, but then, these days, what wasn't? I sank a little lower into the foaming water.

"Do you mind if I ask you something?" the aquarobics teacher asked. She hesitated. "It's for my thesis."

"Ask away," I said, expecting questions about my chosen form of recreation—how often I used the Y, how far I swam every day.

The instructor cleared her throat. "When did your mother die?"

"What?" I asked, not sure I had heard her correctly. How could she know my mother was dead?

"Oh, I'm sorry if that was rude. It's just that the data I've gathered so far shows that forty-one percent of women who have just begun exercising regularly recently lost a mother." My mother had been dead nearly twelve years. Surely, that didn't qualify as a recent loss.

"And the other fifty-nine percent?" I asked.

"Oh, a mix—divorce, cancer, alcohol recovery, the death of a child."

I winced. "I had a miscarriage," I said. "Is that a common reason?"

"No," the instructor said. A good Wisconsin *noooo*, like a soft mooing cow. "That's a new one."

When I snuck into bed that night, Anders moved close, wrapped his long warm arms around me. He nuzzled my damp, chlorine-scented hair. "Hey, Al," he said, and kissed my neck. At my checkup the doctor had told us a single miscarriage was not usually an indication of future difficulties. If we wanted more children, he said, we should keep trying.

"Trying," I said afterward, riding down in the elevator. It was hard for me to believe after six years of trying we were going to get lucky a second time.

"Half the fun," Anders had said, repeating our old, worn joke, and kissed me.

"Feel like trying?" Anders said now, moving up to my lips.

"I'm scared," I said, and as soon as I heard the words, I knew how true they were. What if I did get pregnant again? What if there was something terribly wrong with me? I imagined my womb as a kind of dry-cleaning bag—*this is not a toy*—something that smothered helpless, unsuspecting babies.

"Me too, Alice," Anders said, holding me tight. "Me too." And we made soft, timid love, though whether we were afraid our movements might somehow hurt the baby we had already lost or the one we had not yet conceived, it was hard to say.

That night I swam even in my dreams. But the pool at the

Y was full not of grown orphaned women but of babies. New-borns who swam like porpoises, surfacing only to spit tiny fountains of water. I could tell which one was mine, but no matter how hard I tried to catch her, she slipped from my hands. Finally, the lifeguard blew her whistle and made me climb out of the pool. "You know the rules," the lifeguard scolded me. "No holding on. In this pool the babies belong to themselves."

The next morning when the alarm went off at four-thirty, I groaned. My dream made me think I had already been swim-ming, had somehow done my laps, then ended up back in bed. The alarm beeped again, and I rolled over, ready to get up. But, as soon as my right ear touched the pillow, an amaz-ing ray of pain, like hot light, shot through my head. "Ow," I said, probing the outside of my ear gently with my fingers. Just touching it hurt. Instead of going swimming I waited until Maude was safely oatmealed and on her way and then drove to my HMO's Immediate Care Clinic, hoping to get treated quickly enough to work in at least a half-mile. The doctor at the clinic diagnosed my problem as swimmer's ear. "Here," she said, handing me a bottle of antibiotic and steroid drops. "Twice a day," she said. "And keep those ears dry. Use a blow-dryer or alcohol. Usually I say no swimming for at least ten days unless you're a competitive swimmer. Are you?"

Ten days. "No," I said, shaking my head reluctantly. "I don't compete." *No swimming,* I thought. I would go from here to teach my morning classes, eat lunch, teach my afternoon sec-tions. Then I would go home. It felt like the start of a long, landlocked day.

It was. In the middle of my afternoon remedial English class the campus police came in and arrested one of my favorite students, Mickey, a sweet, quiet Winnebago boy who last year had invited Maude and me to the Native American Student Association Pow Wow in the college gym. He had led Maude

around the circle during the All-Tribal Dance. Maude still talked about it. Now, it seemed, he was the one who'd phoned in
last week's bomb threat. He'd used the phone at his mother's
house, and the police had traced the call. "Well," he said to
the campus police when they cuffed him, "you caught me."

The other students in the class glared at him. Most were
Hispanic or Hmong, new to Wisconsin. They worked nights
to pay for their classes and didn't like the idea of someone
cheating them out of even one. What, I wondered, had Mickey's mother thought when the police came to the door? What
would I have thought if Mickey were my son? That he should
have used a pay phone, for starters. "Oh, Mickey," I said as the
police led him out.

Mickey turned to me and said, "I just want you to know,
Ms. Dahl, I didn't do it to get out of your class. I like writing.
It was math. I'm just terrible at numbers." Mickey smiled at
me, a tall, dark-haired boy in a green and yellow *Go Packers!*
sweatshirt.

As soon as my class was over I went to my office and called
Bibi's husband Lloyd. He was a senior partner in a law firm
so established that it listed two ex-governors on its letterhead.
Mickey wasn't Lloyd's kind of case, but he was my best friend's
husband and the only lawyer I knew. When I told him about
Mickey he sighed deeply but said, for me, he would look into
it. "But I won't kid you, Alice. It's not good," Lloyd said. "If
they want to, they could make this a federal case."

Then, when I got home, Maude handed me a note from
her teacher saying she was having problems at school. Up to
this point Maude had never been in trouble. Well, once: the
first week of kindergarten, for yodeling in the girl's bathroom.
But it was an old school with high-ceilinged, tile restrooms.
With acoustics like that, Anders had pointed out at the time,
who could resist? Otherwise, Maude had seemed to swim easily and brightly through the aquarium that was school, the
happiest of tropical fish. She could read and count, which put

133

her ahead of Mickey, who had managed to graduate from a high school in Milwaukee unable to do either. She had a good dozen "best" friends. The school principal smiled when she saw Maude in the hall.

Her teacher, Mrs. Messerman, now wrote that Maude was not waiting in line, not getting her work done, not following instructions. Acting more like a kindergartner than a first-grader. Maude had given me the note as if there were nothing in the world wrong, then plugged herself into TV and the headphones. She was watching what looked to the outside world like a silent version of *Snow White*. The Wicked Queen offered Snow White her red, red poisoned apple. "She's only six," I said to Anders. "What does Mrs. Messerman expect?"

Anders raised an eyebrow. "What do you expect from your students?"

I sighed. I hadn't had a chance to tell Anders about my bomber. At least Maude didn't need a lawyer—not yet. "I'll write her a note," I said. "Tell her about . . ." I honestly thought I was going to say "the miscarriage" but instead I said "Maude's grief." The words took me by surprise. *Grief.* I felt the press of the old wet sadness. But that was my grief. And Maude's? I looked over at my daughter. Maude was sucking her thumb, something she hadn't done since preschool. If she couldn't be a big sister, I imagined her thinking, then why grow up at all? On the screen, Snow White took a bite of the poisoned apple and fell into a deep, timeless sleep.

Anders was watching Maude too. He shook his head.

Swimming, I thought, *swimming was simpler than this.*

The next day brought a note in return, this one asking if I could come in for a conference. Anders went too, but stayed outside on the playground keeping watch over Maude and Kyle. I went alone and sat in one of the tiny first grade–sized chairs.

"I wish you'd told me," Mrs. Messerman said. She was an

older woman, near retirement, with a soft halo of faintly blue hair. "Maude is worried about you." She patted my hand.

"She is?" I said.

Mrs. Messerman nodded. "I suggested you might need some counseling. But Maude has great confidence in you. She said you would be fine."

I felt my face burn. Which Maude was right? The one who was worried or the one who thought her mother would be A-okay?

"So," Mrs. Messerman said, tapping one finger lightly on the table in front of me, "you wouldn't want to disappoint her, now would you?"

When I came out of the school I saw Bibi standing by the edge of the blacktop, watching Anders push first Maude, then Kyle on the swings. Bibi's dark hair was starting to grow again after her chemo. It looked like the short, luxurious fur of some endangered animal, one that always had poachers after its pelt. I wondered what Anders had told her.

"Well, girl," Bibi said. "You've been making yourself scarce." *Scarce*, I thought. I imagined my new thin self in the mirrors at the Y, heard again Mrs. Messerman's voice: "Maude is worried about you." It was true. Since the miscarriage, I'd scarcely been there—for Maude, for Anders, for Bibi. I thought about how the first lap felt in the morning, that blue rush of the water. I couldn't help it. I wished I were swimming. Bibi held me at arm's length, looked me up and then down. "But, damn, you look great," she said. She touched a finger to my chlorine-desiccated hair. "Except you could use a good conditioner."

"Mom!" Kyle shouted, noticing his mother for the first time. He escaped the swing and came running over, wrapped his long, pale arms around Bibi as if, like some magician's rabbit, she might disappear. Maude was right behind him. She grabbed me around the legs, hugging me almost painfully hard. Kyle had almost lost his mother to cancer. He had good reason to hold her tight. But Maude? What was she afraid of?

Her mother swimming to Cuba, I thought, *and not coming back.*

"By the way," Bibi said. "Lloyd called to say he'd be late. It seems he's representing your college's mad bomber."

That night, Mickey's arraignment was on the evening news. Lloyd, looking nearly presidential in his silver hair and dark blue suit, stood next to him. His mother, a woman I had last seen at the Pow Wow wearing a split doeskin dress, sat behind her son dressed in a nurse's uniform, weeping quietly. At Lloyd's urging the judge released Mickey into his mother's custody, pending trial. There was no mention of federal charges. Lloyd was good, I thought, watching him nod and smile at the judge, shake Mickey's hand. For now Mickey was free to go, but not, it turned out, free to come back to my class. Ted called to tell me the dean of students had expelled him.

"Damn," I said to Ted, though I could see the dean's point of view. The college didn't need a dozen other students, flunking math or welding, calling in bomb threats. But Mickey—what would he do now? Then, again, the way it had been going, how likely was it he would ever pass enough classes to graduate? "Goddamn it to hell," I said, feeling useless and angry. What kind of teacher was I, anyway? And Ted, who had never heard me say *darn* before, listened, speechless.

After Ted's call I paced the living room, Ginger padding worriedly in my footsteps, until Anders actually suggested I go to the Y. I left Anders to put Maude to bed and went to walk on the treadmill, boring myself as I walked five miles by reading a rumpled copy of the previous week's Sunday *New York Times.* Walking in place, swimming in circles, teaching students so far behind they would never catch up, I felt like a woman only pretending she was getting somewhere.

When I got home I found Anders in a slow boil. "Maude's in the tub," he said. "She refused to get out." This was unheard of. Maude was not one to linger near soap. "She said she wouldn't get out unless I carried her. And, on top of that, still sitting in the tub, she announced she wasn't old enough to get dressed by herself. Not even into her pajamas."

"Not old enough?" Maude had been dressing herself since she was three. She had peculiar, Maudish ideas about what went together, and I'd had to learn, when entering a room with a daughter clad in purple plaid pants and a shirt with red polka dots, not to say loudly, "*She picks out her own clothes.*" Besides, in some way that defied all established rules of fashion, the combinations always looked smashing on Maude. Even about what constituted the proper mix of pajama tops and bottoms was normally something only Maude herself could decide. "Where is she?"

Anders nodded at the closed bathroom door. "I gave her a time out."

"In the tub?" I asked. Anders shrugged, his arms folded across his chest, a splendid example of the true dark, Norwegian funk his ancestors had brought with them to this new world of Wisconsin. I looked at the clock. It was nearly nine. "It's past her bedtime." He shook his head, holding his ground.

I went into the bathroom. Maude was scrunched down in the water, playing idly with a rubber duck. She still had shampoo suds in her hair. "What's the matter, Sweetie? Are you sick?" Maude shook her head.

"Daddy yelled at me." Rather than being upset, she sounded oddly pleased with herself, as if she'd accomplished some difficult adult task.

"Well," I said, "you wouldn't do what he asked and . . ." I wondered what to say. *And he lost it?* That hardly seemed appropriate. "Come on now, Maude," I said. "Enough of this. It's late. Let me rinse your hair." I picked up the old enamel saucepan we used for sluicing Maude, and scooped it full of bath water.

Maude covered her head with both arms. "Noooooo," she said, in what I supposed was Maude's idea of loud, mock rage.

I felt a matching surge of real anger. I poured the water over Maude's head. Maude shrieked and kept shrieking. "It's cold!" she said. I felt the water. It was less than lukewarm, but there was no helping that now.

"Stand up and I'll dry you off," I said, but Maude kept screaming, a high odd sound. To my trained mother's ear, Maude's misery sounded fake.

"It was cold! The water was cold!" In the small bathroom, the noise was unbearable, like the wailing of a colicky baby. It was impossible not to react, not to do something to silence Maude.

"Stop it!" I lifted the pan in the air, and for one awful moment I thought I might hit Maude with it. Then I brought it down hard on the edge of the tub. Chips of enamel flew in the air. Maude stopped, stared at her mother, open-mouthed. I moved the pan, trying to see if the chips had come from it or the tub. The pan—as if that was what mattered. Maude slumped back in the tub, clutching the duck.

"Go away!" she said.

I opened my mouth and, from the wasteland of bad parenting I seemed suddenly trapped in, came the words, "For God's sake, Maude. You're six years old. Quit acting like a baby."

Maude heard the word *baby* and burst into genuine tears. Baby. I felt like crying too. Instead, I scooped Maude out of the tub, wrapped her in our largest, fluffiest towel, and carried her to the couch. When Anders came tentatively into the room I shook my head, mouthed the word "later" over Maude's head.

"Why?" Maude sobbed, "why didn't she want to be born? Didn't she know I loved her?"

"Shhh," I said, the way I had when Maude was a baby and woke up in the night, "shhh." I held my daughter tightly, rocking her back and forth in my lap. Maude was so big now, her head bumped awkwardly against my chin, her legs flopping loosely back and forth over mine. It was hard to believe Maude had ever fit inside me. She'd been born by Caesarean section after a monumentally long and unproductive labor. Anders always joked Maude had been so comfortable where she was, the doctor had to go and get her. Slowly, slowly Maude's sobbing eased, gave way to wet, gulping hiccups. I pushed the damp hair out of my daughter's blue eyes. Maude looked up at me.

"I should have talked to her," Maude said, her voice a hoarse whisper. I had a sudden vision of Maude down on her knees, whispering to her tiny floating sister through my navel. "Told her I didn't want to be born either." Maude shook softly. "But it turned out okay."

"It did?" I asked my daughter.

"Sure, see," my daughter said, and spread her hands to take in the warm couch with her mother, her father's tall silhouette in the doorway, our small wooden house, the town, Kyle and Lloyd and Bibi, her teacher and her school, Mickey and his mother, Wisconsin, America, the planet Earth, that big, blue swimming pool. Maude nodded, as if the answer were simple. And who knew, I thought, maybe it was.

Maude rubbed her eyes, yawned wide. "I didn't really know her," she said of the sister she wasn't going to have, her voice faint and sleepy, "but I miss her."

I kissed my daughter's wet head. "Me, too, Maude," I said. "Me too."

Mary

"Let's play hookey," I said to my family. It was late Saturday morning. Anders was at the computer, working on assignments for his beginning photo class. Our basset, Ginger Rogers, lay, sprawled, sleeping on his right foot. Maude was in her room, trying to train a pair of ladybugs that had wandered in from the garden into walking down a pencil balanced between two upturned jelly jars. I'd been proofreading a guide to county parks, a project I'd taken on in the hopes of earning enough to avoid teaching summer school. I had meant to zip right through it, correcting misplaced apostrophes or changing an adjective or two to make the prose more graceful. But I'd found myself reading the booklet as if I'd picked it up at the Wisconsin Department of Tourism. I had no idea there were so many county parks. I had lived in Wisconsin for nearly twenty years and hadn't set foot in a single one.

Outside, it was early spring. The sun was shining through the still leafless trees and the flowerbeds were speckled with the shy colors of crocus. I was struck with wanderlust.

"How can we play hookey if it's not a school day?" Maude asked, carrying the ladybugs into the living room in one of the jars. Maude was in first grade and had only this year learned about the possibility of hookey when two third graders in her school got suspensions for skipping school. Even Maude, a mere seven, had pronounced that ironic.

"Hookey from the house," I said.

"What?" Anders said, not turning his head to look at me, his eyes still fixed on the computer screen.

"Hookey," I said, more loudly, as if my husband were already old and deaf. "Let's get out, have an adventure. Breathe some fresh air." I heard the grating note of irritation in my voice.

Lately, Anders and Maude and I had seemed to draw into our own spaces, our own rooms, our own shells. When we passed each other in the hall on the way to the bathroom or the kitchen we politely excused ourselves to each other. Or sometimes not so politely. As if having to live as a family was a strain on us all. I felt itchy and irritated, and suspected they felt the same. Maybe it was just the result of the long Wisconsin winter, but I was afraid it was a sign of something deeper, a sign that the miscarriage I had had that winter or some other unspoken loss had loosened the sweet, sticky, daily bonds of my family.

Next thing we knew, Anders would be reading the newspaper at breakfast and we'd all be watching the TV during dinner and our lives would take on that awful black-and-white taint of a fifties sitcom. And what was the point of that? Of spending time together as if we were passengers who just happened to be on the same train?

Anders looked up from the computer. I thought he was about to say, "You two go. I've got work to do." But instead he looked at me and something in my face changed his mind. "Sure, always up for adventure," he said, pushing the hair off his forehead. "Where to?"

I held up the brochure. "How about Indian Lake Park?"

"It's too early to swim, Mom," Maude said, as if I had forgotten that just last week she was playing King of the Hill on the icy remains of the snow pile formed by the plows in the school parking lot. After the previous long winter, no lake in Wisconsin would be warm enough for swimming until June.

"Not swim, Sweetie. I want to take a hike. There's this little church you can climb to." I read from the pamphlet. "*Mary of the Oaks.* In 1857, John Endres built this small chapel to thank the Virgin Mary for protecting his family during a diphtheria epidemic."

"You know what," Anders said, looking down at the stamp-sized picture of the church. "I've been there. Years ago with my mother. But I don't think it was a park when I went. The families on the neighboring farms just kind of kept it up." He tapped the picture with his index finger.

Maude sighed and rolled her eyes. I could see she was working her way up to a flat-out refusal. Next would come the list of TV shows she would miss if she left the house, the friends she could be playing with if we would only call and arrange for them to come over. Lately she seemed to plunge, without warning, into some kind of preadolescent angst. Maybe it was a sign she was growing up. But I didn't like it.

Luckily, she could usually be talked into coming around. "Come on, Maude," I said, my voice sounding more sore than inspiring. She crossed her arms over her chest. I looked at Anders and shrugged, tossing him the parental ball.

Anders did his best to spike it over the net. "I'll tell you what," he said. "We'll haul along the eight-by-ten camera and I'll let you take some really big pictures. You can take one of the church and give it to Grams."

"Great," I said.

"Can we take Ginger?" Maude asked.

"Hmm," I said, trying to remember from the pamphlet whether the park allowed dogs. "Better not."

Maude frowned, but Anders put his arm around her shoulders and squeezed her. Maude sighed again, but less heavily.

"But I wanted to play with Spot and Lady," she said, holding up her bug jar. Anders looked down at the ladybugs. In the spring, the red-and-black insects swarmed the southern sunny side of our house.

"How come one is black?" he said.

"I couldn't tell them apart, so I colored Spot with permanent marker."

Anders frowned. "Come," he said, taking the jar from his daughter. "On the way to the car, we'll set them free. Running a ladybug internment camp can't be good for your karma."

So we did go, driving the minivan out of our crowded downtown neighborhood, a family on the move, headed somewhere at last. Anders took the beltline around town, passing the this-could-be-anywhere-in-America pet food warehouses and McDonald's and Walmarts and strip malls full of specialty stores you couldn't help wondering about—House of Dinettes, Just Leather, The Stool Store. *Who shopped there?* I always wondered. Just how many stools did a town our size need?

But this was Wisconsin, so in ten minutes we were past the giant new Home Depot and out into the countryside, passing family farms complete with neat white farmhouses, red barns, silver silos, dairy cows swishing their tails as they tore hungrily at tender spring grass. The land opened up around us, gently rolling, shading from deep brown to pale green. It felt as if we had emerged from a tunnel, dark and concrete, into the daylight. Beside me, I could sense Anders relax, and even Maude, who had been kicking the back of my seat, stopped and began humming softly as the fields rolled by. "Row, row, row your boat," she hummed under her breath. "Merrily, merrily, merrily, merrily, life is but a dream."

Was it? I wondered, as Anders turned off the two-lane highway onto the county road that led to the park. If so, right now it was a pleasant one. I rolled my window down and the spring came in the window in warm damp gusts—the scent of wet, no-longer-frozen earth, of the chlorophyll in the tender plants. Even the usual Wisconsin whiff of cow manure seemed mild, a mere faint promise of ripeness to come.

We passed a cream-colored stone farmhouse that was a dead ringer for Anders's family home. White curtains shining in the arched stone windows, probably built around the same time as the Dahl home, in the 1870s, a dozen years after Endres built his chapel. The road turned right then headed down into a valley.

"There," Anders pointed, and we all saw Indian Lake. A small lake by Wisconsin standards—five acres, the pamphlet had said—but it shone as blue as Maude and Anders's eyes. Anders turned into the park and stopped the van in the small paved lot halfway between the lake and the surrounding hills. There were a half-dozen other cars there, minivans and station wagons mostly, but no one else in sight—just a single empty picnic table with a hand pump next to it and a small brown shed that no doubt housed a pit toilet. It was the complete Wisconsin all-season park setup—no pipes to freeze and burst.

Anders got out and began to unload his tall silver tripod, the bulky wooden box that held his battered antique camera, and the other paraphernalia of large-format photography. Maude unfolded herself from the backseat and stood blinking and stretching on the sun-warmed blacktop as if she had been asleep. "It's this way, I think," I said, pointing across the picnic grounds to the nearest hill. Anders shouldered the camera and tripod, Maude took my hand, and we set out.

The sign at the foot of the trail carried a variation on the text from the pamphlet: *1857, diphtheria, stone hauled by a team of oxen.* Anders put down his camera and studied it. "The chapel was formally dedicated by Archbishop Messmer in 1926," I read out.

Anders poked me. "Don't you mean Messmerized?"

I snorted and Maude laughed too, though she couldn't possibly have gotten her father's obscure pun. The laugh seemed to break some droopy spell, because she suddenly came alive with Maudish energy. "Last one up," she said, hopping on one foot, and then she was gone, bolting up the wooden stairs that climbed the hill.

"Last one!" Anders said, handing me the tripod to even out the race.

I let them tough it out, racing for the top. I swung the tripod across one shoulder like a blunderbuss and took my time with the stairs and the zigzag path beyond. I found Anders almost at the top, resting on a bench by a bend in the path. Maude was crouched a few yards further up the trail, poking at the ground and singing "Merrily, merrily, merrily, merrily." I stopped, trying not to pant. This was a hill, after all, a Wisconsin-sized hill, not an Alp.

Behind Anders the hill dropped away, and I could see how high we were, see the sweep of the valley below. The lake still shone, that bluest eye. The fields turned brown and tan in turns as the shadows of clouds raced across them. I felt the pull of the empty dizzying air, like a bird about to trust its body to the whim of the currents. I leaned forward. Anders took my hand and pulled me down on the bench beside him.

I looked back down the steep muddy path. "I can't imagine what it must have been like, hauling stone up this hill," I said, shaking my head. "Oxen or no."

Anders smiled ruefully and pointed at the camera box at his feet. "I can," he said. "At least I can imagine how the ox felt."

He was joking, of course, but, in his Anders way he was also being dead serious. His ancestors were Lutherans, not inclined to build chapels to Mary, but they had cleared their land and cut and hauled the stones for their houses. Anders had told me his grandfather still kept a team of draft horses when Anders was little, for pulling stumps and other slow hard work. Growing up on a farm, Anders had done milking, mucking, harrowing, and harvesting every day until he went off to college and left all the early-dawn chores and long farm days to his father and brother. He wasn't alone. Almost everyone I met in Wisconsin seemed to have grown up on a farm, to have left behind parents who still got up every day to do the endless chores.

My father had spent thirty years in the army. His father had been a small-town store owner, as had his father before him. My mother had been a housewife most of the time, though she had been a kindergarten teacher in Germany before she married my father and came to America. So, as far as I knew, no one in my family had driven oxen or planted or plowed since they had arrived in the New World.

"Look, Momma." Maude had come back down the path with something in her hand. It was a twig with a single white blossom. She held it to my nose. It smelled sweet and subtly fruity.

"Apple blossom," Anders said. "They must have had an orchard up here." He pointed up the path, and I saw a pair of short twisted trees, still black and leafless after the winter but dotted with a few white blooms, like the first stars at dusk. I looked into the woods and spotted more fruit trees gone wild with no patient farm family to tend them. Was that what would happen to all the Wisconsin farms when the parents got too old and grew tired of their chores, when their children, moved to suburb and town, could no longer imagine living such a life? I tried to imagine Anders's parents' farm overgrown, first weeds then trees taking over the cornfields. I shook my head. Anders's brother, Hal, was there to make sure that didn't happen.

"Come on, Maudie Maude," Anders said, standing up from the bench. "Sit here with your mom and I'll take a picture." Maude flopped down beside me and snuggled under my arm.

I expected he would stoop to unbox his eight-by-ten, which meant we were in for a long rest as he mounted the camera on the tripod, metered the light for the exposure, ducked under the black cloth hood to focus, fitted the wooden filmholders into place in the camera—but then in a place like this maybe old-fashioned patience was called for. If the John Endres family had posed here, looking over their land, they would have had to go through the same long wait to be immortalized. But, instead, Anders whipped out the small Polaroid he sometimes used to check a shot. He set it on a tall stump opposite the bench and clicked the self-timer.

"Say Deep Fried Cheese Curds," he said, naming one of Wisconsin's favorite high-cholesterol appetizers. He flung himself on the bench on the other side of Maude. The bench tipped back with his weight. My heart skipped, ready for a wild tumble down to the valley below.

"Cheese," said Maude.

"Eeek," said her mom.

The flash on the camera popped and with a little satisfied hiss it stuck out our still-developing picture like a rude tongue. The bench did not tip over, hurling us to our deaths.

Anders plucked the Polaroid from the camera and held it out for me to see. Still pale but visible were three people, their eyes wide with what—surprise? terror? We clutched each other as if in fear for our lives, as if the future were racing toward us like a runaway train. Was our reaction all tippy bench? I wasn't sure.

"Not too bad," Anders said, and stuck the Polaroid into his shirt pocket. He shouldered his equipment. "Last one there, rotten egg, etc.," he said to Maude. And they were off again.

When I reached the top, Anders was just coming out of the chapel, which was a rectangle of white stuccoed stone with a roof of tin sheeting. He had left his camera and tripod just outside the iron fence that surrounded it. I could hear Maude's voice coming from what I guessed was inside, singing as muffled as if she were in the tub. I started toward them and in two strides I was there. The chapel was closer than I thought—because it was much smaller than I had imagined. I had the oddest sensation of collapsing perspective, as if I had walked into a mirror thinking it was a door to another room.

The chapel was tiny, about the size of the Sears sheds my father had always had in back of our various houses to hold the lawn mower and rakes, about the size of the elevator in the building where Anders taught. I had imagined something Las Vegas wedding chapel–size—something that would seat, say, a party of eight. This was either a chapel for munchkins or built for a single soul in prayer. A small stained-glass cross shone blood-red in the chapel's heavy wooden door. I lifted the cast-iron latch, swung the door open, and stepped inside.

Inside felt even smaller. The walls were white stucco. A simple wooden altar, more shelf than table, was the only furniture. Above the altar stood Mary, Mother of God, her dainty feet resting on a blue globe spangled with gold stars. There were no pews, no room, really, for even a chair. A single window, cut through the foot-thick stone walls, let in the spring sun. Maude was standing by the altar, the light from the window turning her hair into a halo almost as golden as Mary's. She was looking at a framed picture on the opposite wall, a nearly naked baby Jesus floating on a pair of fat pink clouds. Jesus's bare skin was a faint, chilly blue, as if he felt underdressed for the weather.

"Maudie?" Anders called from the world outside. "Could I borrow you? I need someone just your size to hold the light meter."

"Coming!" Maude yelled back. I squeezed to one side, and Maude shot past me and out the door.

"It's kind of creepy," I heard her say to her father. "There's a picture of a dead baby."

I didn't hear what Anders said in reply. I took the one small step it took to reach the altar from the door. On the altar, at Mary's feet, was a blue spiral notebook. Next to the notebook sat a vase, not of flowers, but pens. I flipped open the notebook. It was filled with handwritten notes—a polite, restrained Wisconsin version of graffiti—or the tiny silver charms—hands, feet, hearts—that Mexican Catholics left behind to remind the Virgin of their needs and their prayers. Some were the sort of messages you might see in any visitor's log left at a tourist site. "Thanks for keeping up such an important historical site. We enjoyed it!" And, "Way cool! I'm here with my best friend."

But many of the messages were openly addressed to the Mother of God, whose chapel this was. "Dear Mary, please help my daughter Kelly Marie who was named in your honor and now needs our prayers," read one in neat blue cursive. Others were religious without being addressed so directly to Mary. Some were thankful. "I offer prayers for all the farmers who work so hard." "Thanks for helping Jack Lehman get along so well in chemotherapy." Some were desperate and direct. "Dear Father, please forgive me for not praying last night and for all the bad things I done in my life. Please take care of Grandma and get her out of the hospital."

Even the groups of schoolchildren, obviously frequent visitors, seemed to catch the mood of reflection, of self-examination. "I hoppe to do better with foloing direshions. Love You, Nick." And, "Please help the kitten we saw on the side of the road, Erica." It seemed rude to read what others had written and not write something. The vase of pens made it seem like a written message was the expected offering, words the coin in the plate. But what would I say? I was stuck between the "lovely historical site camp" and the "Mary, Mother of God." I wanted to write, "Watch over my family. Protect them from all harm." But that always made me feel as if there were a missing postscript to that prayer: "p.s. Let all the bad stuff happen to someone else's loved ones."

When it came to religion, I hadn't been raised as anything in particular. In our travels from base to base I would occasionally get signed up for Sunday School. Presbyterian, Methodist,

Baptist, whichever was closest. Once I made a silhouette for a Mother's Day present. Once a Styrofoam-and-glitter Christmas ornament. But I never seemed to go to any one place long enough to figure out what, exactly, Christians believed.

For a long time I thought that after getting pregnant with Jesus, Mary had divorced God and married Joseph. Who could blame her? In the illustrations in our children's Bibles, God looked like a mean, mad old man, while Joseph was young, blond, and much better looking. I decided the troubles we heard so much about in Sunday School just boiled down to your average, messy custody dispute. Which side would Jesus choose—God or Man? Father or Stepfather? Every kid I knew with divorced parents had to make that sort of choice sooner or later.

I had managed to come out of my muddled religious training with a strong belief in Good—I just wasn't sure about God. Lately Maude and I had taken to attending the local Unitarian Meeting House, where she studied Buddha one week and Jesus the next, and I listened to sermons about being kind to the earth by recycling. Maude loved it. Anyplace where there were people gathered together was her kind of place. And me? Sometimes I felt silly singing hymns with the word *God* replaced by *Nature*, but it seemed the best I could do.

Anders, on the other hand, had been raised with the hard hand of religion at his back, attending Lutheran services without fail with his mother, father, brother, and sister. He knew his Bible by chapter and verse and swore he would never attend a church service again. Not even one where we sang about Light instead of the Lord. As far as he was concerned, Maude could figure it out for herself. She was smart. She didn't need anyone to tell her what to believe. I stole a sideways glance at the blue baby Jesus. Probably, he was right. Still . . .

I heard the fence gate clang open, was aware of someone blocking the light. I turned, expecting Anders, but it was a stranger, a woman. I stepped back from the altar. The woman squeezed by, followed by two girls, twins, younger than Maude. I stood in the doorway, not wanting to be rude, but not quite ready to leave. I hadn't written anything in the notebook.

"What were you looking at?" one of the girls asked me.

"That notebook," I said, pointing toward the altar. "You can write in it if you want. Look, there are pens."

The mother coughed, then went down on her knees in front of the altar with a painfully audible thud. "Girls," she said loudly to her daughters, "this is what you do in a chapel." She crossed herself and bent her head in prayer. The twins stared at their mother, startled. Clearly they had never seen her pray before.

Someone touched my shoulder—Anders. "Lapsed Catholic," he whispered in my ear. "Take my word for it." Then he stepped back. One of the little girls cleared her throat. "Mom?" she said. The mother began a Hail Mary.

I turned and followed Anders out into the thin early spring sunshine. It hadn't seemed dim inside, but I found myself blinking like a mole.

"Kind of the Mercury capsule of religious shrines, isn't it?" Anders said, surveying the chapel with his arms folded across his chest. "You don't get in it, so much as put it on." Anders's camera was already back in its box, his tripod folded and lying horizontal on the ground. I had missed the actual shoot.

"Hey," Maude called. I looked around but didn't see her.

"That way," Anders said, pointing at a clump of birch trees. "There's an overlook."

I walked down the path and spotted Maude sitting on another wooden bench, swinging her legs. This second overlook showed the same view as the one where Anders had taken our picture but from a much higher vantage point. Again it revealed the bright metal of the lake, the rough rust brown of the fields.

"Oh, it's you, Mom," Maude said. "I wanted Dad. I wanted to take a picture of the cows." She pointed at the horizon. On the far side of the road, small white-and-black dots headed for a barn half-hidden by the trees. I knew Anders would try to explain to her just how tiny those cows would look in a photograph, how there might be more suitable subjects, but I also knew she would probably win in the end. No matter how small, when she looked at her picture she would see cows.

"I'll get him," I said, and headed back to the chapel.

Anders was just stepping out of the door when I reached it. Had he been taking an interior shot? Hard to imagine with such a large camera in so small a space. When I told him what Maude wanted he sighed, and headed her way with the camera slung over one shoulder, the tripod over the other.

I checked the chapel. It was empty. I couldn't leave without writing something in the notebook. I was an English teacher, for Heaven's sake. Words were my life. If possible, the interior chapel seemed even smaller this second time, as if God's part of the world were shrinking. I flipped the cover back on the blue notebook and it fell open to a photograph, a Polaroid of three pale but smiling people. A mother, a father, a daughter. Me, Anders, Maude. Us. For Anders, photographer, words were never the answer.

I touched a finger to the cool surface of the picture. Before, we had looked frightened, clutching at each other. Now, fully developed, we looked pink-cheeked and happy. Was this picture the equivalent of my unwritten word prayer: Take care of my family? No, no, somehow it was bigger than that. Anders and I were each hugging Maude, but our spare arms were thrown wide. Maybe for balance, maybe to welcome—who? All souls in Wisconsin, in America, on the planet Earth, that big blue balloon? What could I add to that?

I looked up and was aware for the first time of how steadily Mary was gazing down at me, her face in turns sad, wise, knowing. Mary, a mother too. What could I tell her about the griefs and joys of my family, my husband, my one and only child, that she wouldn't just nod and say, "I know. *Been there. Done that.*"

I closed the notebook. Outside this chapel, my future—our future—was waiting. We would climb down this hill, trying not to slip and fall. We would get in our van and drive to get tall swirled cones of frozen chocolate custard, favorite Wisconsin dairy treat. And, even if we had not survived diphtheria, even if I got busy and the world was as full of little trials as paper cuts, even if I did not have the land or the stone or the oxen or the skill to build a chapel, I would remember to be thankful. I took a deep breath and promised the Mother of God.

Family Portrait

Maude spotted the photograph. She was flopped belly-down on the living-room rug, flipping through one of Anders's innumerable photography books when she saw it. "Look," she said to me. "It's Gram and Grandpa's house."

"What, Sweetie?" I said. I'd been channel surfing through the day's disasters, skipping from twenty-four-hour news channel to twenty-four-hour news channel with mute, trying to catch up on the news without Maude's actually seeing bodies being carried from the scene of the latest earthquake or plane crash or shooting rampage. It wasn't easy.

"Gram and Grandpa Dahl's house," Maude said again, a little louder for her old mother. She turned the book around so I could see.

I clicked the remote, waited for the TV to go black, then bent down and looked, half-expecting to see some farmhouse in New England or Scotland that looked liked the Dahl family home. But there it was—Anders's parents' house, circa 1870. The house's square stone walls, arched windows, and double chimney all looked just as they had the week before when we'd gone to visit Anders's parents. The only difference was the yard. Last week inhabited by only an iron deer and two yard elves, in this photograph the entire Dahl family of 130 years ago was posed to have their picture taken. I counted at least two dozen people, from white-robed babies to an old man who was the spitting image of Santa Claus.

More than people had been turned out of the house to pose for the photographer. The furniture was all out on the lawn, too. Everything in the parlor and dining room had been emptied onto the rough, uneven expanse of the grass. The big mahogany table was set for coffee with the family's best linen and silver. I got down on the floor next to Maude to look more closely at the picture. I recognized the big horsehair couch I'd sat on last week while watching the Weather Channel with Anders's mother, my feet braced to keep from slipping off the slick upholstery and onto the floor. I picked out the claw-foot parlor table and matching chairs, even the mirrored coat stand and the twisted-iron fern stand Anders's mother kept in the hall. Only the large ornate wicker chair was a stranger. The rest of the furniture still lived in the house.

"Hey, Maude," I said, touching one corner of the picture. "There's the big trunk your granddad let you use as a treasure chest." Ginger wandered into the room and came over for a look, wondering what we were so excited about.

"Wow, that's Gram's rocker," Maude said, pointing to the back of a chair that held one of the mothers, babe in her lap.

We all peered at the picture, our rumps high in the air. "Why is everything out in the yard?" Maude asked.

"Good question," I said.

"That's what people did then, Alice," Anders answered. He had come into the room and now joined us on the carpet. "When you wanted to show the folks back in Norway all the wonderful things you owned in the New World, you got a passing photographer to take a picture like this. The glass plates they used then took a lot of light—no way to take a shot like this in a dark formal parlor. So you picked a good sunny day and out everything came."

"Who are all those people?" Maude asked.

"Dahls," Anders said. "But I'll be damned if I know which ones. We'll have to take it with us and ask Dad next time. I think I remember seeing a copy of this in one of the trunks in the lumber room—not in this kind of shape, though. This must be a new print from the negative. Look at that detail." He pointed at the patterned lace petticoats of two girls, posed on the lawn with tall wooden hoops, pretending to play.

"If they're all Dahls, there sure were a lot of them," I said.

"Look," Maude said, "can't you see someone standing in Gram's window? They're waving." We peered at the faint image. Was it a reflection? A shadow?

"It's a ghost," Anders said, and squeezed the back of Maude's neck. She shrieked, delighted to be scared.

The nameless Dahl ancestors all seemed like ghosts, like strangers, though a few had the same high foreheads as Anders and Maude. But the house and the furniture were family we knew, old friends. We might move someday, in spite of Anders's protests, to a new city, a new state. We were talking about getting a new sofa, donating our lumpy old couch to . But the Dahl farmhouse would never change. Looking at the photograph I believed that almost as strongly as Anders did. Here was proof. The house was invulnerable, something time couldn't touch.

Later, I came to think of what happened next as a kind of three-act play: *A Lesson on Life's Uncertainties in Three Phone Calls*. Three weeks after seeing the Dahl family photo, the phone rang and it was Anders's sister, Jean. Of the three Dahl children, Jean had gone the furthest. She lived in San Diego, about as far as she could go from Wisconsin without actually getting on a boat, but somehow she was always the first to get family news, especially bad news.

I heard Anders answer the phone, then heard the tightness

in his voice that was always there when he spoke with Jean, his least-favorite sibling. Then he hung up.

"Gretel left Hal." Gretel was his younger brother Hal's—Halvor Dahl Jr.'s—wife. She looked like a Gretel. She actually wore white pinafores as aprons while she cooked her perfect meals, baked her perfect bread, or cleaned the family farmhouse until it squeaked. Apparently something had not been so perfect after all.

"Left him?" I said. I couldn't imagine this. I thought of Hal and his wife as the gingerbread couple. Now I imagined a cookie, broken in two. But this wasn't a fairy tale. Gretel and Hal lived with Anders's parents, owned and ran the dairy herd. They *were* the Dahl family farm.

Anders pulled a chair from the kitchen table and sat down. "That's not all. She didn't just leave him. She ran off with Lotte Christianson."

I pulled out a chair and sat down too. Lotte Christianson was the wife of the town's Lutheran minister.

I once asked Anders why he left the family farm while his brother Hal stayed. He said he didn't know. I asked him, because he was so obviously bound to Wisconsin as a place and as a landscape, and to me that seemed the same as being devoted to a farm. I asked this right after I met him. Now I think asking why he left shows what a city dweller I was. How little I knew about what went into running a dairy farm, to milking a herd every morning and night every day of the year.

Anders said he just knew he'd never had much interest in the dairy, could never remember which cow was which just by the way she looked or how she sounded, like Hal and his father and his mother could. He liked cows but they were, well, cows. They were more than that to the other Dahls. Well, not to Jean, his sister, but she had hated everything about the farm. She'd even spent her last two years of high school living

158

in town with their Aunt Marguerite, who was principal of the elementary school.

Later, when I met Hal for the first time, he told me a story that was his explanation. When he was five, he said, Anders had talked him into eating dirt from the pasture. Anders told Hal that all Dahl men ate dirt once a week. He told Hal it would give him a taste for farming. Hal ate a couple of big spoonfuls.

It was a joke, of course, the kind older brothers play on younger ones. Anders nearly peed himself laughing, Hal said. "But the truth was," Hal told me, "it was me who got a taste for farming, not Anders." Since he was the oldest, no one ever made him eat dirt.

Anders's mother, Hilda, had another explanation. She said when Anders was three, he'd been caught out in the far end of the pasture during a big lightning storm. For a good year after that he couldn't stand being out in any open space bigger than the front porch. If she wanted to go to the mailbox at the end of their long drive and he was with her, she had to get the truck and drive. Gradually he got over it. He got so he could walk down the driveway or play in the front yard, but he'd never liked being outside, not like Hal. In the end, she was sure, that's why he liked being in a city, with all the cars and buildings so close around.

For his part, Anders's dad, Hal Sr., just joked that Anders, who at six-foot-one was six inches taller than Hal Jr. and a good foot taller than his short, square Dad, was the first Dahl so tall he could stand by the barn door and see clear off the farm, see the cars on the county highway at the bottom of the hill. That was his explanation. I imagined he saw Anders as a sort of Norwegian Columbus, a man who could see beyond the edge of the world. Having had that vision, what kind of man would not be drawn to explore?

Maybe he saw him as a throwback to Great-Great-Grandfather Dahl, who had moved his whole family across an ocean

159

from everything they'd ever known and brought the Dahls to Wisconsin.

Or maybe Hal Sr. only saw his artist son as tall—distant and different and tall.

Call number two came a week later in the middle of the night. It was Hal. "Mom's in the hospital," he said. "She got up to go to the bathroom and when she didn't come back to bed, Pop went looking and found her on the kitchen floor. The doctor says she had a stroke."

Anders left right away, and I followed with Maude first thing the next the morning. The doctors pronounced it a mild stroke, but Hilda seemed dazed and disoriented. When I walked into her hospital room with Anders she greeted me warmly, kissed Maude, good manners hard-wired into deeper parts of her brain than the stroke had touched. Then her eyes wandered over to the window, to the fields of crows and corn just beyond. "Gramma?" Maude said.

"Oh, sweetie," Hilda said, a smile blooming on her pale face, "when did you get here?"

Call number three was from Anders's Dad, Hal Sr. He called to say Hal Jr. was taking a sales job with Archer Daniels in Minneapolis. There was just too much on the farm that reminded him of Gretel. Without Hal there would be no one to help milk the cows, no one to watch Hilda in the house while he was in the milking parlor or the barn or the far field. So he'd decided they would retire to California to be closer to Jean. After 135 years the Anders farm was for sale.

Indeed, it was already sold. A neighbor, Gus Gustafson, had bought the herd and the hay acreage. Gus was the Dahls' nearest neighbor. A couple, the Lyons family from St. Paul, wanted the house. It stood on a high bluff above the Mississippi, close to the Great River Road that was lined with antique shops and was awash with tourists in the summer months. The Lyonses

planned to turn the house into "an historic bed and breakfast." With the farm economy so depressed, I'd imagined the
house would stand empty or, worse, be used as a storage shed
by the Gustafsons, who'd torn down their old family homestead in the '60s in favor of something more modern: an ugly
ranch house with mustard-colored siding.

The bad news was that the Lyonses only wanted the house if
they could have most of the furniture too. A historic bed and
breakfast needed to look the part. They were offering a price
that Anders's parents were in no position to refuse.

"We'll have a farm auction for the equipment Gus doesn't
want and the stuff from the lumber room and attic the Lyonses
don't want," Anders's father said. "Then each of you kids gets to
choose one piece of furniture. I had that put in the contract."

So it was. I wondered if the Dahl ancestors had made their
decision to emigrate to the New World just as quickly. What was
a hundred years in the history of a place? Still, the sale broke
my heart. Anders was sick with it. His father hadn't asked him
to come home to take over the farm. He—we—wouldn't and
couldn't have gone anyway. But still, he was the oldest son in
the generation that lost the family farm. He sawed and ham-
mered away at his art, building shadow boxes full of old farm
photos, miniature cows, and tiny paper tractors, as if trying to
put a vanished Wisconsin inside a museum and then bolt and
lock the door.

Anders and Maude and I piled in our minivan, with Ginger in the back, and drove up the week before the auction to
sort out the stuff in the closets and attic and cellars. There was
an amazing amount of it for a house that had always seemed
to me neat as a pin. Hilda, who had taken a bachelor's degree in Home Ec before she married Anders's dad, had filled
cupboards and drawers and closets with bolts of cloth she always meant to make into dresses or quilts or curtains someday.
There were boxes of dishes, of clothes, of books, and of reports cards from Anders, Jean, and Hal's school days. None of

the clutter was very old, nothing from the generations before Anders's parents. I asked Anders's dad about it, disappointed there were no boxes of Victorian hats, tins of Civil War buttons. He shrugged. "Not room even on a farm to keep everything," he said. "If a thing serves a purpose, that's one thing. But if something doesn't have a use—*fffttt*—out it goes."

I wondered if I could get Anders to apply this more practical manifestation of Norwegian thrift to our house. I made a mental list of all the odd books, old toys of Maude's, art bits and ends that could use a good final *fffttt*, though I knew, even as I thought it, that it was a waste of time. Anders took after Hilda, with her hordes of bright cloth. It looked to me like the last one to apply the *use it or lose it* philosophy to the Dahl homestead had been Hal Sr.'s mother. Hilda had a weakness for bright and pretty but only theoretically useful things. She had enough ceramic flowerpots and vases in the basement to start a florist shop.

Anders and Hal took as gospel their father's injunction limiting them to one piece of furniture each. They loaded the canning jars and old pots and pans onto the semi the auctioneer had parked by the barn for the upcoming sale. They piled up the fabric, the old hats and knit scarves, board games and puzzles from their childhood. Only Jean seemed to think "one piece of furniture" meant that plus everything else she could carry. She made trip after trip to her rental car with boxes of mismatched china.

Hal Sr. himself offered Maude Anders's old bat and glove. He sent her and Ginger off to the now-empty milking parlor to practice bunting.

With each trip from the house to the semi Anders's expression darkened, changing into something mythic and Norwegian. His eyes actually seemed to shift from sky to gun-metal blue. I had seen this gathering of the clouds before, but never so dark, so bitter. Hal Jr., on the other hand, just looked blond and glum. He looked like he missed Gretel, who would have been bustling around with freshly baked cookies. To be honest, I missed her, too. Jean had conveniently disappeared just when it was time to start scrubbing the basement and mopping the kitchen.

The last load Anders's dad carried to the barn was a box of guns. Not real guns, Hal Sr. pointed out, those had gone to a licensed dealer. He snorted just to show me, good liberal Democrat, what he thought of that. These were just pellet guns, ones the boys had owned while growing up. Hal Jr. picked one up, pumped it hard, sighted down the barrel at the wheels of the semi. Anders reached into the back of the truck and pulled out a loosely packed box filled, as far as I could see, with wadded tissues. "Come on," he said, picking another pellet gun out of the box and handing it to me. He handed his brother a box of pellets. "Let's go down to the pasture."

I shrugged and followed, and Hal Jr. did too. Hal Sr. looked at his watch and shook his head. He needed to check on Hilda, who was recovering in a convalescent home in town. It felt odd, clearing out her house without her there, but then no one had really wanted to empty her home in front of her, even if it had to be done.

Anders didn't so much walk as stalk down to the pasture. Hal and I trailed behind with our rifles. When we got to the fence, Anders told us to stay put, then he walked further into the field, angling off to our left until he was hidden by the slope of the land. "Get ready, Hal," I heard Anders call. Hal loaded the chamber with pellets, gave his gun another pump, then raised it to his shoulder. Something bright went spinning in a high arc through the air. Hal followed it with the blue steel barrel, then pulled the trigger. A thousand bright shards exploded in midair.

"What was that?" I called to Anders. Another globe flew into the sky. This time I could see it was a Christmas ornament—something red, with the rusty sparkle of old glitter. Hal was caught with his gun down, pumping.

"Damn, Anders," he said, "that's too fast." He shot at the next one but missed.

"Let Alice try," I heard my husband call from the far side of the pasture.

"Do you know how to shoot?" Hal asked.

"Sort of," I said. I'd watched kids on the rifle range at camp, but I'd settled for archery. The guns had scared me. They were so loud. But then these weren't exactly real guns, were they?

"You got the best one," Hal said. "That's Anders's Crossman. You could kill a cat with this baby." He caught my startled look. "Well, maybe a crow, anyways." Hal showed me how to load, pump. "Lead it," he said, then called out to Anders that I was ready.

I did lead it—it being a star-shaped gold ornament that wobbled awkwardly through the sky. I squeezed the trigger and *pop*—gold fireworks. Anders tossed another, then another. Whether it was the Crossman or beginner's luck, I didn't miss a one. After a while Hal went out to toss ornaments, and Anders took a turn with the Crossman. *Poppity, pop, pop,* went a lifetime of family holidays. *Pop, pop,* the Christmases of his childhood which were never coming back. Sweat ran down Anders's pale face. I watched as Anders, the man I knew so well, a man incapable of getting rid of anything, a man of the most constant affection toward people, places, and things, blew his world out of the sky. I had the feeling, and maybe Hal did too, that if Anders had had his way he would have burned the whole place—house, barn, milking parlor—down to scorched and smoking earth before he would have let a stranger have a single shiny piece of it.

Finally, the ornament box was empty. We were nearly out of pellets. We walked, more lightly now, happy with the finality of ritual destruction, back toward the house. Hal Sr.'s truck was pulling up in the yard, with Jean's rental car right behind it. Hal Sr. climbed down from the cab.

"What's up?" Hal Jr. said, asking for all of us. Before his

father could answer, we saw Jean help Hilda from the rental car, one hand firmly on her mother's elbow. Hal Sr. shrugged. "She wouldn't stay away. She wanted to be here when you picked furniture." Hal Jr. brought a kitchen chair out to the yard for his mother. She sat in it, upright and frail. No one seemed to want to go back inside the house, which now, with a lifetime of Hilda's bric-a-brac removed, felt halfway to being a bed and breakfast already. Maude came running across the yard with Ginger at her heels to kiss her grandmother, who patted her absently. Did Hilda know who Maude was?

Hal picked the walnut halltree, as if what he really needed in his new life in Minneapolis was a place to hang his hat. He and Anders carried it into the yard and loaded it into the back of Hal's old pickup, which was still a farmer's truck even if Hal wasn't a farmer anymore.

Jean wanted the big four-poster bed, but since she had arranged for a shipping company to disassemble its massive frame in order to box and ship it to herself in San Diego, we left it standing for now where it had always stood, in the front bedroom that had been Hilda and Hal's.

Anders and I hadn't talked about what he would pick, but I could have guessed. He and Hal disappeared into the house, then reappeared with the horse-hair sofa from the front parlor, the one the Dahls had posed on for their portrait in this same yard more than a hundred years before. We rolled it in old blankets like a corpse and hoisted it onto the roof of our minivan. Both Hals helped Anders tie it down. I held Hilda's hand as they did this, afraid this last sight might be too much for her.

"I'm sorry," I said. "We'll take good care of it."

She shook her head. Her eyes were sharp, focused for the first time since the stroke. "No tears," she said, though neither of us were crying. "It's not a funeral." She patted my hand. "Take care of my grandchildren," she said. *Grandchild*, I

165

thought, looking over at Maude, but I didn't correct her. Who knew who Hilda thought I was? Or who she thought she was.

When we got home, Anders rousted some neighbors to help with the couch. After they got it off the roof of the van, instead of carrying it inside he had them set it on the sidewalk in front of our house. Then he got out his eight-by-ten plate camera, tripod, and cable release, and prepared to take a picture of Maude and me and himself on the couch, Ginger stretched across all three pairs of our feet. Sitting there in the late afternoon sun, trying not to slide off the horse hair, I felt tired and suddenly queasy, as if the couch were a john boat and we were fishing choppy waters. In that moment I knew that Hilda, from whatever mist she lived in now, had gotten one thing right—grand*children*. I was pregnant again. "Ready, set, go!" Anders shouted, and ran from behind the camera to take his place on the couch. The strobes he'd set up flashed, the camera shutter clicked. There we were: four Dahls in front of our new Dahl Family Homestead.

Night Dogs

I was sorting laundry when the telephone rang. I was pregnant and was moving slowly, just recovering from a bout of morning sickness. It was Steve, a sculptor who taught in the art department at the university with Anders. They met every Monday for lunch to talk about art, life, and the students they had who were either supremely talented, driving them crazy, or both.

When I heard Steve say hello I figured Anders had forgotten about lunch. When he was working on a project he lost all track of time. "He's not here, Steve," I said, before he could even ask. "Did you try the darkroom?"

There was a pause. "I know he's not there, Alice. He is here. *Was* here." Steve was a huge bear of a guy, and I heard over the phone line the distinct whoosh of his drawing in a full, Steve-size breath. "Alice," he said, "Anders had some kind of seizure. One minute we were eating spring rolls and talking about the last department meeting, then boom, he went over backward in his chair, and . . ." I imagined Anders's head hitting the linoleum of the little Thai restaurant where they always ate, his body stiffening, arching.

"What kind of seizure?" I was thinking maybe this was Steve's way of saying *heart attack.* "Is he okay?"

"A seizure seizure," Steve said. "You know, like an epileptic. He came out of it even before the ambulance got here, but they took him to the hospital." I hung up and was grabbing my car keys before I realized I hadn't said so much as thanks or good-bye to Steve.

By the time I got to the hospital, they'd already sent Anders upstairs for x-rays, a CAT scan, and an MRI. The clerk typed in the insurance information I gave her and had me sign a records release form so the hospital could get his medical history from his doctor if they needed it. Then a triage nurse took me into a cubicle.

"How can a grown man suddenly get epilepsy?" I asked her.

She pursed her lips, as if this were a very good question. "Did Anders have high blood pressure?" she asked. "A family history of stroke?" I told her his mom had had a mild stroke. "Had he fallen or suffered any blows to the head recently?" No, I said, not that I was aware of.

All the while, I got the feeling the nurse wasn't really listening to my answers, was making the most minimal of notes. She knows what's wrong, I thought, and she doesn't want to be the one to tell me. I was ushered to a waiting room. After a while Bibi appeared. Steve had called her. Then Steve showed up, and then Lloyd. Their appearance made me feel worse rather than comforted. They wouldn't have come if they hadn't shared my suspicions. They knew this was bad. We sat in the plastic chairs in the waiting room and flipped through old news in the ragged copies of *Newsweek* and *Time* that the hospital provided to distract us from our more immediate concerns.

After a while I closed my eyes, trying to slow the panicked gallop of my heart. With my eyes closed, the rush to the hospital was like a disjointed dream. Like the dream I'd had over and over when I was in college, where I was signed up for a course I never attended. In the dream, the college was an un-familiar maze of vast modern buildings, concrete courtyards, no people in sight. I was always running as fast as I could, panic like a copper penny on my tongue. If only I could find the room where the final exam was being given and take the test, maybe I could save myself from an F, from a scar on my transcript, official record of my life, which would never heal or disappear.

When I finished my dissertation and became a teacher after a lifetime as student, I thought, *Well, at least I won't have that dream anymore.* I was wrong. I still had the dream, at least once a semester. Only now I had somehow forgotten to go to a class I was *teaching*. But if I could only find the room where the students were waiting for me, I could still give the final exam and no one would find out what a lousy, disorganized teacher I was, how ill-prepared I was for my own life.

This was not my only recurring nightmare about school. I also dreamed I never graduated from junior high school—nev-er mind there was no graduation from my junior high school—and I had to go back to my hometown of Jacksonville, Florida, to the sweaty halls of Stephen Foster Junior High, to take a math class I somehow skipped. I did this, all the while thinking, How will they ever find out in Wisconsin? What if I just walk out of here, go back to my life? Will I get fired?

According to a colleague in the psychology department at school, these were very common anxiety dreams. I had a very ordinary unconscious, it turned out, when it came to express-ing my unease. The most common anxiety dream, he told me, was showing up at work or a party, naked. I had this one, too, but in an embarrassingly prudish form. In my dreams I was al-ways waiting for a bus in my pajamas. My friend gave me a list, kind of a cheat sheet, for these dreams. According to him, if I dreamed of biting into a roll only to have my teeth crumble in my mouth, I was having "premonitions of death." If I dreamed

I was being chased through by a tiger through my house or my building at the school, that, too, was "fear of death." Most of the dreams on his list symbolized our collective unease with mortality. Or at least his unease with it. And mine.

Once, in our local Mexican bodega, I picked up a book, *Old Aunt Dinah's Dream Book of Numbers*, that gave the meaning—in Spanish and English—of any object that appeared in your dreams, along with what lottery number you should play. It was remarkably precise. "To dream of yams means you will hear from a long lost friend or relative. Play 995." "To dream of a zebra means you will have snappy clothes and a flashy car. Play 169."

Had I ever, I wondered reading it, dreamed of zinc (your success will come from your talents) or a typewriter (you will be involved in a lawsuit and win) or reindeer (a pleasant surprise in the near future)? Still, I was comforted by the idea that dreaming of mice meant "small worries keep big troubles away."

In my heart I believed in the protective power of worrying. We worriers were the mice of the world, working to keep Big Troubles at bay. But had it ever really worked? What if I were worrying abut the wrong things? Would my worrying still act as a prophylactic?

Once I asked Anders about the list the psych teacher had given me. After he looked it over, he shook his head. "I never remember my dreams," he said.

"Never?" I said, a bit astounded.

"Well," he said, thinking hard, "once I dreamed of a fish." A fish? Of course, I thought. According to the psychologist's list, a fish was "a symbol for life." According to Aunt Dinah it meant, "Be prepared to travel. You will cross a river soon."

After an hour I finally got to see Anders who, except for a wicked bruise on his forehead where he'd hit the corner of the table on the way down, looked great. He had a sort of glow, as if he'd just done a good workout with weights instead of rolling around unconscious on a restaurant floor.

"Oh, God," I said and hugged him.

"Hey," he said and hugged me back. When I let go, he said, "Any chance there's a snack machine on this floor somewhere? I kinda missed lunch and I'm starving."

I sent Steve down the hall with a fist full of quarters—not caring that I was probably breaking all the rules—and we sat and watched Anders eat a late, well-balanced lunch of pretzels, root beer, and bite-size Oreos. Then we sat. And we sat. At three o'clock Bibi left to pick up Maude and Kyle from summer day camp at the Y and take them back to her house. At four, Steve left. At five, Lloyd left to check on Bibi and Maude and Kyle. Every now and then one of the nurses would come in and take Anders's blood pressure and pulse, but they had nothing to say except, "The doctor will be in to see you soon." Anders lay in his bed, and I sat by his side, holding his hand. We watched the local news. We watched the national news. There were at least three civil wars raging at that moment, all with bloody disastrous results. A ring of pedophiles who lured children away from their parents had been exposed by the FBI; two were priests, one a Scout leader, one a former teacher of the year. People were campaigning for president, for senator, for Congress. There was an endless stream of negative campaign ads with menacing voice-overs. "Congressman Blank *pretends* to be for veterans but all the while . . ." I held Anders's hand tighter. When had the world turned so ugly?

We were watching *Jeopardy* when the doctor—two doctors—finally appeared. One was the neurologist, Dr. Sams, who had met Anders earlier and ordered his scans. Dr. Sams was carrying several large envelopes of x-rays with Anders's name and what I took to be his patient ID number stamped on them. Dr. Sams waved his free hand at the mystery doctor and said, "I asked Dr. Mautz to stop by with me. He's an oncologist."

There it was—cancer. An oncologist treated cancer. I knew

we were not supposed to scream or throw things—pillows, the water pitcher, the TV control—at the two doctors to get them to back out of the room and out of our lives, but I felt like doing it anyway. *Go away!* I wanted to shout. *Shoo!*

Anders offered Dr. Mautz a chair. He took after his mother and had politeness hard-wired into him. Dr. Mautz turned his chair backward, sat with his legs straddling the back as if he were a coach and we were his team. "Your tests show a series of a dozen or so tear-shaped lesions in your brain. It's hard to tell exactly what they are, but my guess is they're growing, exerting pressure on your brain, or they wouldn't have caused a seizure. In a way the seizure was a blessing. The brain doesn't feel pain, so sometimes we see very large growths, much larger than yours, that have given no sign of their presence."

I wanted someone to say the word. Anders did. "Lesions," he said. "You mean cancer."

Dr. Mautz said, "Hard to say. At this stage, treatment shouldn't wait on that diagnosis. Rapidly growing lesions, even benign lesions, are not something you want in your brain. Still, I've asked a surgeon to look at your scans, stop by to talk to you. He can determine if it's practical to do a biopsy, whether he can get a good tissue sample. It always helps to know what we are dealing with—lymphoma, carcinoma, melanoma . . ." Another deadly vocabulary list. I squeezed Anders's hand so tightly he winced. "Then," Dr Mautz went on, "at least we would know whether the brain is a primary or secondary site."

"The surgeon is just for a biopsy?" I asked. "Is there any chance the . . . ," I paused for a moment not wanting to say a word I couldn't call back, not wanting to be the first to say *tumor*, "the *lesions* are operable?"

Dr. Mautz looked at Dr. Sams. Dr. Sams looked at us. Then Dr. Sams pulled one of Anders's x-rays from its sleeve, held it to the light for us to see. The lesions appeared like white stars in the night of Anders's one and only brain. A dozen? I thought I counted twenty-three.

"Inoperable," Anders said.

Both doctors nodded. "Inoperable," they said.

They didn't say fatal. No one said fatal. Instead, they said there was the possibility of radiation. They would send a radiologist by. There had been promising advances in chemotherapy drugs that passed through the blood-brain barrier. Dr. Mautz could talk to us about that after we'd seen the surgeon and the radiologist. In the meantime they would put Anders on anti-seizure medication and on steroids to help bring down the swelling in his brain. He should be careful, Dr. Sam said, about bright flashing lights. "And for now," Dr. Mautz said, "it would be better if your wife did the driving."

Dr. Sam and Dr. Mautz stood, nodding in unison. *Tweedle Dee* and *Tweedle Dum*. And then they backed rather apologetically out of the room.

We sat still, holding hands. The room slowly grew dark, but neither of us moved to turn on the lights.

"Why are they sending all these specialists in to see *us*?" Anders asked. "How are we supposed to know what to do?" Suddenly it was my final-exam dream. We hadn't been going to class, and now there was going to be one helluva test.

Anders sighed, "What the hell. I can't complain. I've had a good life. I wouldn't have changed a thing."

I stared at the man who was my husband. Anders looked relaxed, relieved. I, I was suddenly, unbelievably angry. My cheeks turned red. My face throbbed. How could Anders be relaxed about this? Maude needed him. The baby, the one we hoped so hard would be born, needed him. I damn well needed him. How could I live—in Wisconsin, anywhere—without him. I let out a strangled sound, a sort of *mmmrph*. Anders turned toward me, startled.

"You son of a bitch," I said. "Don't you give up," and punched my hospitalized husband in the chest.

After a while, I calmed down. After a while, Anders got angry, then sad. Just that morning Maude had told me an awful joke: "What's red and green, red and green?" Answer: "A frog in a blender." That's what the room—the world, our life—suddenly felt like.

After another long while a nurse came in and gave Anders his anti-seizure medication. "This is going to make you pretty groggy," she said, "but then you could probably use a good night's sleep."

"Why?" Anders asked. I knew what he meant. If he was dying, why should he want to sleep? The nurse just shrugged and watched as Anders swallowed the fat capsules. She refilled his water jug in case he got thirsty, then left us alone.

I didn't want to leave. I didn't want to take my eyes off Anders. My chest felt as sore as if I'd punched myself. My stomach was raw with fear. I didn't want to face the rest of the world outside this room. Maude, I didn't want to have to tell Maude. I pictured her safely asleep in the bunk bed above Kyle. Kyle had been there, done this. Bibi had had breast cancer and she was okay. Anders would be, too. Surely he would be. Maybe we were both just too scared by the word cancer. Bibi had gone through chemo and now she was doing great. But when I put my head on the edge of Anders's pillow and closed my eyes, a negative of his scan kept appearing, the lesions' black holes eating my husband alive.

The pills didn't seem to make Anders sleepy. He was restless, twitchy. The night slept around us, but we sat in a bubble of wide-awake day.

"I feel like a convict on parole," Anders said. I knew how he felt. Tomorrow would bring more doctors, more tests.

"What should we do?" I asked. In novels and movies, people who got the kind of bad news we'd gotten flew to Paris, climbed the Alps, ate foods they had never even seen before to fulfill life-long dreams. But already our schedule seemed too booked for that—see the neurosurgeon, maybe a biopsy this week, then radiation or chemo. Cancer looked like a full-time job.

"I know what I want," Anders said to me. "I want to go ahead with the renovation." We had decided to turn the attic of our house into much-needed extra living space. "I want my new rooms." He pointed his finger at me and actually shook it. "Do you hear me, Alice?" He said this with an intensity I'd never heard in his voice before.

Who wouldn't be intense after a doctor you'd just met told you that you had cancer? But there was something in the tone of his voice, something so, well un-Anders, that I looked at him closely, inspecting him for signs. We weren't in *Invasion of the Body Snatchers*, but there was something different about my husband. It was three in the morning and in spite of the horse pills, he was drumming his fingers. His legs twitched.

It was the lesions, the cancer itself, that was making Anders's body move and had shifted the tone in his voice. I could almost feel the pressure building in his brain. If tumors could turn Anders into a stranger, then how could we have anything eternal, unchanging, in us? If we were just our brains, just the punky stuff between our ears, then what were we? How could we have souls? Anders was still staring at me, waiting for my answer.

"Of course, Anders," I said. "We'll start the renovation. We'll finish the new rooms." Then he relaxed, though groggy was still miles away.

So we spent the rest of the night discussing tile and towel bars for the new bathroom. Paint colors for the new trim. What the hell, I thought as the sun came up on the other side of the double-glazed hospital window. So what if it wasn't practical to go ahead with the construction, with its plaster dust and buzzing saws, on top of everything else? What was practical about cancer? About having another child while your husband was being treated for multiple brain tumors? What was practical or predictable about anything in life? Right now life was all rabbit holes as far as the eye could see.

Just as the room brightened, as the sun made its way across

Anders's rumpled sheets, he fell asleep. For maybe five min-utes he snored, a healthy, vibrant buzz. Then the nurse ap-peared to take his blood pressure.

"Hey," Anders said, as she pumped up the cuff around his upper arm. "I dreamed Maude and I were fishing." He grinned. "I dreamed we caught one helluva muskie. And you cooked it up." Did it mean something different, I wondered, if you both caught and ate a fish in your dream?

Later, at home, I looked it up in Aunt Dinah. "To dream of catching a fish means confusion and trouble. To dream of eat-ing one means a good marriage in the family." Confusion and trouble, that was true enough. And I had a good marriage—if only I could hold onto Anders.

I'd only been fishing once in my whole life and I hadn't come close to catching a muskie. Years before, when Anders and I were living together, we had taken a trip up north, as they say in Wisconsin. Northern Wisconsin is where people from the southern populous parts of Wisconsin and from Illinois and Iowa, nearly waterless states, go for summer vacations. It's dotted with innumerable small, clear lakes, each famous for a different kind of fish: wall-eye, perch, and muskies, or mus-kellunge, a kind of pike, ancient and strange, all bones and great eyes.

We spent a weekend in a cabin in a small resort—a north-ern Wisconsin "resort" being a line of rustic cabins along the edge of a lake where for the price of lodging you got your own short pier, a john boat with an outboard motor, and, if you needed to, the chance to borrow some of the owner's fishing gear. The first day after we arrived we took the boat out but only went sightseeing to an overgrown island in the middle of the lake that had once been home to a grand Victorian resort. Bathhouses stood abandoned on the beach. We spooked bats out of what was left of a boathouse whose high doors were still decorated with ornate woodwork curls. I admitted to Anders that I'd never been fishing in my life. He laughed. "Good," he'd said, "then you won't make fun of me." His grandfather had been the last big fishermen in the family.

The next morning after breakfast we set out to try our luck with our borrowed gear. The sun shone on the lake. The sun shone on us. Anders baited our tiny gold hooks with kernels of canned corn. I laughed. I thought maybe this was the fishing equivalent of hunting snipe—getting a Southern girl to spend all afternoon thinking she was fishing when all she had on her line was a single Green Giant niblet.

As soon as I dipped the hook in the water I got a hit. I yanked up on the pole, too excited to remember how to reel in the line. It was a small rainbow-colored fish about the size and shape of my palm. A sunnie, Anders said, which was a kind of brim. This lake was famous for sunnies. It turned out Anders had no more experience cleaning and cooking fish than I did, so he took the sunnie off the hook and let it go. All morning I caught sunnies as fast as I could bait my hook. Anders too. Unless we were catching the same two fish over and over again, the water below us was teeming, boiling, nearly solid with hungry sunnies. It was addictive, like playing pinball or Nintendo—*bait, hit, bait, hit.* It was hard not to take it as a sign of good fortune, as a generous universe shining as brightly as the sun on Anders and me, together at last in the heart of Wisconsin.

Finally Anders emptied the rest of the niblets over the side for the sunnies, and we drifted, eating our impromptu lunch of Jay's potato chips and drinking warm bottles of Huber beer. I remember asking Anders why he'd became a photographer. Did he have a darkroom on the farm as a kid? No. A camera? An Instamatic, but he'd hadn't taken many pictures with it. He'd taken a photo class in college, the kind he taught now, and it had all just come together, he said. He'd printed his first picture, fished it wet out of the fixer and thought, *This is for me.*

"What was the picture?" I asked. I expected that he'd tell me he didn't remember. Instead he said, "It was a print of a fish—a sunnie—I caught in Lake Mendota. I contact-printed it right in the darkroom. Developed it. And there it was." He opened another bottle of beer by knocking the cap on the gunwale of the boat.

"A photograph is time, stopped," he said to me then. I suspected he told his students this every semester, but I could also tell he meant it. He said that when he was a kid, he would sometimes spend half a day lying on his stomach next to the creek that ran at the foot of their pasture, watching the brown trout. The water never stopped, he could feel it rushing past his fingers when he dangled them in the stream. The fish never stopped. Just watching them made him restless. Restless enough, I thought, to leave the farm, to go off to college with the intention of majoring in art. Then he'd caught a sunnie and frozen it forever on a sheet of light-sensitive paper.

We were floating in the middle of a lake full of sunnies swimming restlessly beneath the aluminum skin of our boat. "Will you marry me, Alice?" Anders asked.

"Yes," I said, "I will."

We took the boat in, drove into Hayward, the nearest town, and went to a place called the Muskie Bar, famous for its record-breaking mounted fish and tableaus of taxidermied animals playing cards and shooting pool. Under the eye of a pair of stuffed possums playing poker we kept up what we'd started in the boat, drinking bar bottle after bar bottle of Huber Bock until, for the only time in our life together, we both got totally and happily drunk. The next morning I didn't even have a hangover. After the night in Anders's hospital room I was sure I had one, even if I hadn't taken so much as a sip of beer. I could only guess what Anders felt like.

I didn't get to sleep until that afternoon, when I dozed off in a chair in the radiology waiting room. Dr. Mautz had decided

Anders needed a whole-body MRI to make sure there weren't other growths hiding somewhere. I dreamed I was on a cruise ship, something impossibly big like the Queen Mary or, God forbid, the Titanic. Anders and I were walking arm-in-arm along the wide upper deck. We were sailing through waters so shallow and clear that I could see what I thought were dolphins swimming alongside us, diving in and out of our wake. I stopped and let go of Anders so that I could lean out over the rail and watch them.

Then I realized that the dolphins were humans. I looked more closely and realized the water was filled with all the people I knew who had died. I recognized my mother and my father. I saw my brother Mark's partner, George, swimming in the foam by the bow. I turned to tell Anders, to point out what an amazing thing this ocean was—a kind of warm, fluid afterlife. But Anders was standing on the railing, ready to take a swan dive. "*Stop it,*" I said. "You're scaring me. You don't even know how to swim."

I woke up to find a nurse standing over me. She was shaking my arm. "Shhh," she said. I must have been yelling. " This is a hospital. There are some very sick people here."

"Yes, I know," I said, still half in my dream. *Do we die and come back as fish?* "One of them's my husband."

On Wednesday, two days after Anders's seizure, the carpenters arrived at seven a.m. and began tearing the roof off our house. I woke to the scream of their saws.

At eleven-thirty the same morning, Dr. Zorn, the neurosurgeon, peeled back a section of Anders's scalp and drilled small holes in his skull. Maybe he used a saw, too, but I couldn't hear any of it in the family waiting room, thank God. Dr. Zorn's job was to mine tiny core samples from Anders's brain for the waiting biopsy slides so the pathologist could study them for errant cells.

When I called Bibi to tell her Anders was out of surgery and would soon be taken from recovery to ICU, she was standing outside my house. She'd stopped by to rescue our basset Ginger from the strangers and noise. "You should see it," she said, holding out her cell phone so I could hear whole sections of the roof decking crash from the top of the house into the waiting dumpster. "It's like they are tearing the place down," Bibi said. I saw Dr. Zorn out of the corner of my eye. He was still in his scrubs and headed my way. He looked puzzled. I thought, *Puzzled isn't good.*

"I've got to go, Beeb," I said, and went to grab Dr. Zorn.

"Your husband's biopsy results are inconclusive," Dr. Zorn said, shaking his head. "The cells are insufficiently differentiated for a definitive diagnosis."

"Does that mean," I said, "it may not be cancer, after all?"

"Oh," he said, "it's cancer, all right. The question is, what kind?" They would send the slides off for a second reading in New York. Just to get a fresh take on the problem. "If we still can't get an exact diagnosis, Dr. Mautz—in consultation with you and your husband, of course—will just have to go ahead and pick a course of treatment, and . . ." he stopped.

"And?"

"Hope for the best," he said.

Before the carpenters attacked the house, I had failed to realize that in order to get a new roof, one with a dormer high enough to allow for a new bathroom and stairs, they were going to rip the old one off. Until I saw Anders in ICU, I had somehow failed to realize that in order to peek into his brain, they would have to shave his head. I looked at his sleeping, sheeted form, and then double-checked the name on the end of the bed. I honestly thought I might be in the wrong room. Without his blond hair, Anders's head looked vaguely pointed, his face unfamiliar. Not to mention how strange the great jagged line of black stitches down one side of his skull looked. Then he opened his blue eyes, and he was Anders again. Or nearly.

"Hi, sweetie," I said, taking his hand.

"Dog. Synagogue," he said to me, and squeezed my hand hard. The nurse swept in behind me.

"He's still medicated," she said. "And after the surgery, there's a lot of swelling. We've upped his dosage of steroids. That'll help, but it means we have to be careful about post-op infection." I must have looked dazed. "Steroids suppress the immune system," she explained, as if that one little bit of knowledge was all I needed to make sense of Anders in the bed, the holes in his head.

The next day, Thursday, we—Dr. Mautz, Anders, me—picked chemo. The radiologist was doubtful he could really zap so many small lesions with his big deadly machines. "The brain is like an egg," he said, meaning, I suppose, that a brain is delicate. I had an image of radiation as boiling water, poaching the delicate white that was Anders. So we chose biweekly doses of intravenous poison. "It will really slow you down," Dr. Mautz told Anders, who was simultaneously pacing the examining room and swinging his arms over his head. As soon as the anesthesia had worn off he'd gotten his words back, but he also, literally, couldn't sit still. Dr. Mautz said it was the steroids.

"I had a round once for poison ivy," he said. "Made me want to jump out of my skin."

But I looked at Anders and I saw the cancer jittering around the room, the cancer making Anders's arms flap like a marionette.

The very first time I ever saw Anders he'd been standing in the kitchen at a party, pouring a bag of Tostados into a bowl. Maybe it was only an optical effect caused by coming out of the dark living room of the house where the party was into the bright kitchen, but the round chips seemed to tumble through the air like golden coins. And Anders's blond hair had shone like the sun.

I'd gone to the party with Bibi, who was deep into her new

love, papermaking. She was taking a master's degree in art and it was that kind of party—an art party. As soon as we got through the front door I was sorry I'd let her talk me into coming. The music sounded like a high-speed dental drill, and everyone was standing around a video monitor watching what appeared to be random shots of feet walking down an urban sidewalk intercut with surgical footage. I watched stiletto heels click by and an appendix get removed.

Almost all the men and women watching the video had their hair dyed coal black. This was early in the body-piercing craze, but there were nose rings and lips studs. Compared to the other people in the room, I felt as soft and gray and shapeless as the sweater I was wearing. I fled to the kitchen, and there was Anders. I busied myself opening the bottle of wine I'd brought. Anders introduced himself and told me he was a new assistant professor in the art department. I offered him some wine. He offered me the chips. It was not a very promising opening. If he'd gone on to ask me what I thought of our host's video, I would have led a very different life.

Instead Bibi came whizzing through, whisked the bowl of chips out of Anders's hands. "Did she tell you about her otherworldly phone message?" she said to Anders, who she either knew or, being Bibi, acted as if she did.

"What message?" Anders said to me. "Did God call you?"

I laughed, hoping this was a joke, then told him about the message I'd found on my answering machine when I got home the night before, one not intended for me. "I just wanted you to know I'm here in the hospital again, Ed," an old man's voice had said. Old and—if my years with my mother made me any judge—alcohol soaked. "I'm going in for liver surgery tomorrow and, well, it looks like I might not make it. If you could get up here somehow to see me, I sure would appreciate it." Then there had been a long pause. "Well, guess you're not there so I'll just say good-bye then." The message ended with the usual loud beep.

I'd already told this story half a dozen times—to Bibi, my roommate, my two officemates in the English Department. What everyone said was, "Wow, how weird." Bibi had also added that it was all very sad. But Anders actually got tears in his eyes.

"Did you try to find him?" he said, wiping his eyes with his sleeve.

"Who? Ed?"

He shook his head. "The guy who left the message. Did you call the hospitals?"

"And ask what? Did they operate on any old guys today?"

Anders had been lounging against the kitchen counter, but now he stood up straight. "Come on," he said. He grabbed the phonebook off the kitchen table with one hand and my hand with the other. He pulled me toward a back bedroom. "There's a phone back here," he said. "It's quieter."

So we called, taking turns. We tried the university hospital first. It seemed the most likely place in town to go for last-ditch liver surgery. I expected bureaucracy, layers of patient privacy. But the switchboard sent me to the surgical schedul--ing clerk who answered every question I asked as readily as if I were Ben Casey. No surgeries that day. No elderly male patients scheduled for the rest of the week. Was there anything else she could do for me? *No. Thank you. Good night.*

We tried the Methodist Hospital, the Catholic one. They were surprisingly closed-mouthed. However, Anders, it turned out, knew an intensive care nurse at the former and an ER nurse at the latter, both on duty. He called them. No elderly male liver patients. Did Anders date only nurses? I wondered.

We sat side by side on our host's bed, the coats of the partygoers piled high around us. "Damn," Anders said, actually striking his forehead with his palm as an idea hit him. "We forgot the most obvious place—the VA Hospital. It's filled with old geezers."

And we found him. "Yes!" Anders said, and gave me a hard

hug that clearly meant "a job well done." Albert Rommer, 69, liver cancer. In recovery in serious, but stable, condition. Anders left a detailed message and his phone number in case Albert needed more information about just how it had happened that his friend Ed had not received his plea for a last visit. In case Albert needed help reaching his old friend.

Then Anders looked at me. Really looked, cocking his head first to one side and then the other, the way Lassie had been prone to in the movies. "Would you let me take some pictures of you?" he said.

I shook my head. "You should take some pictures of my friend Bibi," I said. "She's beautiful."

"I don't want to take pictures of Bibi," he said. "I don't take pictures like that."

"Pictures like what?" I said.

"Pictures of people who look like photographs."

"You want to take pictures of me because I'm *not* beautiful?" I said.

He smiled, his first real smile, and I noticed that his eyes were a fine pale blue. "Well, let's say it's because you're mysterious."

"Really?" I said. No one had ever called me mysterious in my entire life. My first boyfriend had once described me to his best friends as an "adventurous kisser," but that didn't hold a candle to mysterious.

"Like a fish," Anders said, "about to swim away."

So I loved Anders because: A) He wouldn't let an old man go to his grave thinking his friend didn't care. Up until the cancer he had always felt all the right emotions, in the right order. No irony. No distance. Cry when sad. Be happy when you've done something good. This amazed me. I had no idea people could be so good, so honest. It had not been my experience up to that point at all. And B) He thought I was as mysterious as a fish.

And to be honest, most of all, I loved Anders because he loved me.

That very afternoon, Anders had his first round of chemo. He sat in a plaid La-Z-Boy, drumming his fingers and shaking his legs, while what looked like water ran down the slim iv tubes and into his waiting blue veins. I sat next to him and held his hand. The night before, I'd told Maude her father had cancer. Maude and I sat on the couch. I could hear above us the flapping blue tarp that had taken the place of our roof. I'd decided not to mince words. I didn't say, "Your father isn't feeling well" or "Your father is sick." I intended to be honest, to prepare her for what might be coming, even if it might scare her. But Maude, who had seen Bibi go through chemo for breast cancer, lose her hair, and grow it back, had taken the news as a sort of no news. As if I had told her, "Daddy can't go to the park with us today because he has to finish the taxes."

"Poor Dad," she said. "He'll throw up. I hate it when I throw up." I let it go, afraid to use yet another word—this time *dying* —that I wouldn't be able to call back.

But the first round of chemo didn't make Anders nauseated the way it had made Bibi or even knock him out as Dr. Mautz had predicted. Anders came home from the hospital and ran up the back stairs to the attic, stared out the hole down into the dumpster in the driveway. "Fantastic, Fan-cock-fucking-tastic," Anders said. Anders who never even said damn.

Anders couldn't contain himself. He was up and down a dozen times that afternoon, small enthusiastic clouds of *fuck* and *fuckings* trailing after him. "Wow," Bibi said, when she stopped by. "He's doing great. The chemo must be working already." Anders was talking to one of the carpenters, the words spilling out, his arms waving over his head. I made myself nod in agreement with Bibi. The chemo was working. It must be. Anders was here. He was happy. The future, I thought, would just have to take care of itself.

Anders stayed happy. All through August he spun through the house in ceaseless circles, trailing a cloud of happy, if unreasoning, sound. One day cursing, another singing Gilbert and Sullivan. Somewhere in his brain, unbeknownst to me until now, Anders had stored all the words to *The Pirates of Penzance.* "I am a Pirate King. And it is, it is a glorious thing!" The carpenters nailed the new roof in place, taking Anders's enthusiasm in stride, as if nothing a homeowner did or said could possibly surprise them. During the day Anders never stopped and only rarely made complete sense when he talked. Sometimes he scrambled sentences, which seemed like a kind of game, a harmless show of enthusiasm. "Pig peeping purple!" he might say when he saw a new shipment of lumber arrive. And it sounded like scat, an alliteration of excitement. Even the delivery driver clapped his hands like a child when he heard Anders and laughed, thinking he'd brought of load of wood to the door of some jazz poet.

Or he might almost make sense, talking about oil versus latex stain with the contractor, only missing a word or two. "Does the loud door really stand up as well as the oil?" *He's looking so good,* everyone said when they saw him. I nodded. And nodded. And kept my mouth shut. *Don't call him Anders*—I wanted to say—*that's not Anders.* Because it seemed to me the last time I'd seen my Anders, the real Anders, was after his seizure, when we sat up and talked all night in his hospital room.

The nights were the worst. I didn't speak about them to anyone. During the day the house was full of people. Then they all went home to their dinners and their beds. After dinner Anders would swallow the pills that were supposed to make him sleep. He would settle on the couch for a while with Maude, reading her books, telling her stories from his childhood about eccentric neighbors who slept with their chickens, about storms in July with hail the size of baseballs that pounded craters into the roof of his dad's truck. This was the one time in the day he rarely missed a word, never said fuck or fucking. I would listen, too, to these bedtime stories, one warm happy family on the couch we'd inherited from his parents' farmhouse. To lose Anders would be to lose this history.

Our history. All the time we'd shared. No one else would ever know how we met or how my mother died or the name of the Latin professor—Dr. George Washington Boone—who'd sold us this house. How could the world go on without someone as good as Anders, without Anders himself, in it? But, in a way, it already was.

"You're so funny, Dad," Maude said one night after a story about a barn full of popcorn catching fire. "Did you used to be funny?"

"I'm the same me," Anders said. For that moment I could almost believe it.

Then I would tuck Maude into bed, turning on the radio in her room to mask the sounds that would soon be coming, and by the time I got back to the living room, Anders would be up, the medication already losing its hold. He would start pacing and talking and waving his arms, moving faster, his arms swinging more wildly than they had all day. He would ask me a question. "Where are the shaky dogs?" At first I would try to figure out what he really meant to say. When Maude was two, she drove us crazy for weeks saying what sounded for all the word like *pig gown*. At that stage she only had a few words, mostly Bs—*book, bottle, ball*—but she said them very clearly, indeed with an exacting overpronunciation that reminded me of the quiz master at a school spelling bee. She sounded every vowel and consonant clearly. Even strangers understood her when she spoke, something that is rarely true with toddlers.

Pig gown was different. What could she mean? At first Maude would ask calmly, expecting results. Then when *pig gown* failed to appear, she would ask again and again with increasing levels of anger and hysteria. Anders, patient father, man who liked a good puzzle, tried offering her nearly every object in the house without success. Then, one day, we went to the park. Maude ran toward the jungle gym, the swings. "Pig Gown!" she cried.

"Playground," Anders said. "Of course. It's so obvious. Why couldn't we hear it?"

187

Now I started every evening trying to be as patient as the old Anders had been. He wanted shaky dogs. I took a guess and offered him his boots, his slippers, then his sandals. No. Some kind of food? I led Anders to the kitchen. Opened the refrigerator, then the cabinets in turn. He shook his head. "*Shaky dogs!*" he would say, stressing these words that meant nothing to me, trying to make his dim wife understand.

Then, like Maude, he would get angry. Who could blame him? He would move from room to room, asking me about the shaky dogs, then asking himself in a kind of soliloquy. By this stage, any answer on my part would make him scream with rage, he was so angry, so frustrated. I could tell him, his shrieks said, I simply would not. He would circle the house, bumping into walls, asking his question more and more loudly, adding other words, just as out of context, Double heart no shaky dog?

"No," I would say, "no, shaky dog." Or "Yes, double heart." No matter the answer, he would continue his circumnavigation of the house, asking that or some other impossible question.

Once I tried telling Dr. Mautz about the nights, but he simply refused to believe that a man could take as much medication as Anders and keep moving. But Anders did, sometimes resting for a moment on our bed, or the couch, or a chair, only to rise, anxious again, checking, rechecking every room, looking for what I had hidden from him until even Ginger, who loved him with all her saggy basset heart, would growl at him as he came careening through the living room.

Late in the night, Ginger would fall asleep. I would fall asleep. Only rarely, very rarely, did Anders fall asleep. Still, every morning the sun rose and we went on with the daylight versions of our lives.

We went in for chemo on Mondays and Thursdays. We saw Dr. Mautz each Friday. He said Anders was looking good. He said we would know more in October, when they took another scan. With luck the lesions would be smaller. With a dash more luck they would have disappeared, winking out like stars driven out by the dawn of a new day.

Twice a month I went to see my obstetrician. Because I'd had an earlier miscarriage, I'd been assigned a different doctor by Anders's HMO, one who specialized in high-risk pregnancies. Her name, which I found nearly impossible to believe, was Dr. Miracle. That wasn't the half of it, she told me. Her first name was Faith. I liked her. I wanted to believe in her. She was round and short and had an amazing toothy smile, one that showed her teeth clear back to her molars, like rows of bright piano keys. In her opinion I barely rated my high-risk designation after one measly miscarriage. Dr. Miracle smiled her smile at me. Hell, she said, she'd just seen a diabetic woman with epilepsy who was having twins. I was already four months along, and everything was looking great. Still, she didn't say a word when I kept my eyes closed during my first ultrasound. I couldn't bear to see my fetus as an underwater baby. Not yet. Not after losing the last one.

So the weeks leapfrogged on past chemo, past Dr. Miracle. Ginger, loyal basset, spent her mornings following Anders up and down the stairs to the attic until her short legs failed her, and then flopped down beside me on the heirloom couch. I spent the afternoons, Ginger beside me, Anders careening past, trying to prepare for my fall creative writing class. Maude was already back in school, scaling the heights of second grade.

Anders was officially on sick leave from his teaching at the university. At the community college, classes didn't start until the day after Labor Day. I'd thought about taking sick leave, but I only had four weeks of sick pay saved up. With Anders already drawing on his limited pool of leave, I had to think about money. So I decided to teach part-time, keeping a creative writing class which met only two days a week, rather than the five times a week of the composition classes I usually taught. I thought it would be less work, even though I'd never taught creative writing before. I'd see how far I could get into the semester before Anders needed me at home every minute. Or got better, I reminded myself. Got completely, remarkably well. My brother Mark had volunteered to come as soon as he heard the news. He lived in San Francisco and taught comparative literature at Berkeley. But I put him off, keeping him in reserve for that truly desperate day, one I couldn't quite imagine yet but knew was coming. For now Bibi, true friend, was there. She had taken my address book and called everyone who needed calling during that first day when I was with Anders at the hospital.

Like my brother Mark, Anders's dad wanted to come right away, but Anders's mom Hilda was in the hospital in San Diego, recovering from a bout of pneumonia, and he was afraid to leave her. Mark even reached our half-sister Evelina, who we had only met once. She'd just returned to the states from the Philippines, where she'd gone to live with her grandmother right after we met her at our father's funeral. Mark had kept in touch with Evelina, exchanging long chatty letters. I had only managed a Christmas card or two in the ten years since I'd met her. Evelina was about to start a master's in social work at the University of Minnesota. She called me the night following her call from Mark. Just let her know and she could come down any weekend from St. Paul, she said. She had a car. She had plenty of experience in nursing her grandmother. She sounded so grown up. Okay, I said to her, I'll call you.

"Promise," she said. And I promised.

Jean, Anders's troublesome sister, on the other hand, called after talking to Bibi only to doubleguess us and Dr. Mautz. Why didn't Anders go someplace decent, like Sloan Kettering in New York? she'd asked him. It was the wrong thing to ask Anders, with his passionate belief in Wisconsin as the best possible place to be no matter the circumstances, and Jean had gotten an earful of his new vocabulary. The truth was our insurance didn't allow Anders to leave the state and still be covered. If, as we had once been told, fertility treatments outside the blessings of insurance could cost one hundred thousand dollars, how much could a full round of cancer treatment cost? How could we possibly pay for it? How come, I asked Bibi, no one in books or movies ever has to worry about sick leave or restrictions on their health insurance?

After hearing the news, either from Bibi or Mark, there was a constant stream of visitors—friends, former students, colleagues, fellow artists, neighbors—who stopped by to see Anders, to peer into the destruction that was our attic.

I started serving the visitors and carpenters coffee at three in the afternoon. Mostly this was for the carpenters. I felt I owed it to them for putting up with Anders and the visiting friends and neighbors. I thought they must feel like they were demonstrating attic renovation at a World's Fair. And also I just wanted to pretend all this madness was normal. In the presence of coffee and cake, how could anything be wrong with the world?

Coffee hour became the nicest part of the day, almost as nice as the quiet after-dinner moments with Maude on the couch. Anders would sit still, eat a cookie or a slice of banana bread, and drink a cup of coffee that he didn't need to keep him jazzed up. Rick, the lead carpenter, had a wife who was getting her PhD in French. Sonja, the other carpenter, was the sweeper on the local World Champion Women's Curling Team. Curling, she explained, was a kind of cross between ice hockey and shuffleboard. I nodded as if I understood, though it was not a game girls like me from Jacksonville, Florida, had grown up playing. I hadn't even worn a pair of ice skates until Maude was two and Anders taught us both in a single icy afternoon. Maude, tiny Wisconsin toddler, took to skating much more quickly than her mom. Still, with Sonja I talked curling. With Rick, the difficulties of French translation.

Somewhere in the chatter, Anders would put down his cup of coffee and tell us the inside history of some invention. He told us about the invention of the camera, the telephone, radio, and television. As with Maude's bedtime stories, when Anders told these tales his language was nearly normal, no odd outcroppings of jazzy gibberish. But there was more vehemence in the way he spoke than when he was with Maude.

In all cases, there was an unappreciated early inventor who died broke, broken, and unrecognized. Anders felt the unfairness of this like a wound. The other theme was that the world always failed at the time to realize all the invention was capable of doing. The radio was thought useless because you couldn't send a message to just one person without everyone overhearing it. The fact that a radio "broadcasted" its message was, of course, its strength. What were we missing now? How could we be so blind, time and again. What was right in front of us now that we couldn't see?

And whoever was visiting pitched right in. Maybe we were wrong about what computers were capable of doing, our neighbor from down the street would say. No, no, someone else might say. Computers were old hat. It was robots and artificial intelligence that were misunderstood. What's more old hat than robots! the neighbor would hoot back.

On and on it would go. Friends and colleagues in this college town mistaking Anders's insistence—*why, why, why?*—for good intellectual argument. Every day in our house was another mad tea party. Every night, just mad.

August came to an end. The carpenters finished raising the beams for the new roof just in time to knock off for the Labor Day weekend. I drove to my office at school to pick up my class list. In the parking lot I almost ran over a woman struggling to her car with two big bags of books. "Dr. Dahl?" the woman said when I got out of the car, ready to apologize. It was Mickey's mother. "Oh, how are you?" I said. "How is Mickey?"

"Fine," she said. He was working up north in one of the tribal casinos. Now that he wasn't in school, she'd decided she should be. She had her two-year nursing degree, but she'd always wanted a real bachelor's degree, and now she was going to do it. And, she added, the first English class she was going to take was my creative writing workshop. Mickey had told her what a fine teacher I was, how much I cared for my students. She shook my hand, then picked up her two sacks of books and headed for her car. I waved.

I went into my office and put my head down on my desk. I had been trying to come up with a syllabus full of clever exercises for my first-ever creative writing class by borrowing from half a dozen writing books. Now, thinking of Mickey's mom and her expectations, I wondered if that were such a good idea. Just thinking of her in my class made the exercises I'd chosen seem like party games for children.

Now I looked at the class list the department secretary had stuck in my mailbox. I recognized about half the names—my Hmong and Hispanic and Tibetan ESL students. Like Mickey's mom, they had real, sometimes frighteningly difficult lives. And, right now, I did too. Maybe all the creative writing texts I'd been cribbing from had been right about one thing: maybe we should write about what we knew.

So, on Tuesday, when my creative writing class started, that's what we did. I told them about Anders. I told them I was pregnant. I said I would try to be there for every meeting, but I might not be able to make it. If I had to miss a class, I asked, what should we do? Should I just cancel class? I had never asked my students even the smallest question about how a class I was teaching should be run. Now, I was opening my kingdom to democracy. I made myself sit quietly while the class discussed what to do. No, they said. They didn't want to miss any classes. We'll make up a list, they said, and each of us will take one class and agree to be in charge if you're not here. They did that. Then we got out paper and all of us, student and teacher, started to write the story of our lives.

I started my story with this moment, this sentence, then

went back and wrote everything I could remember about the day of Anders's seizure, then further back, to how we met, married. Not in one class, of course, but sitting on the horse-hair couch with Ginger late into my sleep-deprived nights.

I sat and wrote. My husband was dying, raging, and dying. My world was reduced to noise, my house to the sticks and tarps over my head. I sat, selfishly turning it all into words on the page. One night Anders fell down the stairs with a crash like a load of lumber, and my only two thoughts were: *Good, now I can take him to the hospital and they will have to do something.* And *but first, I want to finish this page.* I wasn't ready to let him go, but I would have given anything, *anything*, for a sleeping potion for Anders that would work.

We made it through September, and then it was October. On the first of the month the carpenters finished the new roof and started framing in our new rooms. I left Anders poking at the stud walls and went to my appointment with Dr. Miracle. No ultrasound this time, thank goodness. Just blood work at this six-month checkup, a quick listen for a heartbeat. Dr. Miracle squirted her magic gel on my stomach and rolled her wand around until we could here the baby's amplified heart. *Lub Dub*, went the heart's whooshing rhythms. *Lub Dub*, my baby sang to me from the far shore of my belly. *Lub Dub a Dub Dub.* I closed my eyes. I wanted to put my fingers in my ears. I didn't want to fall in love with someone else I might lose, like I'd lost the other baby, like I was losing Anders.

Dr. Miracle let me sit up and get dressed. Then she looked at me with her arms crossed, no smile now. "You're six months pregnant. After that last ultrasound, I can even tell you with near certainty you're carrying a boy. Don't you think it's time you let yourself be happy about this baby?"

"My husband . . ." I started, but she already knew about Anders. Apparently it was in my medical file because she'd mentioned it at my first visit—our whole HMO medical life an open book.

She shook her head, frowning now. "Women have babies fleeing from war zones, in refugee camps," she said. In the summers, she said, she worked for Doctors Without Borders. "I've seen them. They're happy. Be happy. We're already the past," she said. "Your baby is the future."

Okay, I said to myself. Okay, after she left the room to write out a prescription. I wrapped my arms around my belly. The future. A baby boy. *Lub dub,* my heart went. *Lub dub.* And I started to cry.

The worst night of all was Halloween. Earlier in the day we'd gone in for Anders's long-awaited brain scan. It took all afternoon. Dr. Mautz had ordered sedatives to keep Anders quiet during the scan, but still he couldn't keep still. The technicians had to bring in the doctor on call who increased the dosage as far as he dared. Finally he ordered Anders strapped—head and body—to the machine's cold table.

After dinner Maude, dressed as a black cat, went out trick-or-treating with Kyle and Lloyd. In spite of a cold drizzle, Bibi stationed herself on our sidewalk with a bucket of candy to keep kids from ringing the doorbell. I locked Ginger in Maude's room with a Beatles' Greatest Hits CD turned up on Maude's little boom box to keep her from barking herself hoarse at all the distant childish shrills of *Trick-or-Treat!* But it was Anders who haunted the night. While the kids were out, he ran from window to window, as if he couldn't believe what he was seeing—ghosts and goblins and demons walking the good Wisconsin earth. His whole body shook, hands waving, head nodding, as if he could no longer contain what was growing inside him.

After Maude came home, high on chocolate, and while I was busy scrubbing her black-cat nose and whiskers off with cold cream, Anders got into the shelves of Disney movies and silent classics next to the VCR and pulled all the tape out of each cassette. Then he unscrewed the plates over the light switches in the living room, dining room, and hall and pulled out the wires. When I saw it I couldn't believe he hadn't been electrocuted right then and there. Then he'd moved on to the kitchen, dumping all the cereal out of the boxes, all the spaghetti and rice and noodles and flour and sugar and salt out of their canisters and onto the floor.

I'd spent probably half an hour getting Maude washed, pajama'd, and to bed with Ginger at her feet. But Anders had moved with manic speed. I looked at the living room, then the kitchen, and I followed the trail of floury footprints to our bedroom. I found him in the closet, loudly demanding answers from his bathrobe in some language only clothes could understand.

I called the after-hours emergency number for Dr. Mautz. Then I sat on the bed, listening to Anders scream at our shirts and sweaters while I waited for Dr. Mautz to call back.

When Dr. Mautz did finally call, I held the phone out for him to hear Anders's incoherent shrieks. "What have you got in the house?" Dr. Mautz asked. I went to the medicine cabinet, phone in hand, and read the names off Anders's prescriptions. I could hear Dr. Mautz take a deep breath. Then he made me write down a laundry list of sedatives. "If you can get him to take that many pills, give them to him. If not, call an ambulance and I'll meet you at the hospital."

I expected Dr. Mautz to hang up then, to stumble back to his own warm bed. But I heard him sigh on the other end of the phone. "I looked at the scan," he said. I held my breath. Dr. Mautz sighed even more deeply.

"Not good?" I said.

"Bad," he said. I sat down on the toilet lid. Dr. Mautz had been so optimistic, had stayed so bloody up through it all, that even at this point the worst I'd expected from him was, "It's not what we'd hoped." *Bad* was very bad.

"I think we should consider calling hospice in," he said. "There really isn't any point in going on with the chemo, based on these results. If I call tonight, they'll send a nurse to the house in the morning. She can arrange for medications that will keep Anders comfortable," Dr. Mautz paused. We could both still hear Anders wailing in the bedroom. "And quiet. Arrange for a night attendant, if that is what it takes to keep him at home."

"I can keep him at home?" I asked. No matter how long this moment had been coming, speeding toward us like a train, I wasn't prepared for it. "Home until . . ."

"He can stay home until the end," Dr. Mautz said. "If you want him to. That's what hospice is for. They'll make sure he stays out of the hospital. If you bring him in—even tonight—in all honesty, it may be hard to get him home again. No matter their intentions, hospitals tend to be more, well, aggressive in their approach."

I looked at the clock in the hall. It was three o'clock in the morning. One of my creative writing students, a former Chinese dissident, had written that three was the hour favored by the state police for mass arrests. No one was really thinking clearly, no one was ready to offer resistance at this hour when the tidal flow of our bodies was at its lowest ebb. Ten minutes before, I'd been willing to do almost anything for a little peace, for a good night's sleep. But Anders was my one and only husband. We'd come so far together, I wouldn't give him up now. *Til death do us part.* "I'll get the pills in him somehow," I said.

I did. I mixed the pills with one of Maude's snack-size chocolate puddings and spooned them into his mouth as if he were a baby—a baby crying in his own closet, lost and frightened of this new strange world. Then I half-carried, half-wrestled him onto the bed and kept him there with the weight of my body until his legs and arms stopped thrashing. He fell asleep sprawled across the bed, looking as if he had fallen there from the deep dark sky. I felt his heart, banging away in his chest, still running on overdrive. I felt our baby, nestled between us, turning and turning in restless sleep. Then I fell asleep too.

197

The doorbell woke me up at eight-thirty the next morning. I left Anders asleep on the bed, but Maude beat me to the door, Ginger at her heels. "Aunt Gretel," I heard her say, which helped prepare me for the sight of my ex-sister-in-law standing on my doormat. Gretel had left Hal Jr. and I hadn't seen her since, though I'd heard she was living near the university.

She was wearing a dark green, cable-knit sweater with deer-horn buttons, and her hair hung in two long, chocolate brown braids down her shoulders. She looked fresh out of a fairy tale, which is to say she looked the same as ever. She held a plate of freshly baked almond kringle in front of her at arm's length as an offering and, maybe, as protection. I wasn't angry with her for leaving Hal, just happy to see her, to see anyone with my breakfast in hand after such a night.

"Lotte," she said naming her lover, the ex-minister's wife, "and I are volunteering for hospice. She was on call last night when Dr. Mautz phoned about Anders. I am so sorry. I couldn't believe it at first—when Lotte told me. I thought I was having a bad dream." I took the kringle, and Maude gave Gretel a big hug. She was happy to see her too. We went into the kitchen, and I started coffee.

"Neither Lotte nor I can be your hospice worker—that would violate all kinds of rules about conflict of interest—but I thought I could help you get started. Lotte will come over to help too, if that's okay?" She raised her eyebrows over her deep brown Gretel eyes. Of course it was okay, I said. When Gretel stood to telephone Lotte, I stood, too, and gave her a long hug.

I was wrong not to have liked her when she was my perfect sister-in-law. I hardly deserved her back now, just when I need-ed all the friends and family I could get. I'd been petty and wrong to hold Gretel's tidy domesticity against her, but still part of me was relieved when Lotte arrived. Lotte was nearly as big as my refrigerator and had on a gray sweatshirt over paint-splattered jeans. *No nonsense* was the way Anders's father had always described Lotte when she was his pastor's wife, and from Hal Sr. that was a great compliment.

It would be best, Lotte said, if Anders slept in one of the downstairs rooms so he wouldn't have to manage the stairs. We only had three rooms on the first floor: the kitchen, the living room, and the dining room. I picked the dining room. We could eat in the kitchen.

The choice made, Lotte and Gretel both fell to work with a will. Gretel got Maude fed, dressed, and off to school, while Lotte ordered a hospital bed, helped me shove the furniture in the dining room against the walls, and pulled the pocket doors between the living room and dining room most of the way shut so Anders could have privacy and a little quiet. The bed, which Lotte had somehow ordered express, was there in less than an hour and installed by the window. The medical supply store also delivered a toilet chair, since the only bathroom was upstairs. But I could tell that after a brief trip upstairs, Lotte—who was an RN—wasn't sure Anders was going to be mobile even for that long. There was also a big scary box of adult diapers.

Together we got Anders up, down the stairs, and into the bed. Lotte gave him a warm sponge bath and put a diaper on him. As soon as I saw him in his new bed, the morning light shining on his face, I realized that something more than the combined weight of my body and the baby's or even the drug cocktail Dr. Mautz had ordered had kept him in bed all night. Last night had been like a fever breaking, though with none of the cure that implied. Circuits, switching stations, unfathomable bits of his brain, had flared up like overloaded wiring in an old house, and now they would never work again. His legs and arms, not still in months, were now so much dead weight.

But Anders's eyes were open, and when I looked into them I saw they were calm for the first time since I couldn't remember when. All the frantic madness was gone. The angry stranger in the lurching body was gone. *Blue, blue,* Anders looked out at me. Still in there, still my husband. I sat by the side of his newly delivered bed and held his hand, and he held mine right back. Twice he opened his mouth but nothing came out; no words, no songs—but also no screams.

Anders's official hospice nurse, Mrs. Brown, arrived shortly before lunch. She set to work taking his blood pressure and his pulse. Lotte and Gretel drew up a grocery list after checking my meager supplies. What had we been eating? Lotte asked, checking bare shelf after bare shelf. Cake and coffee was all I could remember. Cereal with Maude for breakfast. Lunch? When had I last had lunch? Dinners had been a blur of macaroni and frozen pizza served mostly for Maude's sake. Anders rarely sat long enough to take a bite, and I was usually too tired to be hungry, though I tried for the baby's sake.

Gretel and Lotte set out for the grocery store with a list three pages long, leaving me alone with Mrs. Brown. I guessed she was at least sixty-five, maybe older, but her face was smooth and, for Wisconsin, oddly tanned, surrounded by wild ringlets of white blond hair. She looked like a secondhand doll Anders had once bought Maude at the Salvation Army Thrift Store. She and the doll had the same hotpink lips. Mrs. Brown had hot pink nails as well. If she had been wearing purple or orange instead of a white nurse's pantsuit I'd have sworn she was one of Bibi's relatives. She had pink shoelaces in her white nurse's Reeboks.

She also came equipped with a Tupperware container full of dog biscuits to make friends with patients' pets, and one full of jelly beans to make friends with patients' children. Ginger got a biscuit, but Maude missed her treat since she was already at school. After dispensing treats, Mrs. Brown got out her folder of handouts and a yellow legal pad and we got down to brass tacks. The first thing she showed me was a signed statement from Dr. Mautz swearing that Anders did, indeed, have terminal cancer and had less than six months to live. "He faxed it over this morning," she said.

"Six months?" I said. "Dr. Mautz said six months?" Thinking of last night, it seemed both impossibly long and impossibly short.

"That's just standard language," she said. "So your insurance will cover your husband's hospice care." She looked at me. "Dr. Mautz didn't give you a prognosis?" she asked. I shook my head. She shook hers, her curls bobbing. "Oh, well, they're never right anyway, are they, the doctors? Anymore than they get it right when they tell you your due date." She nodded at my round belly.

She had a point. I didn't know a single baby that had been born on the day it was due. Still part of me wanted certainty. Should I push Dr. Mautz for a formal prognosis? Make him tell me Anders had three months or twelve months or three days to live? No, Mrs. Brown was right. Whatever he said would be at best an educated guess. *Longer than a day, shorter than six months.* I could do that well myself.

On her legal pad Mrs. Brown started notes for a care plan. Then, as I agreed to each point, she wrote them in on an official hospice form. She would visit three times a week and I could call her if I needed any additional help. She would arrange for a sitter to come weeknights so I could sleep. An attendant would come to bathe Anders every other day. I would have to change his diapers if he couldn't use the potty chair—could I do that? I nodded yes. *Diapers, potty chair*—words from Maude's childhood, words that hadn't been needed in our house since she was two. Well, they were back in the daily vocabulary now, and would stay there for a while—first for Anders, then the baby.

Hospice, Mrs. Brown said, would handle contact with the doctors. No need for me to spend a lot of time calling Dr. Mautz, waiting for him to call back. Most of the calls would be about medications. She checked the records Dr. Mautz had sent. Steroids, antiseizure meds, sleeping pills. Luckily, she said, there were no pain cells in the brain, so Anders wouldn't need heavy medication, but he might need some for the discomfort he could experience as his bodily systems began to shut down, one by one.

She gave me a handout, "The Signs and Symptoms of Approaching Death." "So you know what to look for," she said. The pamphlet listed them as

1. Coolness
2. Sleeping
3. Disorientation
4. Incontinence
5. Lung Congestion
6. Urine Decrease
7. Fluid and Food Decrease
8. Breathing Pattern Change

Then there was a second pamphlet that answered the question, *How Will You Know When Death Has Occurred?* I decided to read that one later.

"This is really the most important handout," Mrs. Brown said as she handed me "Death on the Emotional-Spiritual Plane." "The experience we call death," it read, "occurs when the body completes its natural process of shutting down and when the spirit completes its natural process of reconciling and finishing." According to hospice, in order for this to happen, all of us who loved or needed Anders had to say good-bye and tell him it was okay, hold his hand and stroke his head and say, *It's okay to go.* Go where? I wondered. "Into the next dimension of life," the pamphlet said.

"Hospice is really a religion, isn't it?" I said, looking up at Mrs. Brown. "One that requires a leap of faith?"

She shrugged her thin shoulders. "They try to keep the language open," she said. "I can't really say much about that.

I'm not a big believer myself. All I can say is that I've been a nurse for nearly forty years and I've worked for hospice for the last five. I've seen a lot of deaths in my time—good ones, bad ones. What kind of life a person lived has a lot to do with that, of course. But so does all this—saying good-bye, letting go. I've become a believer in that, at least." She waved a pink-nailed hand toward Anders sleeping in his own dining room. "I wouldn't be working so hard at my age if I didn't think what I did made a difference."

"Are you a widow?" I asked her, then tried to take the question back. "I'm sorry, I've no . . ."

She held up her hand. "That's all right. You've got every right to know what I bring to your house. No, married three times, divorced the same. All of them still alive, as far as I know. So I can't say I've been through what you're going through."

She handed me another list: "Normal Emotional, Spiritual, and Mental Signs of Dying with Appropriate Responses." If Anders saw visions or spoke to people who were already dead, I shouldn't try to contradict him, only affirm his experience. If he was restless, I should hold his hand. If he wanted to see fewer and fewer people as he withdrew, I should understand. I should give permission for him to leave without making him feel guilty. I should say good-bye. I should make sure Maude said good-bye.

Again, so many *good-byes*. So much emphasis on *go*. Could I really bring myself to tell Anders we could all live without him? That we would all be fine when it seemed so far from clear we would be?

"Sign here," Mrs. Brown said, pointing to a line at the bottom of the carefully drawn care plan of our measured response to this bottomless loss called death.

"All right," I said, and signed. *Good-bye my love,* my name in ink said. *Go with God,* it read.

Then things got very quiet. Oh, there was still hammering in the attic, but even that seemed muted now that it was trim work, done carefully with finishing hammers and not with the power nailer. The carpenters crept upstairs in the morning to work. Anders, like a newborn baby or an old old dog, slept most of every day.

The first night that Anders spent in the dining room in his hospital bed, I slept with him. The sitter was starting the next night and then, I knew, I would be too shy to climb, big as a house, into the narrow bed with my husband. It was a tight squeeze, but Anders was thin as a rail. His body curled around mine like a comma around the biggest and fattest of periods. I say *his body curled*, but actually I curled him, moved him, shaping him to my body, and we slept the deep sleep of those who are profoundly weary of this world. Just before dawn I woke up. Anders was moving against me, ever so slightly, maybe all he could move now. We made love—or I made love to him. Lowering my vast self gently onto him. The last time, I kept thinking. The last time.

At least there was this one last time. When had we made love in the busy whirl that was our life before cancer? The night before his seizure? The week? This, at least, I would remember. Remember both the first (on that futon all those years ago) and the last (in a bed with that went up and down at the touch of a button).

After that, the night-sitter stayed next to Anders in those dark hours. I slept the sleep the baby needed upstairs, taking up nearly all our double bed. But I still had the evening hours to spend alone with Anders, after Maude was in bed, before the sitter came at midnight. In those hours I sat next to Anders, our baby turning cartwheels inside me, and whispered all my regrets about the past (why had I taken so long to love him back, to marry him and settle in Wisconsin? Why hadn't we had more children? Made love every day? Why hadn't I spent every minute I could with him? Why had we argued about who would fill the car up with gas? About what was the best way to sort laundry? How long to boil a soft-cooked egg? Why, why, why, why . . .).

Then on to a week of future regrets (that he wouldn't see his new child grow up—if he lived to see him at all. That he wouldn't be there for Maude's growing up either. That he would not be there for her getting breasts, for her needing all kinds of advice, which she might not take but would still need. Would never, in this life, walk into his new rooms.)

Then a good month of remembering (the party where we met, my father's funeral, the long drive up to see his parents when they were on the farm). I remembered that first night in the hospital, Anders saying, "What the hell. I can't complain. I've had a good life. I wouldn't have changed a thing." That night I had taken his tone of contentment for surrender and that had made me so angry I couldn't see straight. Now those words stood in for Anders's side of the conversation we were having, for what he could no longer say. *A good life. Wouldn't have changed a thing.* Not even dying like this? I asked him. He looked back at me—*Not even this.*

That helped me get close to good-bye, though not all the way to *I love you so I let you go.*

Maude followed almost the same path, though with more time on sharing and less on regrets. She sat with her father from dinner until bedtime, holding his hand. She didn't mind the smell of the diapers, the rasp of his breath, or how, after a month, only one eye would open, the other always closed in a sort of twitching sleep. One night when I was tucking her into bed she said, "Do you think Dad will stay like that for a long time?" I wasn't sure how to answer. How long was long in this terminal world?

"I mean," she said, "Teddy Fulton-Mathews's brother, Benny, has been in bed all his life, and Teddy says his brother will live as long as he will, as long as any of us, probably."

I knew vaguely that the Fulton-Mathewses, who lived in a white bungalow near Maude's school, had a severely handicapped son. A wide wheelchair ramp zigzagged its way from their front door to the drive. I had never met Teddy's brother, hadn't known his name was Benny until now. How much constant effort it must be to take care of a such a child, a baby for life. I regretted never offering to take Teddy some evening, never offering Teddy's mother and father the least bit of help—or even interest or concern. On the other side of this awful moment that was now, I promised myself I would be different, I would be better; I would care more for others who lived outside my house.

Maude brought me back to now. "Couldn't we keep Daddy just like he is forever?" Maude asked. "Please?"

"Oh, Maudie," I said. I stopped there, not really knowing where to go after that. I kissed her blond head. I tried again. "Daddy's sick, and we don't want him to feel so bad forever. Let's not wish for that," I said. As I hugged her good-night I thought, remember Maude is there. Remember she needs you, too.

A week later I overheard Maude say to Anders one night, "I don't want you to stay here if it hurts you, Daddy. We'll be okay. I promise. I'll tell the baby all about you. Show him pictures and stuff, right from the very first day." Brave Maude, she was ahead of me on *go*.

Other said their good-byes, too, before I was ready to say mine. First neighbors, students, and former students. Then colleagues. Many of them the same people who had come for our Mad Hatter Coffee Klatches. All through November I sat on the couch with Ginger, sometimes with Maude or Bibi or Gretel, as the visitors arrived, said to Anders what they felt they had come to say. "I got a job," said one student, "in Seattle."

"We're going to stage a retrospective of your photography at the next faculty show," the chair of his department said. "With a four-color catalogue." After they spoke, each would sit a few minutes holding Anders's hand, then leave after stretching their arms wide to give both me and my big baby-filled belly a hug.

In early December, the carpenters nearly done with the renovation, came in one by one to tell Anders some last detail of the work they had continued in his absence. "The oak trim for the doors is stained, and we'll nail it up tomorrow," said Rick, the lead carpenter. "It's going to look just great."

Then Anders's closest friends started coming. They were slower to accept that now was the time to say good-bye. Steve came, then Lloyd. Each week the circle drew smaller. Evelina came down from St. Paul and sat for a long morning with Anders, then left to go to pick up Maude and take her to the mall to buy new snow boots. Evelina stayed all weekend, taking Maude skating and to the movies, fixing us all lumpia and chicken adobo from her grandmother's special recipes. But she didn't enter the dining room that was Anders's room again. "I said good-bye to your daddy already," I overheard her explain to Maude as she left. "It's bad luck to say good-bye twice."

Hal Jr. came down from Minneapolis and spent a night, then drove away, red-eyed. Anders's dad, Hal Sr., flew in the next morning. Hilda, his mom, was still too sick to travel, was not so far from death herself. Hal said good-bye to his son as if he had been practicing for it all his life, as if he were amazed he'd gotten this far without losing a son—to war or a tractor overturning or the country habit of driving too fast on narrow, icy roads. He acted as if having the time to say good-bye to his oldest son were an unexpected gift, something not often granted in this life. And I thought, *he's right.* My mother, my father had disappeared like ghosts, alone in hospitals. The good-byes had been all the more painful for it.

After an hour with Anders, Hal shook my hand, then took Maude out into the backyard to help her hang the bird feeder she'd made in school. The next morning he flew home to be with Hilda, the faint and fading love of his life, and to tell her about her son, to help her say good-bye to him as well.

After that, his sister Jean flew in from San Diego and was

predictably as difficult as ever, badgering Mrs. Brown, refusing to let Gretel in the house. Jean kept it up until I sent her to her room for a time-out like a three-year-old. When she left, a week's worth of Anders's pain medication was missing. "Ah, well," my brother Mark said, when he arrived the next day. "Maybe she's in more pain than she lets on."

Seeing Anders was hard on Mark. It brought back his last awful year with George. He looked at Anders's thin face and saw George, listened to Anders's labored breathing and saw what he feared lay ahead for him someday as well. He said his good-byes, then stayed out of the dining room. He tried apologizing to me for it. "Shhh," I said, "you said good-bye. Our baby sister says it's bad luck to say good-bye twice." Then I wouldn't hear another word. He and Bibi made a great team, organizing the food that people dropped off, taking turns with Maude, buying and decorating a Christmas tree, baking cookies—planning for a holiday I had no room for in my head or heart. Bibi's dark head was next to Mark's, bent over the kitchen table, rolling out dough, cutting out angels and Santas and sleighs. Bibi looked more like Mark's sister than I ever had. Why not? What was Bibi by now if not family?

I overheard them one night, talking over their iced Christmas treats, drinking shots of brandy. "It should have been me," Mark said.

"It should have been me," Bibi said. "Why did I get well?"

God, I hoped she was well. Her own brush with breast cancer was not nearly far enough in the past for me to be sure.

"You don't want to die, Bibi," Mark said. "Not with Kyle so little. Don't even say it."

"What about Maude?"

"It doesn't work that way. You know that," I said, walking into the kitchen, saying what we all knew. "We don't get to pick."

"No," said Bibi, pouring me a double shot of brandy. Mark handed me a snowman cookie. I bit his round white snowball head off and washed him down with the brandy.

"Besides," I said, "it will be us." Tomorrow or years from now, it would be us, and we knew it. But that didn't make it easier for it to be Anders's turn now.

Mark had arrived December twelfth, the day after his last class. His semester ended earlier than mine. I didn't teach my last class until December twenty-third. I'd decided we should spend the last class turning the "books" we'd written into books. Bibi had given me a list of book-binding supplies to ask the class to bring and some quick pointers on how to make hand-bound books. The students streamed into the last class with their revised chapters and bags full of supplies—plastic covers, needles and thread, bright spools of ribbon, markers and crayons, little jars of paint, piles of stiff cardboard. Part of me wanted to say *Stop*, I bet there are still misspelled words in your chapters. *Stop*, let me grade them one more time. *Stop*, this is college, not kindergarten. We shouldn't be using crayons. We shouldn't be having fun. But I ignored that part of me and kept going.

I bound a copy of the chapters I'd written during the previous three months while perched on the couch with Ginger. I bound them in chartreuse cardboard, Maude's favorite color, for good luck. I tied it shut with hot-pink ribbon. These last months were in there, in-between the lines on every page, even when I'd been writing about our life before the cancer and my life before Anders, and I didn't want to look at them again for a while.

Everyone also brought food—a true Wisconsin mix of fry bread and empanadas and Rice Krispies treats and squeaky fresh cheese curds. I'd brought jugs of fresh apple cider from the food co-op. After we all filled our paper plates, the students made me close my eyes and count to ten before I opened them. I heard the classroom door open, a brief hurried rustle of wrapping paper. "Surprise!" the class shouted. In front of me was a very large bundle, wrapped—swaddled really—in about two rolls of pink and blue wrapping paper.

"Open it," Mickey's mother shouted. "Tear into it," another student yelled as I started timidly unwinding the paper from one end. I did.

Inside was a white wicker baby bassinet, the kind that lets you keep your baby right by your side no matter where you are for those first fleeting weeks. It was impractical—all that expense for just a few weeks!—and lovely and absolutely touching. This from a class where one woman had written about putting her babies down for the night in banana boxes from the grocery store.

Part of me wanted not to take it—it was too much, too expensive, how could I? But the smarter half of me knew it was not a gift I could turn down. I took it in the spirit it was given. One of the Hmong women had made a quilt for the bassinet out of strips of midnight blue and parrot green and sunflower yellow. When the class was over we went out into the night—me with my newly bound book, my bassinet, and my bright quilt; they with their empty dishes and bound volumes of their lives. All of us warm in spite of the cold. Mickey's mom followed me to the car for one last hug. "I didn't want to tell you in class," she whispered in my ear. "But Mickey was in a car accident—a drunk driver hit his truck, and he rolled into the ditch."

I stiffened, my mouth opening to let out the softest *no*.

"He'll be okay," she said. "They're not sure they can save his leg. He's here in Madison, at the university hospital. They brought him down on the Medflight helicopter. If you have time, he'd love to see you."

"Time?" I said. "Of course I have the time."

As it turned out, I didn't.

On the day Maude was due, I'd been ready—eager—to feel the first cramping pain of labor. Instead I felt a pluck, like the twang of some guitar string hidden in my body, and then a gush of water soaked my underwear, my jeans, everything.

My water had broken. From jokes I'd heard over the years I'd assumed that was the usual first sign of labor, until the instructor in the childbirth class Anders and I took told us differently. Usually, she'd said, your water—your amniotic sac with its amniotic fluid—did not rupture until well into labor. If it did, you should go to the hospital. Labor would begin within a couple of hours.

I'd called the triage nurse at the hospital who said to come, but not to hurry in. I took a shower while Anders paced nervously back and forth in the kitchen, looking at his watch, as if Maude were a train he was afraid we would miss. Then, wearing several layers of sanitary napkins to keep my pants and the car seat from being soaked with the salty sea that our Maude was swimming in, we left for the five-minute drive to the hospital.

The triage nurse joked when she checked me to see if I was dilated. "Not yet, but any minute," she said. We settled in and watched a late movie. Then a later one. No labor. "By morning, you will be," the doctor on call assured me, "if it doesn't wake you up—*boom*—before then." Anders slept on the fold-out couch in the maternity suite, which was really just a hospital room with blue-and-peach-flowered wallpaper in place of the usual medicinal green paint. I tried to sleep on the bed, which was really just a rock-hard delivery table with sheets. But no matter how often I turned over, the weight of Maude inside me made my legs go numb, my arms fall asleep.

The next morning a new doctor, another obstetrician from our HMO, came in. Late February was prime doctor winter vacation time, and I was becoming aware that I would see a new doctor every eight hours. I didn't know yet that the one doctor I was fated never to see was my own OB/GYN who was, at that very moment, on the beach in Cancun. I groaned when I rolled over for my exam, feeling like a whale beached on the world's hardest sand.

There was a Jacuzzi in the tub, the new doctor told us, but

since my water had already broken, I couldn't use it. Once the amniotic sac was ruptured, he said, my womb wasn't a hermetically sealed, germ-proof environment anymore. If we weren't careful, Maude could be born with an infection, even pneumonia. As long as I went into labor soon we wouldn't have to worry about that.

And if I didn't go into labor? I asked. Then, he said, they would start a round of pitocin, a hormone that induced labor. With enough pitocin, he said, I could make a rock go into labor.

They put in an IV drip that afternoon and also hooked me up to a fetal heart monitor, a web of wires attached to my round belly by small sticky pads. Pitocin often induced strong contractions, said the nurse, and so she would sit with me and watch the monitor to make sure Maude wasn't getting squeezed too tightly, that she had enough oxygen flowing to her tiny, vulnerable brain.

Yet another doctor turned on the pitocin. The first drip went visibly drip, then drip, drip. "We'll start you at a low dose and work up," he said. He waited a moment. I waited. Where was the boom? "It may take a few hours," he said, and left Anders, the nurse, and me to watch Maude's heartbeat roll merrily along.

It took all afternoon, all evening. The local PBS station was running back-to-back episodes of Ken Burns's epic documentary of the Civil War. Lincoln was elected, guns fired on Fort Sumter. The doctor kept stopping by, upping my dosage. The war went one way, then, after Gettysburg, dramatically the other. At midnight, shortly after Lincoln's assassination, the new doctor on duty gave up, and had me unhooked from both the IV and the fetal monitor so I could sleep. We'll try again tomorrow. It always works, he said. With enough pitocin . . . Anders stopped him. "I know, I know," he said, "you could make a rock go into labor."

Any rock but me. Six doctors tried for three days. Each day, the new doctor on call would call for a new bag of pitocin—as if he suspected the last one of being mere water. We would start again, the dosage climbing, the nurse watching the monitor, Anders and I watching old movies on the cable movie channel. The doctors had ordered me kept off solid food. I could only have fluids—water, popsicles—for fear I might need an emergency Caesarian section. At dinnertime on the fourth day, I did. Maude's heartbeat took a nosedive—though it wasn't because of any contractions—and they had me unhooked and rolling so fast toward the operating room Anders had to run to keep up.

They put him in scrubs while the anesthesiologist gave me an epidural. "It's like Novocain," the anesthesiologist said. "It numbs you below the waist so you won't feel any pain, though you may still feel some tugging or pinching." This way, he explained, I would be wide awake when Maude was born. I nodded. My daughter's birth was not something I wanted to sleep through.

Anders appeared next to me and took my hand. He was wearing blue surgical scrubs that matched his eyes. "We're starting the incision," the surgeon called out. The nurse drew a little white cotton curtain across the table just below my ribs so I couldn't see my own blood. I could feel the incision. It was more than a pinch and more than a pull, if not quite screaming pain. I took a deep breath and squeezed Anders's hand hard.

"She hasn't dropped at all," I heard the surgeon say to the intern. "I can't get her. Apply some pressure to the uterus to force her down my way, will you?" The intern went to his task with a will. I had a sudden flash of an old Samsonite commercial featuring a fully grown gorilla jumping up and down on a suitcase. That suitcase was me. *Ooophh*, I said. *Ooooo*. Could I faint lying down? Anders, who fainted when he got a tetanus booster, who couldn't bear to see blood when I cut myself in the kitchen, was peering bravely over the curtain, watching his wife get "sectioned," as the doctor called it, as if I were a Florida grapefruit.

"I've got her," the doctor said. Then Maude cried, just like in the movies. For once they had it right, though I didn't see anyone slap her bottom. Instead, they whisked her away to do who-knew-exactly-what in the far corner of the operating room while the surgeon and the intern started the tedious business of sewing me shut, layer by layer. I could feel the prick and tug of needle and thread. But now I didn't care. The nurse handed Maude to Anders. She wore a tiny stocking cap pulled low over her forehead like a salty old fisherman.

"Here," Anders said, and handed her to me. I stared down at her. She stared up at me with astonished eyes. Both of us were surprised to see a stranger's face on this person we knew in other ways so well. It was like meeting a lost uncle at a family reunion. *Hello, I've heard so much about you.* And here you are. Here you are.

My heart gave a sudden jerk like a boat about to tear loose of its mooring in a riptide. In one overwhelming rush, I loved her. Without a second's hesitation I would have thrown myself to the lions, in front of tanks, off the planet itself to save her. She was my baby. It hurt how much I loved her, as if I were using muscles I'd never used—never even knew I had—before. "Welcome to Wisconsin, Maudie. The best place in the world," Anders said, and kissed his daughter on her tiny forehead.

"*God,*" I thought, still woozy from all the sewing and tucking, "*I love that man.*"

The afternoon of the day Anders died, I was sitting next to his bed, holding his hand. I put my head down, my forehead to his palm, closed my eyes, and fell sleep. Slowly my body floated as his must have being doing on his drugs. I was out at sea, and Anders was there already.

Together we tumbled on the swells, up and over, far away, until we landed, the sand of the beach a faintly warm surprise.

If only his cancer were all a dream, I thought, we could fish this salted water, look up and see only white gulls, blue sky, then the gulls again, see the harmless moon, a jellyfish which, like death, had lost its sting.

Then I woke, and the dreaming ended. The shadow of Anders's death came closer, block by block, the blade which would sever everything. His hand slipped from mine. His one good eye, which had looked and looked, was slowly closing too.

Wake up, Anders, I wanted to say, in spite off all my hospice indoctrination. *Don't be hasty.* We can rearrange your trip. Let someone else go ahead of you this time. I kissed him on his dry cracked lips, his forehead, his lips again.

Instead I said, *It's okay, Anders. Everything will be okay.* I said *Go.* I let go. He let go. His breath not an awful sticky rattle, but a long, long sigh.

Oh God. Death was here, right inside this room. "I won't look," I said. "I won't." Then I did.

Anders was gone. The lights twinkled on the Christmas tree in the living room. From Maude's room, from her boom box, came the faint sound of Jose Feliciano singing "Feliz Navidad." Five o'clock Christmas Eve and Anders was gone.

No need to check the hospice list to tell me death had occurred, he *was* the list—

—no breathing
—no heartbeat
—eyelids slightly open
—eyes fixed on no certain spot
—no blinking
—jaw relaxed and mouth slightly open

As for the last sign—release of bowel and bladder—his diaper saved me from having to think about that.

"Death is not an emergency," the hospice guide said. "The body does not have to be moved until you are ready. The family may assist with preparing the body by bathing or dressing. The police do not need to be called. Hospice will notify the physician. When you are ready, call the funeral home to have the body moved and identify the person as a hospice patient."

"Body." For them always it was "the body." A word chosen to drive home their view that the person inside had flown home, crossed over, was gone for good. But Anders was not just a *body* to me yet.

I bathed Anders. Before I would have been afraid to touch a dead man, wash his hair, feet, hands, genitalia. But I had touched Anders every day as he made the trip from health to emaciation. Now I wished I had rushed across the lake to see my dead, still-warm mother in her hospital room, had gotten to Florida before my father was neatly turned to ash. To give one last bit of care seemed the best good-bye. I bathed Maude and I would bathe my new baby. Didn't my dead deserve the same?

Mark helped me dress Anders, picking out a color-coordinated ensemble of socks, shirt, tie, and suit that matched far better than anything Anders would ever have chosen himself. "I know," Mark said, reading my mind. "Take it as my gift. Anders deserves to look a little snappier in death than life. It's a grand occasion."

When we had him ready, Maude came in. I wasn't sure this was a good idea, but Maude insisted. She'd done her hospice homework too. She just stood by the bed and looked, turning her head, first to one side, then the other. She didn't seem to want to touch her father, and I didn't suggest it. Maybe he was already a body to her, the only one she'd ever seen. "He still looks sick," she said. "Somehow I thought when he died, he'd look all well again." She shook her head. "I think I'd rather remember him fat," she said, meaning when he was healthy

216

and merely tall and thin, before he was bony as a bat with skin drawn just as tight. "And with hair," she added. She handed me a drawing to tuck inside his suit pocket. "Don't look," she said.

I didn't, though I had seen her drawing it the night before. It was our family—Anders, me, Maude, and her soon-to-be baby brother—in front of our house-in-progress. The picture that was pure imagination, a portrait of something that would never be. But then what is art but pure longing, our heart's desire in bright colors?

It was nearly six o'clock and already dark when we called the funeral home. It was snowing outside, and when two workers arrived with their gurney, they were lightly dusted as if with powdered sugar. "Nice Christmas tree," one of them said to Mark, as I signed the paperwork. "Blue spruce?"

Mark nodded. "We cut it ourselves," he said.

The worker nodded too. "They last longer that way."

Then the two men rolled Anders onto the gurney, covered him with both a sheet and a blanket, as if he could still catch cold, and strapped him down. I followed Anders to the door, stood watching until the van was out of sight. By that time it was snowing hard, not confectionery magic anymore, but a full-out December snowstorm. I stood there staring into the night until I noticed the snowdrift building up in the hall, noticed how white and cold my hands and ankles were. I made myself shut the door and walk back into the living room of a house with no Anders. An empty, empty house, no matter who was in it. I sat down on the couch, and after a few minutes I noticed Mark had slipped a cup of hot cider into my hands. I took a sip. Maude came and sat next to me with her own cup of cider, and we sat looking at the blinking lights on our freshly cut blue spruce. The house was completely still. No raspy breathing from the dining room. No sounds from Mark or Ginger, wherever they were.

Even the noises from outside were muffled by the snow. The

storm would make for a very white, very slippery Christmas. It would have made a funeral difficult, the flying in and out of Madison a nightmare, but we weren't planning on a funeral, not right away. Anders's father had asked that Anders be buried in his hometown cemetery next to the Lutheran church, buried in the family plot that had a view of the old Dahl farm. Letting Anders join the other Dahls seemed right to me. But there was no burying anyone there in late December. In the old days, Anders had once told me, they'd just set the coffins by their plots, let them rest covered by blanket upon blanket of snow. Only in the spring, when the ground thawed, could they be buried in the ground, their graveside services conducted.

After talking to his father I decided to have Anders cremated. Then, in the spring, we would all drive up for a funeral, stand in the high grass above the farm and the Mississippi. There was talk of a memorial service at the chapel on campus, sometime in May perhaps, before the rush of graduation.

"Good thing we don't have to go anywhere tonight," Mark said, coming into the room with more cider.

"Oh, damn, I forgot Mickey!" I said, standing up. "I promised his mother I'd go to the hospital to see him." Maude stood too, ready to go, ready to get out of this quiet, quiet house.

"Not in this storm," Mark said, nodding at the frosted windows, "we're not driving to the hospital."

Then, with an ironic bit of timing no one would dare put in a play, I felt the familiar faint pluck inside my belly I'd felt with Maude, and my water broke. Only this time, instead of days of waiting in vain for the faintest sign of labor, I hardly had time to take a breath when it was on me, hard and fast and hurting like hell. I bent over to grab the arm of the sofa. Man, it hurt. I tried to remember my Lamaze breathing. I'd learned it for Maude and never used it. I'd meant to take a refresher childbirth course, but . . .

Maude squeezed my hand and talked to me while Mark went to call an ambulance. After a life in warm and snowless places, he was afraid to risk driving me in such a storm. But Bibi appeared in her four-wheel-drive SUV before the ambulance arrived, and we made it to the hospital after sliding through only one intersection. Mark came too, leaving Maude with Lloyd and Kyle. I lost track of what happened after we got to the hospital. It was Christmas Eve, then Christmas day, and then night again. Dr. Miracle, who I wanted to see now more than anything, both as a sign of things to come and as a doctor, had Christmas off.

Christmas. I hoped someone, somewhere, remembered to open presents with Maude, to eat the cookies Bibi and Mark had so carefully made. The nurse took over from Bibi as my labor coach. I'd already worn out Mark. I was not doing so well on the breathing, and my labor pains came without stop, with none of the promised rests in between. At first I almost didn't mind. The worse it hurt, the better. Now my body felt the way my heart did, the way my whole soul did. I could yell and sweat and swear, and no one expected me to just accept all the pain I was feeling. Or, if they did, I didn't fucking care. My husband was dead and I was in more pain than I had ever known I could be.

My breathing got better, the nurse a better coach than Bibi (who kept flinching), or Mark, who looked like he might faint. I moved into another stage of labor. I could feel the baby coming down, getting closer to being in the world with us. The morning after I'd delivered Maude by Caesarean section, I met another mom who'd also had a C-section. She joined me for our mandatory first hobble down the hall and said to me, "Hell, it's not so bad. At least this time I got a baby. Last year, I had my gall bladder out, and all I got was a test tube full of stones."

This pain, I told myself, was going to get me a baby. This pain was worth every bit of agony. Then a resident came in to check my progress. I'd hardly dilated at all, he said. I wasn't having productive labor. Then he whispered to the nurse, and I caught the word "section." Oh damn, I thought, here we go again. Why couldn't I get this right?

Thinking of the operating room made me wish Anders were there. Suddenly, I missed him. Not the Anders, drawn as a mummy, who I had bathed that morning, or the mad Anders of the attic renovation and that God-awful Halloween, but my Anders. The Anders who was here last time to hold my hand when the surgeon cut me open and who'd been there with me to see Maude for the first time. He had been everything good and normal and stable in this world.

I started crying, great choking sobs, and then I couldn't get my breath. I heard the fetal monitor alarm go off, and the next thing I knew I was being rolled fast as a stock car down the hall toward the operating room. "C-section," I heard my nurse call out. If last time with Maude had been an emergency then this was a ten-alarm fire.

The operating room doors swung open to receive us, and someone called, "We need a general," and a hand appeared from nowhere and slapped a mask down on my face. A voice that went with the hand whispered, "You'll be out for a while, but I'll bring you around as soon as the baby's here. I promise."

Then I felt a hand touch my cheek—a cool thin hand. It was almost certainly the anesthesiologist. I closed my eyes and said *Anders. Anders touched me.* I willed myself to remember it that way. *As I went under, I felt Anders touch my cheek.* And, who knows, maybe I did.

There was a moment, a good long dark moment, when I was trying to wake up and not getting there. Maybe awake was not some place I really wanted to be. I thought about just drifting, down into the darkness, following Anders up or over or under, wherever that place he had gone might be. Then I heard the most annoying noise—half buzz saw, half alarm clock. What was that sound?

In *Through the Looking Glass* Alice grabs the Red Queen and shouts, "I'll shake you into a kitten, that I will!" Then there are two of the shortest chapters in any book:

Chapter X
SHAKING

Alice took her off the table as she spoke, and shook her backwards and forwards with all her might.

The Red Queen made no resistance whatever: only her face grew very small, and her eyes got large and green: and still, as Alice went on shaking her, she kept on growing shorter—fatter—and softer—and rounder—and—

Chapter XI
WAKING

—it really was a kitten, after all.

I realized in my dream that the alarm clock was someone crying like a baby. Was it me? Anders? Who was it? Why couldn't they shut up?

I woke to find it was a baby crying like a baby. My baby, in Mark's firm big-brother grasp. "Your doc was right. It's a boy," Mark said to me. Next to Mark was Dr. Miracle, brought in by plane or Santa's sleigh, but there at last.

"Take your baby," she said to me. "He needs you."

I looked around first. I was in recovery with tubes running every which way into me. Then I took the baby, because it was, clearly, my baby. Why else would my brother hand him to me, and Dr. Miracle tell me to take him? I looked into the baby's face, expecting to feel the electric jolt of motherhood, the fierce and instant love I'd felt for Maude. Instead I felt this: he was a nice-looking baby. Someone should take him home. Then I fell asleep.

When I woke in my room, the baby was in a clear Plexiglas bassinet next to my bed. Bibi saw my eyes open and buzzed the nurse, who hustled in and handed the baby to me to breast-feed, which I was glad to do. I was glad when he latched on like a little land shark and sucked for all he was worth. I felt a general motherliness. But I didn't feel like *his* mother. It was more like being handed someone else's baby and being glad that, as an experienced mother, you could be of help, because you'd done the same for your own babies.

Then the baby looked up at me and I saw Anders's eyes. Damn, I thought. He is my son. What am I going to do? I would have to learn to love him. Well, maybe "have to" was the wrong way to put it. I *would* learn to love him. The way I'd learned to love Anders, learned to love Wisconsin because of Anders, learned to *love* because of Anders. I switched my son to my other breast, cupping his soft warm head in my palm. He was a little guy.

"Six pounds," Mark said, reading my mind once more. I felt a small tug at my heart, the first nibble of love, like the small-est sunnie striking the hook. I did learn to love him, of course. Day by day. Until I loved him like I loved Maude, which is to say, more than life itself.

"What's his name?" Bibi said. "Dr. Miracle asked me but I said I didn't have the faintest. I'd have suggested Santa Claus but he missed being born on Christmas by two hours."

I looked down at his bobbing head. He was still busy ran-sacking my nipple for his first-ever breakfast. "Nils," I said. Anders had always loved that odd, old-fashioned Norwegian name, though there hadn't been a Nils in the Dahl family since the old country. Now it seemed right to give Anders the last word. And, to be honest, if it had to be Norwegian, Nils was a name I could take. I couldn't have stood a Halvor III, or even, though it had crossed my mind, another Anders. Anders was Anders. Nils would be himself.

I drifted off to sleep again, this time holding Nils. Mark and Bibi disappeared to make phone calls to friends and relatives. This time they brought the best and the worst of news for the price of one. A man had died, a boy was born. *The King is Dead. Long Live the King.*

I woke just as Maude came in, followed by Lotte and Gretel. Maude looked at her brother, and I saw the switch flip and the light go on. Maybe I hadn't felt that fierce surge of love for Nils because such a connection only needs to be made once. Maybe, after that first one, your heart is always open. For Maude, seeing Nils was truly love at first sight.

She took her brother's tiny hand and wrapped it around her big finger with its ragged, nibbled, second-grader nail. She beamed at him. "I'm Juliet, Mom," she said, "and he's my Romeo." I nodded, knowing exactly what she meant. I left it for some other year for my advanced reader to discover Shakespeare's play was not about a sister's undying love for her brother.

The night after Nils was born I dreamed I brought him home, but we passed through the front door of our house without touching the knob, passed through walls, room to room, without bothering to find the doors. I stood in the kitchen, holding him in my arms, and felt the house around us more transparent than glass, like some soft permeable membrane with light and life moving through it as easily as air. I thought, *this is the truth.* Everything *is* light. We floated up the stairs, headed for the remodeled attic, for a first peek at our new rooms. But just as we reached the top of the stairs I woke up.

The next day when Mark came to the hospital we talked about an urn for Anders's ashes—his one last earthly need. Mark said a colleague from the art department, a glass artist, had called to ask if he could make something. Then a cabinetmaker called to make the same offer, and still another, a potter.

Later, I said to Mark. Let me sleep on it. I had time to think it over—this wasn't my father, already late for his funeral. I had all winter to come up with the right vessel for what was left on this earth of Anders. I could choose glass, for transparency. Or wood, in honor of the boxes Anders made. Or a pot made of good Wisconsin clay. But I wouldn't mistake the decision for more than it was—the urn was not Anders, the ashes were not Anders. Whatever, wherever Anders was or wasn't didn't depend on this choice. It was mere set decoration for his funeral, a choice designed to make those of us still weighed down by our flesh feel better about his fleshlessness.

Mark told me that Gretel and Lotte and Mrs. Brown had opened presents with Maude at our house on Christmas morning while I was in labor. Mrs. Brown had even brought along a nylon chew bone gift-wrapped for Ginger. Only later did I hear that Maude—maybe guessing Mrs. Brown had nowhere else to be and so was a soft touch—had curled up on the couch with her and made her read *The Night Before Christmas*, over and over until Maude fell asleep.

Maude told me my presents were waiting under the tree. No one mentioned any for Anders, and by the time I checked there weren't any. I know I hadn't thought to buy him anything. He was so clearly beyond the need for anything material. Had no one believed he would last into the New Year? It made me sad to think not even Maude had made him a card or a painted handprint in clay. He seemed to have slipped from our lives too quickly.

I stayed in the hospital the required six days after my emergency C-section. With Maude I'd lobbied to get out early, sick to death of the place after the days I'd spent waiting to go into labor. Besides, I had Anders there to help me, I told the doctor. Anders would be there to hand me Maude when my incision hurt too much to lift my infant daughter. The doctor had

224

relented and let me go after three days. Now, I bided my time, making myself eat every cube of Jell-O, drink every glass of milk, building my strength for the climb ahead.

On my last day Mickey came to see me, trailing his IV stand, his mother pushing him in a wheelchair, one leg stiff in front of him. There'd been a bunch of surgery, he said, but in the end they'd saved his leg. Now the doctors said he'd be okay, though he had a lot of therapy ahead.

"It will be hard work," his mother said, in her best nurse's voice. "It will hurt," in a softer mother's tone.

Mickey snorted. "Like I'm going to complain about a few months of lifting weights," he said. "As long as it's not math." Maybe, he said, as long as he was laid up, he'd think about getting back in school.

"You should, Mickey," I said. His mother nodded. "I'll talk to the dean of students for you, if you need me to."

Mickey nodded, noncommittal. There was still all that math between him and any diploma. "I'll think about it," he said.

Mickey said Nils, who had just woken up, looked like a little bruiser. His mother said he had a lovely head. "The shape," she said, forming a perfect oval with her hands, "shows a lot of balance." We hugged before she left.

On the morning of the sixth day Dr. Miracle signed my discharge orders. It was December thirty-first, New Year's Eve. One more day and it would be January. Twelve years before, my mother had died in January. Last year in January I'd discovered I was pregnant—though with a baby who would not be born. Now, another year was about to burst into the clear night sky over Wisconsin's frozen lakes.

Lloyd and Bibi came to get us in Lloyd's Mercedes. I deserved the royal treatment, Bibi said. Lloyd and Bibi's baby gift, a brand-new infant car seat, was buckled safely to the Mercedes's leather seat. Maude and Kyle and Mark were waiting at the house. The living room was full of baby gifts and flowers. The Christmas tree still stood surrounded by red and green packages near the fireplace. Someone had even remembered to plug in the little blinking lights.

Beyond the tree, the pocket doors to the dining room were thrown wide open. Anders's bed was gone. The toilet he'd never used was gone too. The dining room table was back in its place. Its oak surface—which Anders had stripped and re-varnished the year we bought the house—reflected the bright colors of an It's A Boy! balloon bouquet. Not exactly a house in mourning, but then maybe the one gift of passing away after a "long illness," as the obituaries said, was that some grief came before the death, not after.

"You haven't seen the baby's room," Bibi said.

Mark took Nils. Lloyd took my arm and helped me up the stairs to the attic, with everyone following behind. I closed my eyes at the top for a second, at the very spot where I had woken from my dream of the house with the translucent walls. Then I opened my eyes to see what Anders had not lived to see—our new upper floor with its three new rooms. Here was the office for me—light streamed through the tall windows onto the freshly varnished oak floor. The walls were fresh crisp white, the ceiling too, and the light seemed everywhere at once. It was wonderfully empty, letting me imagine a new desk, tall bookcases, maybe a red Persian rug in all their imaginary splendor—never mind they would soon be littered with papers, with books I'd pull down to use for a class and never find the time to put back on the shelf. For now the room was perfection.

Beyond my office I could see our new bath with the white-and-green tile Anders and I had chosen on that long night after we learned he had cancer. Someone—Mark, Bibi?—had already hung fat, fluffy bright green towels on the chrome towel bars.

On the other side was the baby's room. It was white, too, and nearly empty, except for an oak rocking chair and

Maude's old crib. "I wanted to tear into it and do it all up in bright colors," Bibi said. "But Maude said you should see it this way first. 'Mom's not chartreuse, she said.'"

No, I was the one who liked gray. No—correction—I was the one who *had* liked gray. Gray was for tomorrow, gray was for the long haul. For now, I thought, white was the color. Today, everything in Wisconsin was snowdrift white, inside and out. White rooms, bright light. My baby wrapped in his warm, new white blanket. Tomorrow? These new rooms were mortgaged. Maude and Nils needed taking care of. There was money to earn and work to be done. I would miss Anders like the ache from a dozen broken bones. But that was tomorrow.

This morning I looked past Nils to the window of the nursery, out into the sky beyond. White flakes blew up past the window into the white winter sky, into the air over Wisconsin. Today, even the snow was too light to fall.

In the Prairie Schooner
Book Prize in Fiction series

Last Call
By K. L. Cook

Carrying the Torch
By Brock Clarke

Nocturnal America
By John Keeble

The Alice Stories
By Jesse Lee Kercheval

UNIVERSITY OF NEBRASKA PRESS

Also of Interest in the *Prairie Schooner Book Prize in Fiction* series:

Last Call
Stories
By K. L. Cook

K. L. Cook's debut collection of linked stories spans three generations in the life of one West Texas family. Events both tender and tragic lead to a strange and lovely vision of a world stitched together in tenuous ways as the characters struggle to make sense of their lives amid the shifting boundaries of marriage, family, class, and culture.

ISBN: 978-0-8032-1540-5 (cloth)

Carrying the Torch
Stories
By Brock Clarke

The stories in this collection occupy a world at once as familiar as a suburban backyard or a southern college's hallowed football field and as strange as a man who buys Savannah, Georgia, and tries to turn it into the perfect Southern city as part of his attempt to win back his estranged wife.

ISBN: 978-0-8032-1551-1 (cloth)

Nocturnal America
By John Keeble

This collection of loosely connected tales returns readers to the American Northwest so finely observed and powerfully evoked in John Keeble's previous, celebrated works. Nocturnal America occupies a terrain at once familiar and strange, where homecoming and dislocation can coincide, and families can break apart or hone themselves on the hard edges of daily life.

ISBN: 978-0-8032-2777-4 (cloth)

Order online at
www.nebraskapress.unl.edu
or call 1-800-755-1105.
When ordering mention
the code BOFOX to receive
a 20% discount.